Edward The Exile

Fen Flack

Fen Flack

Flack Publishing

Flack Books, 23 Stourport Road, Bewdley,
Worcestershire DY12 1BB, UK

www.flackbooks.weebly.com

First edition 2017

Cover design by Head Desk Graphic Design Studio from
illustration by Bhavin Mistry

Printed in the UK by A. & G. Printing Co. Ltd of
Stourport-on-Severn, Worcestershire DY13 9AX

ISBN 978-0-9564961-6-4

Characters

In England

Edmund, King of Wessex
Frida, his wife
Edward, their young son
Eadwig, King Edmund's brother
Ealdwine, King Edmund's chaplain
Hild and Edith, Frida's women
Cnut, a Dane, King of the rest of England
Queen Emma, Aethelred's widow who married Cnut
Eadric Streona, Earl of Mercia
Godwine, a thegn with lands near Chichester
Lord Valgar, a Danish nobleman and merchant
Cnut's sons – Swein, Harold and Harthacnut
Edward, son of King Aethelred and Queen Emma
Alfred, his brother

In Denmark

Harald, King of Denmark (Cnut's brother)
Gunnhild, Lord Valgar's wife

In Sweden

Olof Skötkonung, King of Sweden
His sons, Anund and Edmund
Jakob, in Lord Valgar's employ
Swen, a sailor

In Russia

Yaroslav, Grand Duke of Russia
Irene, his wife (known as Ingegerd in Sweden)
Olaf Haraldson, deposed King of Norway
Astrid, his wife and sister to Irene
Wulfhild and Magnus, Olaf's children
Harald, Olaf's half-brother (later known as Hardrada)
Levente and Andrew, exiled Hungarian princes

GLOSSARY

Aetheling – a son of the King, one of those considered worthy to succeed to the throne

Fyrd – a fighting force, raised locally

Reeve – a local official, sheriff is a corruption of "shire reeve"

Seax – short sword

Shieldwall – a battle formation created by men standing shoulder to shoulder with their shields locked together making an almost impenetrable wall

Thegn (pronounced thane) – a lord, of lower rank than an earl

Wergild – payment made by a criminal to those against whom he committed the crime

Witan – the King's council, which included bishops, earls and thegns

Royal Family Tree

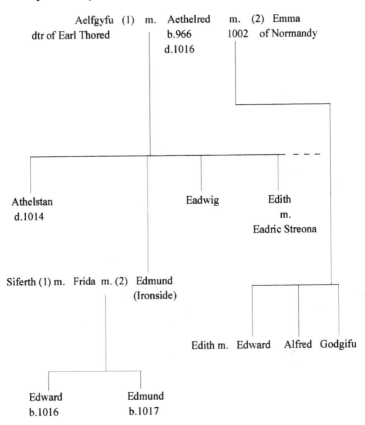

Aelfgyfu (1) m. Aethelred m. (2) Emma
dtr of Earl Thored   b.966   1002   of Normandy
                         d.1016

Athelstan   Eadwig   Edith
d.1014   m.
                                    Eadric Streona

Siferth (1) m. Frida m. (2) Edmund
                      (Ironside)

                                    Edith m. Edward   Alfred Godgifu

Edward   Edmund
b.1016   b.1017

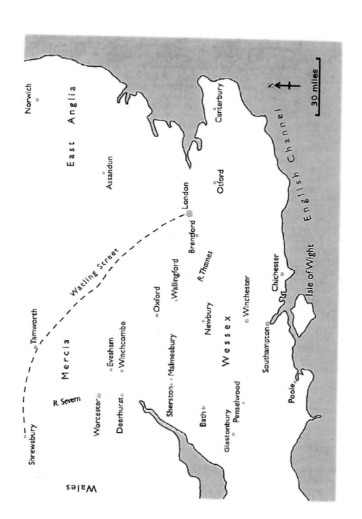

Map of Southern England

Contents

The book could not have been done without the help of:

The ACW group in Leamington Spa, Bewdley Bards,
Birmingham Central Library, Britta Flegg for
information about Sweden's early history, Martin Flegg
for the maps, Margaret Hawkins, The Hive at Worcester,
Julie McCarthy, Liz Munslow for proof reading and
support, Barbara Viney and the David Wilson Library at
the University of Leicester

PART I – ENGLAND

CHAPTER 1

Winchester, November 1016

"Wulfgar, I need you to write a letter."

I stood as soon as I heard his voice in the doorway.

"Yes, sire."

He slumped onto a stool, his feet scuffing the rushes on the earth floor. He ran his hand nervously through his light brown hair, making it more tousled than it was. He looked across at me.

"Do sit," he said.

I obeyed my King, but couldn't take my eyes from his face. He was pale despite the sun tan of a long summer, and his eyes were bloodshot.

"Sire, are you alright?" I enquired anxiously.

He sighed.

"I've been sick in the night." He grimaced. "At least I have no battles to fight today."

At that moment, my stomach churned over and I felt sick too. I couldn't explain why, but I had a horrible premonition that it wasn't just something he'd eaten the previous evening.

"I could do with Lord Godwine here in Winchester," he explained.

He pulled the stool across to where a brazier gave out some heat before he dictated a short letter and left me.

When he'd gone, I sat staring at the stone wall of the small room that I and his chaplain, Ealdwine, used.

I had begun serving him when he was simply Lord Edmund, one aetheling among several. That was back in 1013, when I was ten. I had been there through the Danish invasion when we'd hidden in a monastery, and at the restoration of his father King Aethelred a year later. I'd witnessed the traumatic events of the Oxford Witan of 1015, which had led to his marriage to the beautiful Lady Frida. Then, later, he'd become King when his father died, but we were harassed by the Danes again. He fought a valiant campaign in 1016, but had lost the battle at Assandun in October and been forced to make a peace treaty with Cnut. Now he was King only of Wessex and we were living in a fine house in Winchester.

"It's only a few weeks since he stopped fighting," I muttered. "Perhaps he's just tired. A few more weeks with Lady Frida and his baby son will help."

Edward was now about six months old and I could see the King adored him nearly as much as he did the child's mother. Sometimes the couple had eyes for no one else. It was good that he could relax a little now. Being King only of Wessex, with Cnut ruler of the rest of England, was a bitter blow, but he wasn't a man to give up. I knew he was determined to make the best he could of the situation. After all, his ancestor, the great King Alfred, had fought the Norse and won back his kingdom. This time of recovery was important for the future, a glorious future we still dreamed of.

Ealdwine came in and interrupted my reverie.

"Daydreaming again, Wulfgar. Haven't you got anything to do?"

"Yes, father, I've a letter to send for the King. He wants Lord Godwine here."

"That's good. He could do with some support."

"There are many who are loyal still. Now there is peace, the thegns down here don't have to choose."

"Yes, the support in the south and in the west country is fairly solid, for King Edmund commands more respect than his father," Ealdwine agreed. "It is hard for those in the midlands and north. They bear the Danish yoke."

"For now."

He raised his eyebrows and gave me a hard look.

"We are silent about the future," he said quietly. "For the present, we work with what we have."

"Well, one person who won't mind that he's under Danish rule is Earl Eadric. I suppose he's an earl again."

"We haven't heard yet how Cnut intends to rule, but it's likely Eadric will get back his position as Earl of Mercia."

"The more I've thought about it the more sure I am that he only pretended to support our King and that all along he planned to run away at Assandun and leave us to be beaten. After all, he changed sides once before."

Ealdwine sighed.

"You may well be right, Wulfgar. I don't know how

3

that man can live with his conscience."

"If I ever get near enough to use my seax on him, he won't live!"

Ealdwine said nothing. He'd told me before that I should forgive, but treachery such as Eadric's was not something I could forget. I hated that man.

"The letter, Wulfgar."

Ealdwine brought me back to the present.

"Yes, I must find a rider."

I sealed the letter and went in search of a suitable messenger.

Lord Godwine was with us in two days, for his estate was near Chichester. He had proved a good friend and had held London with Lord Eadwig, the King's brother, after our defeat at Assandun. The treaty caused them both to leave the capital, Lord Godwine returning to his estate and Lord Eadwig making his home at the King's former residence near Newbury. Nowhere was far from Winchester if the King needed any of his men.

"Godwine!" The King hugged him tightly. They were about the same age, though Lord Godwine was more stocky and of a darker colouring.

"Sire, it's good to see you. I trust you are well."

"Yes, my wife and son give me great joy. I recommend marriage!"

He certainly looked better than he had when I did the letter, but by the way Lady Frida watched over like a mother swan as he ate, I suspected he wasn't fully recovered. I noticed too that he didn't eat much and that his ale cup didn't need refilling as often as it usually did.

I soon discovered the reason for Lord Godwine's visit.

"We are going west," Ealdwine announced the next day. "The King wants to visit Bath and Glastonbury, and Lord Godwine travels with us."

In fact, Lady Frida came too, leaving Edward with his nurse. The King and his wife had spent so little time together since their marriage the previous year that I think every minute was precious. She could bear to be parted from her son, but not from her husband.

I had been to Bath before. Back in June the King had fought his first battle at Penselwood and then made for Bath, where we had briefly stayed before having to fight the Danes again near Malmesbury. We were more welcome this time, as, previously, the King had been raising troops to add to his army and there were mouths to feed and pressure on resources. Now we were a small party in comparison, but including retainers and a bodyguard.

One of the leading men in Bath gave us hospitality. His hall was lit by numerous candles flickering in the dark of a mid-November evening. There was a large fire in the centre, which spit sparks when a new log was thrown on and whose smoke climbed up to the thatch, seeking a way out. All the shutters were tightly closed against the murky cold.

The King sat well away from the draughty doorway on

a small platform next to his host, with Lady Frida at his side and Lord Godwine nearby. The rest of us mixed with the thegn's own men, except for me, as my job was to hover near the King, awaiting instructions.

Our host entertained the King with good food and with minstrels playing on lyres and pipes. There were riddles to solve and jokes to share. The atmosphere was relaxed and jovial, with smiles and laughter. It was a long time since we had been like this and I hoped the King would feel better.

"I travel next to Glastonbury," I heard him say.

"This isn't a good time to travel, sire," our host responded. "The roads are muddy after a week of rain and it could be difficult to get through if there's flooding. You might need a boat!"

King Edmund smiled slightly, as he picked the meat off a bone.

"Several boats," he admitted.

"Can't your visit wait for better weather?"

"It's a special place. I need the prayers of the monks."

"I presume your lady has not been there before?" the thegn asked.

"No, I haven't, but my lord has spoken of it and I know he has a longing to be there," Lady Frida replied.

Her voice was sweet and soft, calming and encouraging her husband. From where I stood behind them I could not see her pretty face, but she had turned her head towards him and I guessed those pale blue eyes were fixed upon his handsome profile. There could be no doubt of her devotion to him.

"My father remembered the saintly Dunston enlarging the monastery when he was abbot," the thegn responded. "That is many years ago now." He paused. "It is good that it's within your kingdom, sire."

The King said nothing and continued to pick at his bone.

It must hurt, I thought, that he is King only of Wessex and cannot even travel to other parts of England. As an aetheling, he had travelled through most of the land and met many of the leading thegns, but now his freedom was restricted. What did being King only of Wessex really mean?

"It's good that the King can travel safely," Lord Godwine interjected, "and know he is among friends."

"Indeed," the thegn agreed. "Can I tempt you all to stay and hunt for a few days? There are plenty of birds wintering here."

"Not at this time," the King answered. "We must press on in the morning."

That night I lay across his doorway, as I had often done in the past when we travelled. I wasn't there to protect him, more to be available if needed. I was rarely disturbed, for he lay in his lady's arms and they satisfied their need of each other. But, that night, I was woken by his stumbling over me.

7

"Help me, Wulfgar!" he groaned. "The courtyard. Quickly!"

We had no light, but I knew the way. He leaned heavily on me and was gasping and coughing. The fresh air gripped my throat, but gave him release to empty his stomach. I watched, distressed and wretched.

Ealdwine said mass the next morning and prayers for our journey, but there was a tension in the air. Everyone knew the King had been ill in the night and no one knew what to say. Lady Frida was pacing about and fidgeting with the ends of her sleeves, as we packed ready to travel. When Lord Godwine came to say the horses were ready, she grabbed his arm.

"This can't go on," she urged.

"My lady?"

"Someone is poisoning the King," she whispered.

"No! Surely not?"

He was frozen to the spot, his face registering the horror of her suggestion.

"Then why is he ill?" she demanded, and I could see tears in her eyes.

"I don't know," Lord Godwine admitted.

"Someone must taste his food. He must not die."

The anguish in her voice was too much for me.

"I will!" I cried.

CHAPTER 2

My whole body went cold as I realised what I'd said. If someone really was trying to poison King Edmund, I was going to die instead.

"Wulfgar, would you?"

Her beautiful voice brought me back from my nightmare. Her eyes were still swimming, but the look on her face! It wasn't love, but it was gratitude. She clasped my shoulders, her face close to mine.

"Oh, Wulfgar! God bless you!"

I never saw Lord Godwine's reaction, for my eyes were fixed on Lady Frida. I had offered to die for my King, but I think in my heart, I was offering to die for her. I wanted to remember her expression for as long as I lived – and that might not be very long.

The first test came later in the day when we received hospitality from a thegn as we made our way southwest. A meal was prepared and I had to sit and eat part of it, with Lady Frida watching me. Each mouthful felt like sawdust; I felt sick just at the thought of being ill. I finished the tasting and Lady Frida took charge of the platter and its contents. She would give them to the King if I wasn't ill. But how long should we wait? She decided on about two hours. I showed no signs of being sick, so the meal proceeded.

In fact the King wasn't ill that night. Had the poisoner taken fright about being discovered? Lady Frida was taking no risks. Everything offered to the King, food and drink, I had to taste. If I had felt more sure of living, I might have enjoyed the good things that came my way, but I was scared that each mouthful might be my last.

We completed our journey to Glastonbury, where we received hospitality from the monks. I thought my job might be over now, but Lady Frida insisted I continued.

I hadn't been to Glastonbury before and found the church there impressive. It was a huge building made of stone. The area inside was far too big for the number of monks that seemed to constitute the monastery, but, of course, when their voices rose in praise, the sound drifted up and filled the vaulted roof space, and was awesome. The interior had whitewashed walls with images depicting scenes from the Bible. It smelt holy, I suppose it was the remains of incense that permeated everything.

"The King's grandfather is buried here," Ealdwine told me, pointing out a stone sarcophagus near the High Altar. "It is a very holy place and the King will find balm for his soul in the prayers of the monks."

Would he also find healing for his body? I wondered. He hadn't been sick for two days, but his face was pinched and he looked weary.

"Some of our saints served in Glastonbury," Ealdwine continued. "St. Dunstan was here and did much to improve the religious life, before he moved to Canterbury. Aelfheah too. He spent time at Deerhurst and here, before becoming Archbishop."

10

"Isn't he the one who was killed by the Danes with ox bones?" I asked.

"You know that story?"

"I heard it a while ago, but I've never forgotten it," I confessed. "It was Easter Day, four years back and they were drunk and they battered him with the bones."

"Canterbury suffered much from the invasions, though this place is vulnerable, with the sea being close and the many waterways round here," was his response.

"But wasn't it somewhere near here that King Alfred hid from the Norse? In those days, the waterways kept him safe."

"Yes, Athelney is an island a little to the southwest, I believe."

"So it's happened before," I urged.

Ealdwine frowned and said nothing.

"King Alfred was pushed to the edge, a bit like us now," I continued. "The Norse had the upper hand, but King Alfred fought back and eventually he beat them. That's what King Edmund will do. He'll make Wessex so strong that we'll crush Cnut and get England back."

"Wulfgar, I've warned you not to talk like that."

"But I'm sure it's what our King plans to do. He won't be content with Wessex."

Ealdwine wouldn't comment. I could see he believed I shouldn't voice my thoughts, but I was sure the King would fight back – somehow. He was not a man to take defeat easily.

For the time being though he wasn't thinking of battles. Rather he was immersing himself in the prayer and worship of the monastery. One day I went with him to a holy well and had to drink the water first before he too drank some. I was tasting his food without any ill effects, but it worried me that he still didn't eat much of what was declared safe and showed no signs of recovering his full strength.

The next day we climbed the tor, Glastonbury's hill. It sticks up in the landscape like a shield boss. The way was steep and we had to keep stopping. Back in the summer, the King could have raced up it, but now he was struggling to get his breath, while I dutifully paused at his side and pretended to admire the extensive view. But I was concerned because the lack of food was making him weak. Our party rested on the summit.

"This is my kingdom, Wulfgar." His tone was sad. "Marsh and water."

"They yield a lot of fish, sire," I responded, in an effort to encourage him. "And elsewhere in Wessex there are fields which grow good crops."

"I don't have London," he countered.

"You have Winchester and that's more beautiful than London and full of your family's history."

"But the trade, Wulfgar. Winchester is not a port."

"Southampton is," I argued.

He smiled and patted me on the shoulder.

12

"You are a good servant, young man." He paused and then added quietly, "You have been risking your life for me. I appreciate that."

He turned to gaze back at the watery landscape and the few naked trees.

"If something happens to me, look after my lady for me, will you?"

"I ... uh...nothing will happen to you, sire!"

"None of us knows how long we have on this earth. Think of Athelstan. I was never meant to be king. It should have been him. He would not have lost at Assandun."

"That wasn't your fault!" I cried. "It was the traitor's fault, going off in the middle of the battle!"

He snorted at my mention of Eadric.

"You are a fine king," I asserted. "The people love you and one day you will retake the whole of England."

What I said was true – he was a fine king and he was loved. His father, King Aethelred, had made too many bad decisions and had sometimes been unjust. As a result, he had briefly lost his kingdom and had only been welcomed back on the basis he would rule more fairly. King Edmund was *not* like his father. He didn't look like him and he didn't act like him. The nickname his people had given him was Ironside, for he was a strong and brave warrior.

Right now, however, he wasn't strong. I kept wanting to believe he would soon be his old self – fit, energetic, undaunted by any challenge. But his pale complexion and dull eyes made me fear.

That night he was really ill and kept to his bed the next day. The monk in charge of the infirmary came with remedies he hoped would help. I was glad I didn't have to try them first. Lady Frida trusted the monks and I was sure she was right, for I heard their fervent prayers for his recovery. Indeed, all of us were praying.

I spent most of the day sitting in the shadows of his room, in case I was needed. Lady Frida never left him. She held his hand and spoke gentle words. I couldn't hear what she was saying; nor could I hear the King's response. Ealdwine brought him consecrated bread and wine, as a reminder of the death of Christ, but we also believed in the healing power of the sacrament.

The next day, the scene was repeated. As far as I knew, the King had taken no food. The monk gave him some liquid, which I think he kept down, but without food he could only get weaker. I was frightened. I felt we were on the edge of a great pit and there was nothing to stop us all falling into its unknown depth.

"Wulfgar, go and get Ealdwine!"

Lady Frida's command had me running to find the priest. We were back in the room very quickly.

"Father, hear his confession," she urged.

I crept back into the shadows and found I was shaking and I couldn't stop, however hard I tried. Ealdwine bent over the King and I heard the murmur of their two voices,

14

one presumably seeking the forgiveness of God for his mistakes and failures, the other assuring him of the saving power of Christ and the victory of the cross.

Time seemed to stand still. I had no idea whether it was day or night, for the windows were shuttered in an effort to keep the room warm. I only left to relieve myself and to find a little food, though I had no appetite. I brought some bread, cheese and ale back with me for Lady Frida, but I don't think she touched it and the King certainly didn't. He appeared to be asleep.

Ealdwine came again with the sacrament.

"Sire, it is St. Andrew's day," he said. "We are pleading with the saint to intercede for you."

Everyone was praying, I was sure of that, including all the saints, and while the King still breathed, there was hope.

Later that day, the Abbot came, together with Lord Godwine and Ealdwine. By then the King's breathing was laboured and I knew it couldn't be long. The room was heavy with prayer and a strange light I couldn't describe. It really felt as though we were in another world, that the veil between us and God was very flimsy.

"My lady, he's gone," I heard Ealdwine say.

Lady Frida began to weep. Her world had died, and so had mine.

CHAPTER 3

Lady Frida's crying filled the room and, for a moment, I was taken back to the scene in Oxford more than a year earlier when she had bewailed her first husband's murder. Her screams then were about justice; her weeping now was desolation, the loss of her deeply loved husband.

We had lost our King. We couldn't really believe it. He had fought the Danes five times and come through those battles unscathed, but some unknown illness had sneaked up on him, like a traitor in the dark, and ended his life.

I couldn't weep – I felt numb. I simply stayed in my corner and watched as the prayer for the King's soul began.

The next few days were a blur. I was probably busy though I can't think what there was I had to do, for the monks took charge of the funeral preparations and Lord Godwine took charge of Lady Frida. I was glad he was there, for he was a man who could keep a cool head in a crisis. And we certainly had a crisis. What were we going to do? Who would rule Wessex now? Edward was only a few months old. Perhaps Lord Eadwig, the King's brother, would be chosen. Or ... No, surely not? I couldn't believe the southern thegns might take Cnut as their leader.

No one spoke of what would happen in the coming days, for all our energy was concentrated on the present, and giving our King a royal funeral. I wondered if we would take his body back to Winchester, but soon found a decision had been made, by whom I've no idea, to bury him here in Glastonbury, next to his grandfather, King Edgar.

The church was heavy with the smell of incense, the monks using thuribles to waft the perfume across the wooden coffin. We surrounded our King with our prayers and the monks chanted numerous psalms. Candles burned everywhere and cast muted shadows against the high walls. The smoke from both the candles and the incense drifted up into the gloom of the lofty roof, but our spirits did not rise, for our hearts were heavy and nothing could lift them.

The climax was the lifting of the coffin into a stone-built sarcophagus. Our King was finally at rest.

The next morning we began our journey back to Winchester. The hours of daylight were few, the mist and rain making our travelling even more gloomy, so it was several days before we reached our destination. I think Lord Godwine must have sent word, for everyone already knew of the King's death, and within a short time, Lord Eadwig arrived.

"Godwine!" he exclaimed. "Is it true? Is Edmund dead?"

"Yes, my lord. He died in Glastonbury, so we laid him to rest there, beside your grandfather."

"But how? The last time I saw him, he was fit and well. Battle-weary, yes, and bitterly disappointed. But he gave no appearance of being sick."

"He wasn't well when we left Winchester," Lord Godwine told him. "Wulfgar, I think you said he had been sick?"

"Yes, my lord," I answered, "but we hoped it would pass."

"The monks at Glastonbury tried everything," Lord Godwine continued, "but nothing could be done to save him."

Lord Eadwig was flushed and clearly troubled by the news.

"Poison?" he asked.

"I don't think so, my lord," I volunteered, "for I was tasting all his food and I wasn't ill at any time."

"Oh, God, what are we going to do?" the aetheling cried.

"The word has gone out calling the thegns to Winchester," Lord Godwine replied. "There is little we can do until they have met – and made a decision."

Lord Eadwig looked at him sharply.

"You think they may not choose me?"

Lord Godwine shrugged his shoulders.

"I've no idea, my lord."

Lord Eadwig groaned.

"Oh, God, what a mess!" he muttered. "And Lady Frida? How is she?"

"Grieving," was Lord Godwine's laconic response.

"Of course she is, man! I meant, how is she coping? She has a tiny child and a dead husband. I hope she hasn't gone mad."

"You can visit her. She will probably be pleased to see you. Wulfgar, take Lord Eadwig to her."

Lady Frida had been given a room for her and Edward and two ladies who attended her. We hadn't seen much of her since our return and I was glad of the opportunity to take her a visitor.

Her pale face brightened when one of her ladies introduced us.

"Eadwig and Wulfgar, welcome. Oh, Wulfgar, don't go."

I had made a move to leave them, but turned back at her request, happy to be in her presence again. I slipped onto a stool near the door, while the King's brother seated himself close to her.

"Dear lady," he began, "I grieve with you. I cannot believe what has happened."

"Nor can I," she responded. "Every time I wake, I think I will find him at my side, but the bed is cold. A light has gone out."

"A light has gone out in our land as well as in your life," he asserted, "but I hope to relight the fire and continue his good work. My brother was a fine king."

They fell easily into talking about King Edmund, Lady Frida, it seemed, being very pleased to talk about her late husband and relish the happy memories she had. When Edward woke and started to cry, his mother took him in her arms.

"Here, Edward, here is Uncle Eadwig come to see us."

"He has your colouring, dear lady."

"But he has his father's eyes," she responded proudly. "I had hoped he would be king one day."

"It's still possible," Lord Eadwig responded.

Lady Frida was quiet for a moment.

"If the thegns choose you as king, you will want your own sons to succeed you," she said softly.

"King Athelstan never married and then ensured his nephew succeeded him."

"But you would want to marry. You are a man like any other."

It crossed my mind that, at some point in the future, Lord Eadwig might marry her and that would mean there would be no squabbles over the succession. When King Aethelred had died in April 1016, there had been question marks about the next king, for his second wife, Queen Emma, wanted her son Edward to be chosen, but he was only eleven at the time, whereas Lord Edmund was well into his twenties and had already got experience in warfare.

Their conversation over, Lord Eadwig rose to leave and so did I.

"Don't go, Wulfgar," Lady Frida said. "I want to talk to you."

So they took leave of each other and I stayed, puzzled she should have some message. She took my arm and pulled me over to where Lord Eadwig had been sitting. I wasn't used to sitting next to her like this.

"Wulfgar, I'm so glad you brought Lord Eadwig to visit me," she began. "I've been wanting to see you."

I couldn't take my eyes from her beautiful face and being so close made me tongue-tied.

"You risked your life for the King and I will never forget that."

Her words were like honey. I would have done it again to hear her praise me.

"You have no lord now, even as I have no husband. I do not know what will happen. If Eadwig becomes King, then I think he will be my protector. If he doesn't, I ... I fear for the future. I have no wish to retire to a nunnery and anyway, there is Edward. I couldn't bear to be parted from him."

I couldn't think what to say. Her position was awkward, if not perilous. Much would depend on who became King of Wessex. If it were Cnut – then the future was bleak.

"You served my husband," she continued. "I remember you were there when the news came that Swein had taken Gainsborough. You were there through all the ups and downs of King Aethelred's later years and you were at the new King's side all through this summer of conflict." She paused. "And you were there at the end."

21

I could see tears in her blue eyes.

"I'm not sure what I can offer you." Her voice was on the edge of breaking. "But I want you to serve me. I would be your new lord."

CHAPTER 4

I was speechless! Lady Frida was asking if I would be her servant, part of her household.

"My lady!" I gasped, my voice coming out as a squeak, "I would be honoured."

"You understand I don't know what will happen," she warned.

"For as long as you need me or at least for as long as I am allowed to be your servant, I will be there, I promise."

She clasped my hand and lifted it to her lips. A tingling sensation surged through me.

I was in a daze for the rest of the day. I moved my mattress to a new place outside the door of her room. Lord Godwine simply raised his eyebrows when I told him – he had no power to stop me, for, in legal terms, I was lordless. I now had the job of delivering food to Lady Frida and her two women, whose names I discovered were Edith and Hild. I also brought fresh logs to put on the brazier that gave them some warmth.

"Wulfgar!" I was accosted by Lord Eadwig. "I hear you are serving Lady Frida."

"Yes, my lord."

"That's good. This is a terrible time for her and it's good that she has people around her whom she knows and whom she trusts."

He paused and glanced around him.

"This is a perilous time," he whispered. "You

probably know the local thegns were here yesterday."

"What did they decide, my lord?"

"I think they will back my claim to be King, but they weren't all very vocal. I noticed some said nothing at all. A couple of voices were raised in support of me, but the silence of others bothers me. They have now gone to London to meet Cnut and the thegns from the midlands and perhaps the north too."

"But your claim is good, my lord. The King's son is too young and what other aethelings are there? Lord Edward is eleven, I think. He wasn't chosen in April, so he's not likely to be chosen now."

Lord Eadwig sighed.

"We don't quite know what Edmund and Cnut agreed at Deerhurst," he admitted. "When they divided the country, did they make provision for one of them dying?"

"I doubt it," I responded. "The King was, what? 27 and Cnut very much younger. Neither would be expecting to die just yet."

He sighed again.

"Yes, I suppose you're right. But I'm still not sure whom I can trust beyond the few retainers that I have."

The conversation disturbed me. I think I had assumed the southern thegns would back him, for the only other option was Cnut and surely they wouldn't want him as their King. Lord Eadwig, however, had never been as prominent a figure as his brother Edmund. He hadn't been involved in fighting the Danes in 1014 and then, this year, he had helped to hold London while the King had gone through Wessex raising an army. Would the thegns reject him because he hadn't been at Assandun or any of the previous battles? We would have to wait for word to come from the capital. I thought he was wise not to risk going in person. There were other men out to please Cnut besides the treacherous Eadric, and Lord Eadwig wouldn't necessarily know who they were. Indeed the death of King Edmund had rocked our world and made everything uncertain. Men who had stood by him when he was alive might now decide to change sides. I knew I didn't want to serve Cnut, but might I have no option?

I pushed such thoughts to one side. Right now, I was serving Lady Frida and I would do that as long as I could. When I was not busy on some errand, I could sit in the corner of her room and watch her. When the light was good, she tried to do some embroidery, but I noticed she couldn't concentrate and often the work lay untouched in her lap and her eyes were fixed on some far-off point. Edward's needs helped her to focus. She would take him on her knees and talk to him. Sometimes she had me play with him, for he was beginning to explore his world, grabbing at objects and pushing things into his mouth. I learned how to make him laugh and his gurgles of delight would bring a faint smile to my lady's face. The child had no idea he was fatherless and that he was cast adrift in a dangerous and uncertain world. Just how uncertain, we were about to discover.

Lord Godwine returned to Winchester, but without any of the other thegns. I saw him and his retainers ride into the courtyard of the complex of buildings we occupied in Winchester. Stable boys took charge of the tired horses; it looked as though they had travelled fast.

"Wulfgar!" he called. "Can you find Lord Eadwig and bring him to the hall and then ask Lady Frida to join us too?"

I eventually found the King's brother talking to his sword-polisher. Lady Frida was in her room as usual. We gathered in the hall, where a servant had brought some ale, bread and cheese for Lord Godwine. One or two retainers were hanging around; after all, the hall was the centre of everything and in it blazed a big fire. So I decided I would hang around as well and hear the news from London.

"What is the news?" demanded Lord Eadwig.

"Let Godwine take his breath," Lady Frida interposed. "He is hungry and weary after his journey."

Lord Eadwig fiddled with his belt, while fixing his eyes on Lord Godwine's face. The latter had eyes only for the food, but at length he glanced up.

"It isn't good," he said softly.

Every muscle in Lord Eadwig's body appeared to tense; he was like a wolf waiting to pounce.

"The King met with the thegns," Lord Godwine continued.

"The King!" Lord Eadwig exploded.

Lord Godwine now returned his gaze.

"He is the King in London and he is King of all but Wessex."

Lord Eadwig snorted.

"Let Godwine speak," Lady Frida urged. She briefly touched his arm, but his mood didn't change.

"The case was made to Cnut that Wessex should now be ruled by you, Lord Eadwig, as the aetheling most fitted to take the crown."

"I should hope so."

Lady Frida touched his arm again.

"Cnut, however, declared that the treaty he made with King Edmund at Deerhurst made provision for the early death of either of them ... and that they agreed the survivor should be king of the whole country."

"Rubbish! Edmund would never have agreed to that."

"His bargaining position was weak," Lord Godwine reminded us.

"Yes ... I suppose it was, but I'm sure Edmund would have wanted his son to rule."

"Of course, he did," Lady Frida responded, "but he knew it would be many years before Edward would be old enough."

"Did you talk of it?" Lord Eadwig demanded.

"Yes," she admitted. "We both wanted our son to take the throne, but we knew much could happen before he was of age."

"Did Edmund tell you he'd agreed Cnut would be King if he ... if he died?"

She hesitated.

"No, he didn't actually say that."

"You see, Godwine. If they'd agreed that, Lady Frida would know!"

Lord Godwine sighed.

"Whether that was part of the treaty or not," he continued, "it is irrelevant. Cnut means to be King of all England."

"But how can he – without the support of the thegns?"

"He has got their support," was the quiet response.

"What?!"

Lord Eadwig was on his feet, his face growing red with anger.

"He told them the country was now his – according to the treaty – and he was taking it. If anyone opposed him, he would confiscate their lands."

"Did no one speak up for me?"

Lord Godwine was quiet.

"Didn't you?"

"These are difficult times."

Lord Eadwig grabbed Lord Godwine's tunic and tried to shake him, but the slightly older man stood his ground.

"Stop this!" Lady Frida cried. "Eadwig, let go of him and sit down."

She sought to prise them apart.

"You've ratted on me," Lord Eadwig growled, as, reluctantly, he released the thegn and sat down.

"We have no power," Lady Frida urged. "Cnut is too strong for us."

"And the thegns don't want more fighting," Lord Godwine added. "They have fought the Danes for a year now, seen their lands ravaged and their people killed. The taste of peace is sweet."

"Peace! What does that mean with a tyrant on the throne?" Lord Eadwig snorted.

"Cnut may prove to be a good ruler," Lord Godwine responded. "We don't know yet."

"His legitimate claim is weak, so he resorts to threats." Lord Eadwig would not be pacified.

There was silence for a moment, a silence heavy with uncertainty and fear.

"There is more," Lord Godwine reported.

"More? News worse than this?"

The thegn's eyes were on his ale cup, which he fingered nervously.

"There really is something worse, isn't there?" Lady Frida whispered.

Lord Godwine still did not look up.

"Yes," he said quietly. "Cnut has ordered you, Lord Eadwig, to leave England."

The aetheling's face was frozen in horror and his red complexion slowly turned pale.

"I ...," he stuttered, "I ... am banished?"

Lord Godwine nodded. He still did not meet the young man's gaze.

No one in the room moved and no one seemed to be breathing. Banished? The only surviving son of Aethelred and his first wife would be a fugitive with a price on his head, in danger of death if he returned to his homeland.

"I'm sorry," Lord Godwine spoke eventually. "It is not what we wanted, but as Lady Frida says, we have no power. Cnut can do what he likes."

"How ... how long have I got?" Lord Eadwig's voice was barely audible.

"He commands that you be gone by Christmas."

"By Christmas?!" He was on his feet again. "That's but a few days. This is outrageous."

"Eadwig, please." Lady Frida too was on her feet. "Please, don't do anything foolish."

"I am a King's son and a King's brother. I am a member of the House of Cerdic."

"Go to Normandy," she urged. "Surely they will treat you kindly there."

"There is something else," Lord Godwine interposed, and there was a chill tone in his voice.

Lord Eadwig and Lady Frida both sat down again, suddenly aware that the nightmare was not over.

"Cnut has ...," Lord Godwine said slowly, "... has commanded me to ... to take Lady Frida and her son to London."

There was an audible gasp from everyone in the room.

CHAPTER 5

We had more time to prepare for our travelling than Lord Eadwig, who chose to leave Winchester immediately. He may have returned to the homestead near Newbury to gather what he could of his belongings and portable wealth and even a few faithful retainers, but I wasn't privy to that. My job was to work with Lord Godwine to prepare for Lady Frida's journey to London.

"I fear for our future," she confided to me. "If Cnut has banished one aetheling, what will he do with Edward?"

"He is a tiny child, my lady," I tried to reassure her. "He is no threat to Cnut."

"You will come with me, Wulfgar, won't you?" she pleaded. "I feel so alone."

"For as long as I can serve you, my lady, I will."

If she and Edward had also been exiled, I would have gone with her.

"Lord Godwine has not asked you to serve him?"

"No, my lady."

All of us who had served the King now had to find new lords. Thegns like Lord Godwine already had a large retinue and, anyway, I knew where my heart was.

The journey to London was miserable – three days of riding through mist and drizzle along muddy roads. Hild and Edith took care of Edward between them, while Lord Godwine and several of his men acted as a bodyguard.

We were not troubled by robbers, only by our gloomy thoughts.

I had tried to reassure Lady Frida, but, if I was honest, I too feared for the future. Cnut had rejected Lord Eadwig's claim and so must reject little Edward's. I wondered what had happened to King Aethelred's other sons. Queen Emma had borne him Edward and Alfred and a daughter. The girl wouldn't count, but the boys surely did, for Aethelred had become King when he was twelve, and Edward was maybe eleven or twelve, so old enough to be a king in theory. And that got me thinking about the Queen – where was she?

When we had gone to fight Cnut in Essex in mid-October, we had left her in London. After our defeat at Assandun, London had held out. The treaty at Deerhurst had left King Edmund with merely Wessex, and London, traditionally, was not part of Wessex. It wasn't really part of Mercia either, as it stood between the two great provinces, but Cnut had taken it anyway. Was Queen Emma still there or had she fled to her homeland, Normandy? I thought she must have fled and taken her children with her, but no one ever mentioned her and I did not feel bold enough to ask Lord Godwine. After all, it was irrelevant, or so I thought.

We reached London two days before Christmas and as the light was failing. Enquiries made by Lord Godwine revealed where we were to stay, at least for the present. It was a small room with only basic furniture and little warmth, but we were in no position to complain.

"You cannot sleep outside the door," Lady Frida told me.

"It isn't right that I sleep within," I responded.

"We will put up a screen to give us ladies some privacy. I insist, you cannot sleep outside."

I didn't argue after that, so had my mattress in a corner. It was a far cry from our accommodation in the palace in Winchester.

The next day we were summoned to meet King Cnut. He was in the grand hall. I remembered it well, for this was the place where Lord Edmund had been declared King by the Witan back in April. Now a stranger sat where he had sat, a man who could not even speak our language.

Lord Godwine led Lady Frida forward.

"Sire, this is the Lady Frida, the late King Edmund's widow," he announced.

How those words hurt! I could not see her face, but she held herself erect and proud. After all, she was an uncrowned queen.

"Velcome to London."

The Danish accent was obvious. I had only seen him in the distance, when the leaders met on the Island of Olney. Now I could see him more clearly. What struck me was his youth! He looked like a boy! He had very little facial hair and his cool green eyes were wide with interest.

Lady Frida gave him a slight curtsey, but did not bow her head.

"You come in time for Christmas," he added.

"I come at your command." Her voice did not quiver.

A smirk flitted over his face and he made some comment in his own language to a man who hovered at his elbow. This man now spoke.

"The King will make you more comfortable in a few days' time and invites you to feast with him and his court on Christmas Day."

"I accept his invitation, of course," she said, quite sweetly I thought, considering she really had no choice.

The King said something else to his translator, who then indicated the rest of us were to go forward.

"Your people?" the King asked.

"My son Edward, my ladies Hild and Edith, and my servant Wulfgar."

We bowed our heads to acknowledge the King, all except for Edward who was asleep. We were soon ushered back to our temporary quarters, each of us deep in thought. I realised he hadn't offered any condolences to Lady Frida for the death of her husband, but, then, he was hardly likely to, for King Edmund's death had been to his advantage. I suppose I had to be glad he wasn't playing the hypocrite.

I still couldn't get over how young he was – and yet he was now King of all England, he had beaten us at Assandun and he had since cowed all the thegns into submission. He might look little more than a boy, but he had a man's head on his shoulders and knew how to get his own way.

That was what frightened me – that we had absolutely no control over our future. We were now his subjects and he could do what he liked with us. No one had really stood up for Lord Eadwig, so no one was going to stand up for Lady Frida. The young Edward could prove to be an embarrassment.

I didn't relish the thought of feasting with the enemy – that's how I still thought of them. Little more than two months earlier, we had been trying to kill each other and now we were expected to sit side by side and appear to enjoy eating together.

On Christmas Eve, I accompanied Lady Frida to St. Paul's church, where the mystery of the Incarnation was rehearsed again and we were reminded that the name Immanuel means God with us. It didn't feel like it! We were the losers and the Danes made us feel as though God was on their side, not ours.

Ealdwine wouldn't have agreed. He would have told me off for my lack of faith and reminded me of the sovereignty of the Almighty and how right always triumphs in the end. How I missed Ealdwine! We had known each other for more than three years, and for much of that time, I had worked closely with him. I now could read and write as well as he could, though my Latin wasn't anything like as good. Like all of us he'd had to find a new role after the death of our King and had chosen to stay in Glastonbury.

I sighed and tried to concentrate on the liturgy and let God raise my spirits, for they were very low.

The next day, in the late afternoon, we were summoned to the hall where all of the King's court had gathered. I say "we", for the ladies and Edward were expected to be there, though they sat with the other ladies, while I was with some Danish servants.

I saw the King greet Lady Frida warmly and indicate she should sit by him, on his left. I was surprised at how gracious he appeared to be. I was much too far away to hear what they said, so watched them out of the corner of my eye, while listening to my companion's broken English.

I was shocked by what happened next. People stopped talking and looked at the latest guest to arrive. The Earl of Mercia strode forward with a lady's hand on his arm. Eadric the traitor was here – the man who had run away at Assandun and who encouraged the devastating peace treaty. I felt my body tense. I wanted to kill him, but I had no weapon and anyway he was too well protected.

Eadric bowed deeply to King Cnut and presented his lady. She too was warmly greeted. I had never seen his wife and therefore expected an unfamiliar face. The King indicated she should sit on his right, and as she turned, I saw someone I instantly recognised – none other than Queen Emma, wife of the late King Aethelred. I nearly fell off my stool!

The assembled court settled down to eat – venison, duck, salted pork, with fresh bread to soak up the delicious sauces. I made sure I ate well, but I could see that Lady Frida wasn't doing the same. The King tried to make conversation, but his English was clearly inadequate, as he frequently had to ask a translator to help. I could read all that from their body language. Occasionally, Lady Frida gave him a slight smile. I guessed she was being polite, but not effusive.

The King also talked to Queen Emma, but here there seemed to be no language barrier. She was a Norman and would know Norse as well as English. Unlike Lady Frida, she was very liberal in her smiles and it looked as though she was laughing at something the King said, appreciating jokes he was making. The ease with which they chatted meant the King said less to Lady Frida, but others around her were making conversation, so she was not totally ignored.

Queen Emma touched the King's arm and even leaned close to whisper something in his ear, something which made him laugh. I suddenly realised what I was watching. She was actually flirting with the King!

CHAPTER 6

I was so shocked at what I was witnessing that, for a moment, I stopped eating.

"You not like?" my neighbour asked.

"Oh, no." I pulled myself together. "The food is good."

"Ya, England good place for food," he commented.

I dug in my memory for what I knew about Cnut. He had come over to England with his father, Swein, when that Dane had conquered us in 1013. In fact, I was sure Cnut had married someone, an English woman who was part of an important northern family. Surely she had borne him a child, hadn't she?

"Tell me," I asked, as casually as I could, "is not the King married? I do not see he has a wife here."

"Ya, he married English woman. He has two sons."

"Two sons?"

"Swein and Harold."

"And where are they?"

"They live in the north."

Well, that explained why they weren't here, I thought. But why would Queen Emma be acting in such a familiar way if the King already had a wife? I had seen young girls acting like this with young unmarried men, but once a man was married, he was meant to have eyes only for his wife. King Cnut was clearly enjoying the attention she was giving him.

She must be nearly ten years older than him, I thought, but you'd never guess from the way she's behaving.

I was surprised that a former queen of England was acting like a silly girl, and was very pleased Lady Frida was being far more sensible. But there was a world of difference between the two women. Emma had been much younger than Aethelred and there were rumours it was not a happy marriage and that he had many mistresses. He had now been dead for eight months. Lady Frida's marriage to Lord Edmund was a love match; I knew that, for I had seen for myself how devoted to each other they were. She was in her early twenties I guessed, so a few years younger than him. Another big difference from the Queen was that Lady Frida had been a widow for less than a month. I couldn't imagine she felt like flirting with anyone.

A few days later, I was summoned to escort Lady Frida to visit the King and as she sat near him to converse, I sat well away, at the other end of the hall. Lord Godwine saw me and stopped.

"Is all well, Wulfgar?" he asked.

"Yes, my lord."

"I think the King is trying to find some more comfortable accommodation for Lady Frida," he commented. "I see he is talking to her now."

Their body language suggested the conversation wasn't easy, because the King was having to use his translator quite a bit. Lady Frida looked very serious.

"I noticed, my lord, that Queen Emma was at the feast on Christmas Day. I was very surprised to see her. I thought she would have returned to Normandy."

"I'm also surprised she's still in London," he conceded. "She was here at the time of Assandun, but I don't know what happened after that. When we got news of the treaty, I left and returned to Compton, my estate near Chichester. Then, of course, I accompanied the late King Edmund to Bath and Glastonbury."

"So, are her children here too?" I asked.

"No. Someone told me only yesterday that they left the country a few weeks ago, before King Cnut took control of London, so it is puzzling that she didn't leave too. I'm sure her brother in Normandy would give her a home and he might even find her a second husband. In about four months, she could marry again."

"Four months?" I queried.

"It is usual for a widow to wait a year before she marries again." He looked at me and grinned slightly. "But we both know someone who was only without a husband for a matter of days."

Lady Frida! I thought. Lord Edmund had heard of her husband's murder and rushed to rescue her from her imprisonment in Malmesbury Abbey. They certainly hadn't waited a month, let alone a year!

I returned his half-smile. A widow was vulnerable, she needed a protector if she had no property and Lady Frida would have lost all her first husband's lands if Lord

Edmund had not claimed them so rapidly. The estates were in the north, so truly lost to both of them after the treaty, and now Cnut had Wessex too, she had nothing. She was totally dependent on his goodwill, but from what I could see, he was trying hard to be pleasant.

We got other invitations to eat with the King and his court and I noticed he was always very gracious to Lady Frida and gave her a place of honour. I noticed too that a place of honour was given to the arch-traitor, the man who, in my eyes, had cost us victory at Assandun. Eadric was certainly sucking up to the King and appeared to have ingratiated himself with the Danes. Well, if he was responsible for their victory at Assandun, that was hardly surprising! Before he pulled his men from the battle, we English had outnumbered the Danes.

I was engrossed in such bitter thoughts, when I was joined at the eating bench by another Englishman.

"You were part of King Edmund's household, they tell me," he began.

I nodded.

"It is said he was murdered."

"No, it's not true," I replied. "He was ill and there was concern he was being poisoned, but I tasted all his food and drink and never had a problem, so he definitely didn't die from poisoning."

"Oh, I hadn't heard about the possibility of poison," my companion responded. "I heard ..." He looked around

41

and lowered his voice. "I heard he was attacked while he relieved himself."

I simply stared at him.

"A man is very vulnerable when he's pooing," he added.

"Well, that's not true either!" I was genuinely shocked at the suggestion. "He died peacefully in his bed."

"So no one stuck a spear up his arse?"

"No, they did not!"

"Oh."

He looked disappointed. I was horrified, partly by the nature of the story that was being spread and partly that some people hoped it was true. The picture of my young, brave, noble King being so shamelessly attacked and killed in such a painful and brutal way made me feel sick and I picked up my ale cup and moved to join another bench.

The horrific picture wouldn't leave me and as I gazed across the hall at Eadric's greasy, grinning face, I began to form a plan. He always had a couple of burly retainers with him, against whom I with my seax stood no chance. I needed to find an opportunity when he was alone and vulnerable, and the tale told me about my late King was giving me an idea as to when that might be.

I first had to find out where he lodged. To do that I singled out a few of his henchmen and casually followed them. It only took a couple of days to establish the location of his accommodation.

Does he use a piss pot in his room? I wondered. Or does he come out to the midden round the back? There was a pit across which a bench with a hole in it had been placed. But even if he did use this, how could I make sure I was there at the right time?

I wanted to pray for God's help, but I had a nasty feeling he wouldn't want to give it to me. If Ealdwine were around, the priest would tell me I was plotting murder and God had commanded we did not kill like that. It was one matter to kill a man in battle when your own life was in danger and your country had been invaded by foreigners, but it was another matter to murder someone in cold blood.

I didn't care, for this man deserved to die. He had taken his men from the battlefield at Assandun, causing us to be defeated. In my eyes that meant he had been responsible for the huge number of Englishmen who had lost their lives there and he should pay the price for his treachery. King Edmund could have brought a charge against him, but Cnut appeared to condone what had happened – which was hardly surprising! I thought Eadric felt he, and he alone, had gained the throne for the Dane. If I chose, I could spread rumours that the Mercian Earl had murdered my King, except that quite a few people had already heard me say the death was natural.

Having located the midden, I also planned how I would escape, because I knew from my experience at Assandun that he would scream like hell and I would have to run. I soon knew my way through those back alleys. But would I get the opportunity?

I watched Eadric as he feasted that evening. He was eating plenty of rich food and washing it down with either ale or mead; from my seat, I couldn't tell which. Surely he would need to relieve himself of all that? In a few hours I reckoned he'd need the midden and decided to take my chance.

I hardly slept that night and was up long before the wintry sun had made an appearance. I blackened my face with wood ash from the fire and tied my cloak in such a way that my head was well covered. I didn't want to risk being recognised as I made my way through the silent streets and alleyways.

I had worked out a good place to hide within a few yards of the pit. An hour passed and only one man had come and I could see, even in the dim light, that it wasn't the man I was waiting for. The stench was beginning to get to me and make me feel sick. Perhaps I was right about the piss pot.

Then I heard a belch and saw someone else was coming – a man, and he had a rush light with him, which illuminated his face. It was Eadric and he was alone. Surely God had delivered my enemy into my hands.

CHAPTER 7

The Earl had no idea he was being watched as he put the light down on the ground. He belched again and then drew up his tunic to sit on the bench. My seax was ready. He farted and began to empty his bowels. Now was the moment.

I sprang forward, every muscle in my body ready to thrust the blade hard into his bare buttocks. But he must have heard me, for he moved quickly and his arm hit my weapon broadside, deflecting it from its target. He was on his feet and swung to face me. He had no sword, but he was a big man and somehow he managed to hit my head with his fist, making me stagger back.

I still held my seax, but I had lost the moment, and in a straight fight, I stood no chance against this bulky warrior, so I took to my heels and fled, never looking back.

Eventually, I stopped running and gulped in the cold dawn air. No one was about and I was able to slink back to our base unseen. I had hoped to creep into our room without disturbing the others, but as I gently pushed on the door, it was pulled wide open by someone inside.

"Wulfgar, where have you been?" Lady Frida demanded. "And look at you!"

She pulled me in and held a rush light near my face.

"Oh, my God, what have you been doing? Your face is black and your forehead is bleeding."

She pushed the door to and dragged me over to a stool, where I was made to sit. She stood over me, still holding the light.

"You've been out for hours," she said. "I know because I rose and found you gone. I've been worried sick. Now, I want the truth, the whole truth. Where have you been?"

It was hard to meet her eye, as I felt both a fool and a failure.

"You stink like a midden too," she added.

"That's where I've been," I confessed, "lying in wait by the midden used by Eadric."

I sensed her body stiffen.

"Where's your seax?" she demanded and, fumbling under my cloak, she pulled it from my belt and held it in the light to inspect it carefully.

"It's clean," she said. "Were you trying to kill him?"

"Yes, but I failed. He was ... unprotected, but he must have ears like a wild cat. As I lunged forward, he turned and deflected the blow."

"And pissed on you," she added. "That's why you stink. Did he recognise you?"

"I don't think so. I had blackened my face with ash from our fire and I kept my hood up. It was all over so quickly that I don't think he saw my features."

I looked up to see her staring at me, her forehead creased with anxiety.

46

"Let's pray he never knows who it was or you will pay a high price." She sighed and sat down opposite me. "Whatever were you thinking of?"

"He's a traitor, my lady. It's all his fault we lost at Assandun. If he hadn't run away with his men, we would have won and King Edmund would still be King of all of England."

"I'm not sure he would," she said quietly. "His sickness might still have claimed him." She sighed again. "But I know what you mean and I understand your anger, but, Wulfgar, you must not try to kill him. Promise me you will never be so foolish again?"

The look of pleading on her face melted my heart. I couldn't bear to see her so distressed.

"I promise," I said, "but I still hate him and can't forgive him."

"You must learn to let go of your hate because it is you it will eat and destroy, not Eadric."

"Don't you hate him, my lady? After all, he had your first husband killed, as well as acting as a traitor to King Edmund."

"His men did kill Siferth, but I'm sure that was on the orders of King Aethelred. Eadric is a weak man really. He bends in each wind. He seeks only his own gain." She paused. "I do not hate him. I pity him."

"Pity?! He's a rat! He needs no pity!" I exploded.

"He does. He has no true manhood and apparently no conscience. I wouldn't want to be in his shoes when he faces the Day of Judgement."

"Well, sadly, he didn't face it this morning," I groaned. "I doubt if I even drew blood."

"But he did." She stood up and bent over me. "He hit you and I think he must have been wearing a ring, for you have bled. I will dress the wound and you must stay out of his way until it has healed."

She found some water, salt and a clean cloth.

"It looks worse than it is," she commented, after bathing the wound. "How did you know he would be there?"

"I didn't," I admitted. "I took a chance and had to wait ages. But then he came and it was like a godsend, as though God was putting him in my power."

"You may have been praying you would get the opportunity to kill him, but back here I was praying you'd come to no harm and get into no trouble."

I didn't tell her I hadn't dared to pray that because I knew in my heart, it was wrong, so it was no wonder God had perhaps answered her prayer and frustrated my efforts to commit murder.

She was now using the water to wipe the dirt from my face. She was wonderfully close to me, but I couldn't relish the moment, for I could smell my clothes and so could she.

"Now change out of these clothes and I'll get Hild to wash them," she ordered, as she moved away. "It was a blessing Eadric had no dog with him or you might not be alive."

That was a sobering thought. I doubt if I could have outrun a dog.

The rest of the day passed quietly and we all kept away from the court. If I had killed him, Eadric could have done nothing, but he was alive and could even now be seeking the identity of his attacker. If he found out it was me, or rather, if he *suspected* it was me and accused me, it would be his word against mine, the word of his supporters against the word of mine – and I had none, no lord to declare I couldn't possibly be guilty of such a crime. I wouldn't stand a chance. A moneyer discovered making false coins had his hand cut off. What might they do to me?

I had been foolish, but it was too late now. I had tried to kill an earl, and failed, so my future looked bleak.

The only comfort I had was that the light had been poor, my features unclear, and the encounter very brief. Surely I was not the only man who hated him for his treachery, but some knew I had served the late King and now served his widow. I would be a prime suspect.

The following day, I was doing my usual chores when a messenger appeared at our door.

"Are you Lady Frida's man?" he demanded.

"Yes."

"The King wants to speak to you. You are to come with me."

My heart started beating faster. I looked across to where Lady Frida sat by the brazier. Our eyes met. We didn't need to say anything – we had but a single thought.

I said nothing. I grabbed my outer cloak and went with him. My mouth was dry with fear. How could Eadric know it had been me? I'm not a good liar, but I was going to have to bluff this one out.

Too soon I was being ushered through the occupants of the hall to stand and bow before the King. Again I was struck by the fact he looked so young. Might he have pity on a foolish youth who now regretted his hot-headed action? I doubted it. He might look young, but he had a cool head. Three years ago he had mutilated his English hostages by cutting off their noses, ears and hands. What might he order was done to me?

His icy green eyes bore into me.

"You belong Lady Frida?"

"Yes, sire," I managed to say.

"Your name?"

"Wulfgar, sire."

I was not surprised he didn't remember being introduced to Lady Frida's people.

"You with King Edmund too?"

"Yes, sire."

The eyes barely blinked.

"You loyal?"

"Of course!"

I had been trapped. I'd confessed to serving the late King and to being loyal to him and his widow. I had virtually admitted my guilt.

CHAPTER 8

The King was still holding my gaze. I dared not look away, as I had to make myself look innocent, but I could feel my face was beginning to burn. He turned to his translator and spoke in his own tongue.

"The King says," his translator began, "that he respects loyalty. He has found a new place for your mistress and asks you to arrange the removal of all persons and of all your goods."

I blinked. I nearly opened my mouth in amazement. He ... he wasn't accusing me of attempted murder after all!

"W ... where are we ... to go?" I stuttered.

"Vestminster," the King answered.

"The King is putting Lady Frida and her son into the care of the Abbot of Westminster," the man added, "and hopes she will be more comfortable there."

"Th ... thank you, sire," I managed to mutter, and bowed again.

"Also, the King asks that you take good care of her."

"Oh, I will!" I replied warmly.

This was the end of my audience with the King and I was free to go. Free! I could hardly believe it! A little voice did say I shouldn't relax just yet, but another voice argued that if Eadric was going to accuse me, he would have done so by now.

Lady Frida was thrilled by my news. She, too, had feared the call was the result of my attack on the Earl and was relieved that, at least for the moment, I was not under a cloud of accusation.

"The King said he respects loyalty, my lady, but how can he, when he rewards Eadric for his treachery?"

"Maybe it serves his purpose to turn a blind eye to Eadric's lack of loyalty," she replied. "But you are to put Eadric out of your thoughts, Wulfgar. This move is good news."

She was delighted when she saw our new accommodation. We were to have two rooms, the one accessible from the other. The inner room would act as a bedchamber for her, Edward, Hild and Edith, while the outer room would be our living area and the place where I would sleep. The Abbot would supply our food from his kitchen and there was a well, which gave fresh water, in an easily accessible courtyard. We were further from the King's court, perhaps a mile or more away, and so the Abbot also provided Lady Frida with a horse from his stable.

I say the Abbot, but really I mean his servants. He visited us briefly to bid us welcome, though he was not effusive in this and I did wonder if he'd been put upon by the King and was expected to look after us out of his own income. Clearly, Lady Frida had no money or resources and was dependent on charity.

"Perhaps the King will give you an estate, my lady," I suggested, "and then you can be independent."

She had a wistful look on her face.

"What a blessing that would be," she sighed, "but I fear it's unlikely. If I had no child, my future would be in a nunnery, but because my son is an aetheling, I cannot be allowed my independence. The King wants me where he can control what happens to Edward."

"I don't think the Abbot will be very pleased if he has to provide for us for the next twenty odd years," I commented.

She gave me a rare smile.

"I think you are right there, Wulfgar. He does not strike me as a man given to long-term charity."

It was a situation none of us relished, but we were powerless to change it. We continued to be invited to eat with the King and he was always polite and gracious to my lady.

"Wulfgar, I have some good news," she reported one day as I escorted her back to Westminster. "Do you realise we have not seen Eadric since ... you know when?"

"I certainly haven't seen him, my lady," I agreed.

"That is because the day after your ... encounter, he left London."

"Left?"

"Yes. The King has made him Earl of Mercia, as everyone expected, and he has gone home to Shrewsbury to ensure his area does not rebel against Danish rule."

"That is good news!" I agreed. "At least for us, though maybe not for the people of Mercia."

Shortly after, still in the early part of January, something happened that would prove to be very significant, though we didn't know it at the time.

I took my lady to court, but as she dismounted, she caught my arm.

"Oh, Wulfgar, I am a little dizzy today," she complained. "Let me lean on you as we go in."

I was happy to oblige, but hoped her dizziness was nothing serious. As we came to the entrance to the hall, we saw Lord Godwine talking to an older man, who still retained his good looks and held his frame erect like a man who knows himself and is not ashamed of what he knows.

"Lady Frida!" Lord Godwine greeted us. "Are you alright?"

"A little faint that's all."

The handsome stranger's deep-set blue eyes were fixed on her face. His blonde hair had streaks of white in it, adding to his air of nobility. I reckoned he was probably in his forties.

"Let me introduce you to the latest addition to our court," Lord Godwine continued. "This is Lord Valgar, recently arrived from Denmark." He turned to the Dane. "Lady Frida is the widow of our late King Edmund," he added.

Lord Valgar bowed his head, but without taking his eyes from her face.

"I am honoured," he said warmly. "I have heard much about your husband's bravery."

55

His English was remarkably good for a foreigner, but there was still the hint of an accent.

Lady Frida gave him a warm smile and, without realising, revealed what a beautiful face she had. Lord Valgar was still staring at her and now returned her smile.

"I hope King Cnut is good to you."

"Yes, my lord, he has given me and my son rooms at Westminster."

"Vestminster? Is that far?"

"A mile or so, but the Abbot provides me with a horse to travel here."

"And so he should," was the warm response.

Lord Godwine had been completely forgotten in this exchange and now spoke.

"Shall we go in?"

"Dear lady, let me take your arm," Lord Valgar offered, and I had to stand aside.

From my corner in the hall, I watched my mistress and saw how attentive Lord Valgar was and how easily he engaged her in conversation. Lord Godwine was elsewhere, talking to other thegns and King Cnut wasn't there that day.

Later, Lord Valgar delivered Lady Frida back to my care.

"I did not know I would find...," he struggled for the right English words, "... such sunlight in the winter," he said, smiling.

Lady Frida returned his smile and thanked him for his attention.

I was carefully scrutinising his face and knew what I saw there. He admired her, that was obvious.

He's falling in love with her, I thought. He is not the first man to find her so completely captivating.

As we made our way back to Westminster, I wondered if that was where our future lay. Some man would seek her hand in marriage, for she was very beautiful and still young. Then she would have a protector and provider. But could that happen when she had an aetheling as her child? Might she abandon Edward? I couldn't imagine that, but ... in dark times, we can make unnatural decisions.

The next day, Lady Frida did not stir from the room. She was quieter than usual and lethargic, but didn't complain of dizziness. However, the following morning, I could see she was very pale. She picked at her food and then suddenly rose and made for the door.

"Wulfgar, your arm!" she cried, and I was immediately at her side. "The courtyard, quickly."

I helped her into the fresh air. There was a raw breeze and the threat of snow. She leaned against the wall and began to retch. I was back with my King, agonising over his sickness. Could my lovely mistress be about to suffer the same fate?

After a few minutes, she stopped and began to breathe deeply. Her eyes were closed and her whole body was against the cold wall.

"My lady?"

She reached out her hand and I took it in mine. It was icy cold and I began to rub it, hoping thereby to warm it.

"My lady, are you ill?" I whispered, eaten up with anxiety.

"No." Her eyes opened and I could see how bright they were – surely not the eyes of a woman about to die?

"Wulfgar, I am with child."

CHAPTER 9

"With ... with child?" I stuttered.

"I have lost my dear husband, but he has left me a precious gift." She smiled. "I am carrying his child."

"Oh!"

I was truly shocked. It had never occurred to me that she could be pregnant, but, of course, she and the King had been inseparable since the late part of October. In the six or so weeks before his death, she had conceived his child.

"Oh, that's wonderful!" I gasped.

"Yes, it is wonderful," she answered quietly. "God has blessed me, but say nothing – not yet. Hild and Edith know, but I want no one else to know until I cannot hide the fact."

I frowned, but nodded.

"It may make things worse," she explained. "If the child is a boy and he lives, that means two aethelings to snap at Cnut's heels, not just one."

"Yes," I said slowly. "I see."

Another child, especially if it were a boy, could make things even more difficult.

"Pray for me," she said. "Pray for my child too."

She laid her free hand on her stomach.

"Of course, my lady."

She had given birth to one healthy baby, but we all knew how dangerous childbirth was. Her husband hadn't been with her for the birth of Edward because he'd been with his dying father. He couldn't be with her this time either, but for a very different reason. It struck me again how alone she was and how desperate I was to do my best to serve her.

Once past these early stages of pregnancy, Lady Frida began to be much happier and she had an aura I hadn't seen before and a freshness and bloom to her features, which enhanced her beauty.

Lord Valgar must have noticed, for whenever she went to court, he made sure he spent time with her. It was obvious to me that he was in love with her and I wondered if the rest of the court could see it.

Occasionally, Queen Emma was also there. She never spoke to Lady Frida and always tried to monopolise the King. There was still an element of flirtation in her actions towards him – an arching of the eyebrows, the secret smile, the whispered comment. However, the King was also attentive to Lady Frida, and at such times Lord Valgar had to step aside and wait patiently until the place at her side became vacant again. Two events changed all this.

We were in Westminster, when Lord Godwine suddenly arrived and interrupted our quiet day.

"I think you should know," he said, once the formalities of greeting had been completed, "Lord Eadwig has returned to England."

"No!" Lady Frida cried. "Where is he?"

"In the West Country, doing exactly what we hoped he wouldn't do – raising a rebellion."

She gasped.

"There is some support, of course," Lord Godwine continued, "but there won't be enough."

"Has the King sent a force to crush him? Will he go in person? Oh, Godwine, what is going to happen?"

"The King will not go," Lord Godwine replied. "He will not want to make this look serious, so he will send a force. He has plenty of trained men who can deal with such a rebellion."

"More bloodshed!" Lady Frida moaned. "There was so much last summer and now there will be more. Oh, foolish Eadwig, why did you not stay abroad?"

"He has the late King's courage, but perhaps not his wisdom," Lord Godwine sighed.

"My lord was impulsive sometimes and did not always think through the consequences of his actions," she countered. "But ... but the situation is so different now. King Cnut is tightening his grip on England, is he not? I pick up some bits of news at court."

"Eadric was given responsibility for Mercia, and Thorkell has been sent to East Anglia. There is more Danish sympathy in the north – there always has been, as you know. The King's man there is Eric of Lade. The King, I believe, intends to concentrate on Wessex, rooting out any English support that may be lurking there."

She nodded.

"As I thought," she sighed. "Any rebellions will be crushed. Eadwig doesn't stand a chance. Oh, why could he not have made a new life for himself abroad?"

Lord Godwine cleared his throat and Lady Frida looked at him sharply.

"Is there more?" she asked.

"Only rumours, my lady."

"What?" she demanded.

"Some people are saying that Lord Eadwig was ... was enticed back to England."

She stared at Lord Godwine, but said nothing.

"That the King paid men in the West Country to ... to pretend to pledge their support. Once Lord Eadwig was back on English soil, he could be ... be killed without impunity, because he would be in breach of the order of banishment."

"That is a foul plan!" she exclaimed.

"We don't know it's true," Lord Godwine countered. "It is merely a story, but ..." His voice trailed off.

"You believe it could be true, don't you?"

He nodded.

"The King is very clever and very ruthless," he said. "Having gained the throne of all England, he will not let it go. We need to realise ... and I'm sorry to say this ... realise that the House of Aethelred has no future here."

Lady Frida's hand instinctively went to her stomach, as though seeking to protect her unborn child. I noticed this action, but I don't think Lord Godwine did. Her face went pale – that he could see.

"I'm sorry, my lady," he apologised, "but I think you need to know that your son might one day be a ... a problem to the King."

"Yes, I see that. I have always known it and I pray constantly for God's protection. However, I am grateful for the information you bring."

Soon afterwards, Lord Godwine left and my lady was very quiet for the rest of the day. Much of the time I suspect she was praying, silently pleading with God for ... what? By now, for all we knew, Lord Eadwig might already be dead, because it took days for news to travel from the West Country to London.

We were not at court for the next few days and I wondered if the King would ever invite her back, in view of her brother-in-law's rebellion. However, for Candlemas, we went to St. Paul's as we had done for Christmas and were to dine at court the next day.

I remembered so clearly the Candlemas service of three years before, when I had been in York with Archbishop Wulfstan. Then we were a conquered country as we were today, Swein having been accepted as King by all the thegns and even London being under his control. Shortly afterwards news had come that Swein had died, his life snuffed out at the very moment, it seems, we snuffed out our candles. I couldn't see King Cnut dying though – he was far too young – but King Edmund hadn't been that much older and yet no longer lived, and that was the cause of all our present troubles.

I escorted Lady Frida to the hall and she was given her usual place on the King's left, the right side being occupied by Queen Emma. I couldn't see that anything had changed, except I did wonder if the King said less to my lady than usual.

Lord Valgar was there and took every opportunity he could to talk to Lady Frida.

He must know about the rebellion, I thought. They all must know, and do they know Lord Eadwig's fate?

I did not raise the subject with the group of retainers with whom I sat. We were trying to outdo each other with riddles, the ruder the better. The Danes, I discovered, loved our earthy humour.

"England good place for rude jokes," laughed my companion, slapping me on the back.

Being with women most of my time, I liked this male company, even if it was a bit bawdy. I missed having a lord as my master, but I would not have left Lady Frida, even if offered a small fortune.

As I escorted her back, I noticed she was very quiet.

"Are you tired, my lady?" I asked.

"Tired, yes, but tired of men's ambition," was her soft answer. "Wulfgar, why can we not learn to live in peace?"

"I don't know, my lady."

"Yet I understand Eadwig's rebellion, because he should have been King. I do not believe my husband agreed to Cnut taking the whole kingdom."

"Is there news?" I asked tentatively.

"Yes and it is the worst." She paused. "He was killed and has been buried at Tavistock."

CHAPTER 10

The invitations to be at court now became infrequent and I was sure the King was cooler towards Lady Frida when she was there. By early April, she could not hide her pregnancy and now the King did not have her sit by him. It was good that Lord Valgar was there to take care of her, for I sensed the thegns in general were wary. They didn't want to appear to favour anyone who might be a threat to the King. Lady Frida herself was no threat, but she was inevitably linked with the failed rebellion led by the late King's brother and she was the mother of one aetheling and the potential mother of perhaps another. Even Lord Godwine seemed less willing to be seen in our company.

Our position was more difficult than ever and I had grave misgivings about the future, but *that* was beyond our control. In the meantime I had to watch the outrageous behaviour of Queen Emma.

Her year as a widow was drawing to an end and she had redoubled her efforts to flirt with the King. He was totally engrossed by her, but I was puzzled, for he could not marry her, so what was going on?

In late April, it all became clear. The King announced he was to marry the late King Aethelred's widow.

"How can he?" I cried, as soon as I was alone with Lady Frida.

"He is the King and believes he can do what he likes," she answered. "Lord Valgar says he will probably put aside his first wife, or may even continue to keep her somewhere."

"The bishops won't like that, will they?"

"No, but what can they do?" She sighed. "It's political, of course. Lord Valgar says the King hopes by this marriage to neutralise any challenge from Queen Emma's sons."

"What do you mean, my lady?" I genuinely didn't understand.

"Edward and Alfred are in Normandy with their uncle, who could decide to back their claim to the throne of England, but he will give no military aid if his sister is married to the King."

"Oh, I see, but I'm still surprised the Queen chose to stay here rather than seek refuge with her children."

"She has abandoned her children in favour of again being Queen of England." There was a tone of disapproval in Lady Frida's voice. "She may well enjoy being bedded by a man much younger than herself," she added.

There was nothing more I could say.

The wedding was to be in July and that was also the month when Lady Frida's child was due. We stayed in Westminster all the time now and I could feel my anxiety growing. She, on the other hand, seemed remarkably at peace, as she sat with her hands laid over her swollen abdomen, silently praying. Sometimes I went with her into the church, which was much cooler than our accommodation. One of the ladies would come too, while the other played with Edward, who was beginning to walk and get into everything, so that he needed someone with eyes only for him. Soon, we hoped, he would have a healthy sibling.

Thus it was that while London celebrated the unlikely marriage of King Cnut and the former Queen, a former King's child was entering our uncertain world.

"Wulfgar, get some clean water," Hild ordered.

When I looked a bit puzzled by the request, she added, "Lady Frida has gone into labour, you idiot! Oh, and when you come back, you'll need to look after Edward. We don't want him under our feet at a time like this."

I did as I was told and remained playing with little Edward and within shouting distance for the next few hours, while, in the inner room, the women were doing what women do at such a time. Never having seen the birth of a human, I had no idea what that involved, but I heard the groans, which turned eventually into agonising cries and I feared for my lady's life. Then there was a frightening moment of quiet before I heard different cries – those of a child! Even then, I had to wait ages for Hild to emerge with a bowl of bloodied cloths.

"Is all well?" I asked anxiously.

She smiled, yes, she *smiled*!

"A boy," she announced.

"And my lady?"

"Tired, but happy."

I took that to mean she was not in imminent danger of death, but I was still anxious, for I knew that sometimes there was bleeding which could not be stopped.

It was the next day before I saw Lady Frida and her new son. She was paler than usual, but couldn't stop smiling, as she looked at the tiny bundle in her arms.

"Wulfgar, I'm going to call him Edmund," she said.

"That is very fitting, my lady," I agreed.

It was wonderful to see her smiling, but, of course, her joy must have been tinged with sadness that the child's father would never see him.

We had been in our own little world for several days, hardly aware of what was going on in the rest of the city, but news of the birth must have reached the court, for a basket of honey cakes came as a gift from Lord Valgar, and then something much more sinister happened.

I was having to keep Edward amused because the newborn was so demanding. I often took him into the courtyard to play, but, one day, I thought I would take him down to the river and show him all the boats.

I came to the gateway that gave us access to the street and found a burly man blocking my path.

"No kint leave!" he ordered. "King says kint to stay."

"I cannot take this child for a walk, is that what you're saying?" I asked, genuinely puzzled.

"King's orders. Kint ... child to stay. You can go."

I felt my insides going cold. Had King Cnut really ordered the children to remain in the abbey precincts? I took Edward back to the courtyard and found some games to play. I didn't want to worry Lady Frida, so decided at some appropriate moment I would go to the court to find out for myself.

The next day, I suggested I find Lord Valgar and thank him for his gift, and Lady Frida agreed, so I went to court in search of him. Eventually, he appeared and I took my opportunity.

"Lord Valgar, Lady Frida has sent me to thank you for the cakes," I began. "She is very grateful and thanks you for your kindness."

"Is she well?"

"Yes, and the child is too. She has named him Edmund."

Lord Valgar smiled.

"That is very appropriate. How hard it must be for her that her husband is not here to see his son."

"She views the child as a precious gift."

"Tell her I pray for her and her children."

I glanced around, but no one was taking much notice of us.

"She needs it," I said quietly. "I think the King has put a guard on us."

He raised his eyebrows.

"How so?"

"I tried to leave with Edward, but a Danish retainer ordered me not to take the child out. He said the King had ordered the children to stay."

"I have not heard that," he replied in a low voice. "Stay in the court awhile and I will see what I can find out."

So I chatted to some of the young men with whom I often ate.

"We haven't seen you for a while," one said.

"The court's been a bit busy, hasn't it?" I responded. "Celebrating a wedding."

"Ah, we had good food that day. Shame you missed it. We told a lot of rude jokes that night," he added, winking.

I could imagine, though I reckoned people would be very careful not to make direct allusions to the fact that the Queen was a good ten years older than her husband. Nor did I imagine anyone considered the fate of her children by King Aethelred, for whom permanent exile now seemed likely. And certainly no one was thinking about the children of the late King Edmund – except Lord Valgar.

Quite some time passed before I saw Lord Valgar. He caught my eye and then left the hall, so I casually followed him until he came to the butts and joined other men practising archery. I too took up a bow and some arrows. A moment came when we were both retrieving our arrows from the targets.

"I have news," he said without looking at me.

I concentrated on my arrows.

"You are right," he told me. "The new wife – she doesn't like to see the children of King Edmund."

"Are their lives in danger?"

"They may be. Take care of them, young man."

That was all he said and we both pretended to practise for a little longer before going our separate ways.

CHAPTER 11

I went back to Westminster in low spirits. I would have to say something to Lady Frida, for she needed to know the situation and how serious it was. I noticed our "guard" today was a much younger man, who gave me a pleasant smile, which I returned. At least, I thought, he doesn't look like a child-killer.

"You have been away a long time, Wulfgar," Lady Frida noted, and I could see her scanning my face. "Was Lord Valgar hard to find?"

"No," I admitted, "but I asked him something and the answer took a while."

"There is something wrong, isn't there? I know that look on your face."

I tried to look away.

"Is it something to do with the Dane, who now stands outside our gate?"

"You've seen him?"

I couldn't stop myself from glancing at her.

"Hild saw him. There was a different man there yesterday, she says."

"They are there on the King's orders," I confessed, "charged with making sure the children do not leave. I tried to take Edward out the other day and was stopped. Lord Valgar confirmed what I feared and added that the measure might be laid at the feet of Queen Emma."

"Ah, I did wonder," she sighed. "She is a woman who thinks only of herself."

I said nothing.

"When she married King Aethelred, she insisted her children take precedence over those of the King's first wife, but, of course, her Edward was far too young when Aethelred died, and the Witan chose Edmund."

"The best choice, my lady," I responded warmly and was rewarded with a gracious smile.

"When Edmund died, she had to make a decision, go into exile or ... try to defeat the new king. She had no sword; she had a far more subtle weapon."

I remembered her flirting at Christmas and thought how she hadn't wasted any time in her assault on Cnut.

"If she were Cnut's ally rather than his enemy, then he had less to fear from her children by Aethelred," she explained.

"I think you said Normandy won't fight for Edward and Alfred while their mother is married to King Cnut."

"Exactly. The alliance benefits them both. Cnut can be sure Normandy won't attack and Emma gets to be Queen of England again." She paused. "She will not want her position threatened by any aethelings."

"And since Lord Eadwig's death, there are only two aethelings in England – your sons, my lady."

She was quiet for a moment.

"Our situation is grave indeed."

"Lord Valgar says he's praying for you."

"God bless him for that. At least I have one friend."

Once Lady Frida was fully recovered, she resumed her visits to the court. If the King was there, he was usually engrossed by his new wife, but others were more polite and Lord Valgar seemed not to fear being seen as her friend, for he often sat by her. I continued to escort her there, but we left Hild and Edith with the children with strict instructions to take great care of them. Lady Frida didn't like leaving them, but felt it was important she maintain her position among those at court.

The talk now was of a coronation, though no one knew when it might be.

"All the opposition's been eliminated," one of the young Englishmen commented to me. "King Cnut's got control of the whole country and there'd be no point rebelling. Who'd lead a rebellion anyway? A snotty-nosed lad?"

I thought of twelve-year-old Edward in exile in Normandy. I had spent several weeks as his "minder" the previous summer and thought him spoiled and arrogant, hardly likely to inspire men to fight for him. I agreed there was no one, but couldn't trust myself to say so.

"No one's likely to invade, either," I remarked. "Denmark is ruled by the King's brother and Normandy by the King's brother-in-law. What do we know about Norway?"

"Norway? The King there is Olaf Haraldson. He's only held power for about two years, so he's not likely to try and extend his kingdom yet."

"I remember Olaf Haraldson. He fought for King Aethelred back in 1014 and used his boats to bring down Southwark Bridge."

"I remember that!"

We reminisced about the way the King had overcome the Danes and recaptured London.

"It's the only time I can remember King Aethelred leading his troops," my companion remarked. "He made a lot of mistakes after that and left his successor a bitter legacy."

"But King Edmund rose to the challenge."

"Don't defend him too loudly in the present company," he replied in a low voice and winked.

I grimaced. We were a conquered people with a foreign king and no hope of seeing an English monarch back on the throne for many a year. Even if Queen Emma gave Cnut no sons, there were always the two he'd already got, unless they were now regarded as illegitimate. The King was playing a very cunning game. What had Lord Godwine said? Clever and ruthless. Was he so heartless he would have two small boys killed in cold blood? I wasn't sure, but I had a nasty feeling his wife would do it and have no conscience. How could we save these aethelings from an early death?

Back in Westminster, I found there was a glimmer of hope.

"Wulfgar, come here."

I hurried to my lady. She pulled me down onto a bench by her side.

"I need to talk to you," she whispered.

I nodded, though I was at a complete loss as to what was so secret.

"You know Lord Valgar is our friend?"

I nodded again, my eyes fixed on her pale face.

"He wants to help us."

Because he loves you, I thought.

"He has estates in Denmark," she continued, her voice barely audible. "He will give us a home there."

"But how ...?" I stopped. What madness was this? I found my voice again and whispered, "We are the King's prisoners."

"I know," she acknowledged, and sighed. "He has two boats on the river. We would leave with him under the cover of darkness. We would be out of the Thames before dawn. He says his boats are fast, his oarsmen strong, and if the wind were from the west, we would be safe within a few days."

"We? Is he willing to take all of us?"

"Yes, I said I would not go without you."

I was stunned. Escaping from Cnut in Danish boats! What a great enterprise!

"But, my lady, how can we leave here undetected?"

"I don't know," she admitted. "Try and think of something, Wulfgar. Lord Valgar can only help us once we are out of Westminster."

Here was a challenge, a big one. We had the offer of a refuge, a safe place beyond the clutches of the King, but how could we escape our prison? Lady Frida was not really restricted in her movements, but her children were and there was no way she would leave them. That would be pointless anyway, because her life wasn't in danger. It was the two young aethelings who posed a threat to Cnut, or might be a threat when they were older.

I lay on my straw mattress, gazing up into the darkness.

"Lord God," I prayed, "thank you for Lord Valgar, but how do we get out of here unseen? Please help us."

One of the children whimpered in the room next door; otherwise there was only silence. I cherished my lady's trust and I desperately wanted to find an answer. I wanted to be a hero in this desperate situation, but, at the moment, my hope was very faint.

CHAPTER 12

"Wulfgar, a word with you – where we can't be seen."

Lord Godwine's soft voice surprised me, but I didn't show it.

"Back of the bakehouse in a little while," he added, and was gone.

I sauntered to our meeting place, which was quiet at this time of day. He was waiting in the shadows. I couldn't see anyone was watching us, but he kept glancing around nervously.

"Your lady is in danger," he whispered. "The Danes want her children dead."

I nodded.

"I'm not sure how to save them," he continued.

"You are the King's man now," I responded.

"Yes, I am, but would have given my life for the previous King."

I noticed he didn't mention his name.

"And I want to save Lady Frida and her sons."

He sounded so sincere and troubled that I found myself saying, "It's in hand. There's a plan."

"There is?! How?"

Should I say more?

"Lord Valgar is also concerned."

He was quiet.

"Valgar," he muttered. "Can he be trusted?"

"She thinks he can," I said, and quietly added in my

head, 'Can you?' "So don't worry, my lord. I think they will soon be safe."

I sounded more confident than I was. I still had to think of a way of releasing the prisoners.

We parted and, as far as I could tell, no one had seen us. And, I thought, I don't think I said too much. He had seemed genuine in his concern and, certainly, while in King Edmund's service, he had been completely loyal, but, like so many, he was now Cnut's man, working hand in glove with the conquering Danes.

I said nothing of our meeting to Lady Frida, but found I was more wary in general. I sometimes wondered if I was being followed, but I never saw anyone obviously tailing me. Was I just being over-sensitive? I wasn't in the court much, but when I was, my eyes were everywhere, trying to see if anything was different. I did not fear for Lady Frida's life, but for her children, and they were in Westminster. She did not often leave them, but her only way of meeting Lord Valgar was by being at court and mingling with its members.

"I am so worried, Wulfgar," she confessed, "that I cannot sleep. Edith has given me some poppy juice and that helps. Lord Valgar says his boats are nearly ready."

My heart began to beat faster.

"Poppy juice, my lady? Does it have a strong taste?"

"No, mixed in a drink, it has no flavour." She looked at me. "Why?"

"I've had an idea, my lady."

For my idea to work, I had to be more friendly towards our "guard". Lady Frida and her children were not locked in their room, but a Dane was always at the entrance onto the street. Most of the time it was the same young man, the most friendly of our jailers.

So I made sure I chatted to him. He wasn't much older than me and I discovered his name was Eric. I got him to teach me Norse words and in return I told him riddles. He loved our earthy humour and especially the riddles with double meanings, the ruder the better.

"Here's one for you," I said.

*"A young man made for the corner where he knew she was standing; this strapping churl had walked some way –
with his own hands
he whipped up her dress, and under her girdle
(as she stood there) thrust something stiff,
worked his will; they both shook.
This fellow quickened: one moment he was forceful,
a first-rate servant, so strenuous
that the next he was knocked up, quite
blown by his exertion. Beneath the girdle
a thing began to grow that upstanding men
often think of, tenderly, and acquire."*

"What's that?"

"What I'd do with a pretty girl any time I could," he guffawed.

"No, no!" I cried. "It's making butter in a churn!"

He laughed loudly.

81

"Butter-making! Yes, of course."

The plan was working well. I now shared it with my lady.

"Oh, Wulfgar!" she gasped, cupping my face in her soft hands and making me tingle. "That's wonderful! Bless you."

All we needed was the word from Lord Valgar that he was ready.

I had gone with my lady to court and while she was talking to some of the ladies, I suddenly became aware of someone close to me.

"Can you do it tonight?" a Danish voice whispered.

"I'll do my best," was my quiet reply, and Lord Valgar moved away.

Tonight! I prayed Eric was on duty and not the morose older Dane, who sometimes replaced him. I prayed that on and off for the rest of the day. Surely God would not want the death of two small boys? Surely he would want this plan to succeed? I knew, however, that the Almighty did not always do as I hoped. The death of King Edmund had been like a knife in my back, but I wanted to believe God would help us now.

Eric was on duty and a silent prayer of praise went up.

"I've smuggled out some mead," I told him.

He shook his head.

"I'm not meant to take strong drink," he said.

"A small amount will make you more alert," I argued. "Come, friend, drink with me."

I pulled him down to sit next to me and we leaned our backs against the wall.

I poured him a draught.

"Have you heard this riddle?" I asked, as I handed him the drink.

"The deep sea suckled me, the waves sounded over me;
rollers were my coverlet as I rested on my bed.
I have no feet and frequently open my mouth
to the flood. Sooner or later some man will
consume me, who cares nothing for my shell.
With the point of his knife he will pierce me through,
ripping the skin away from my side, and straight away
eat me uncooked as I am."

As I spoke, I noted he had downed the liquid. I pretended to drink some too and then refilled our cups.

"What was that?"

"I got something about bed."

"Not the sort of bed you're thinking of," I laughed. "It was the sea bed. The answer is an oyster."

He hiccupped slightly.

"I have another one," I teased.

While he struggled to understand the riddles, he drank more and more, as though the mead would help him to guess them. He didn't notice I wasn't matching his intake. We laughed and shared stories. He told me about some of the girls he'd met. I wasn't impressed by his Danish morals, but let him ramble on. Gradually, his speech began to slur and he was struggling to keep his eyes open.

The poppy juice in the mead was working. His head sank onto his chest and the cup rolled out of his hand. I rescued it, checked he was asleep and crept inside.

"It's done, my lady," I reported.

She was ready. Hild and Edith each held a sleeping child and I wondered if she had given them poppy juice too.

"Should we bind him?" she asked.

"No. I think it best to leave him sleeping. He may not think to check on us when he wakes. I think we have a few hours."

"Then we go? Now?"

"Now. Follow me."

I picked up my pack, the few things that were mine. Lady Frida also had a bundle, which I guessed were some basic things. The ladies had the children, so between us we had hardly any baggage. We were relying on Lord Valgar to have the food we'd need on this journey. I had some rush lights, one of which I lit before we ventured outside.

The darkness of the night was softened by a half moon, so we could see our way to some extent. Eric was snoring as we passed him and I prayed Cnut wouldn't punish him too much. I also prayed he would sleep for a long time, as it would take us at least an hour to walk to Greenwich, where the boats were moored.

We made good progress through the quiet city, but I hadn't thought about the gates through the walls. I

84

expected them to be unguarded because our country was now at peace and we had no enemies who would seek entrance under cover of darkness. Indeed the gate was ajar, but as we got close, a man suddenly appeared from the shadows.

"Stop!"

The instruction was in English, but the accent was Danish.

"No one leaves," he announced.

My heart was thumping in my chest and I didn't dare to look at the women. Lord, what should I say?

"Sickness." My voice was firm and clear. "We have sickness. They are ill. I'm taking them out of the city to keep others safe."

He stared at me.

"Don't come close," I warned, and put up a hand as though to prevent his coming near us. "They are ill," I repeated.

He stepped back and, in the dim light, I saw fear on his face.

"Go!" he ordered, pointing at the gate and stepping even further away from us.

We quickly obeyed and I sent God a prayer of thanks. Now all we had to do was get to Greenwich and the waiting ships.

There were houses here too, though all was quiet and in darkness, but, as we passed the corner of one building, a figure confronted us, sword drawn.

CHAPTER 13

My lady gasped and my hand went to my seax.

"Don't touch your weapon," the man hissed.

"Godwine!" Lady Frida's voice registered her shock. "Would you betray us?"

Lord Godwine! Cnut's man now. I wanted to run him through, but I knew he could kill me before I could kill him.

"My lady, I am a loyal servant and have always been," our confronter replied.

"Loyal to the Danes," I sneered. I was desperately wondering how we could escape from him, but even if I managed to fight him for a while, the three women couldn't run for safety.

"Loyal first to Edmund," he answered quietly. "I've come to make sure you reach Lord Valgar's boats in safety, but I dare not let the King know what I've done. Come. My lady, what can I carry for you?"

We were stunned and watched Lord Godwine sheath his sword.

"I couldn't risk your killing me, Wulfgar," he quipped. "I know you're like a she-wolf guarding cubs. My lady, how can I help you?"

"Help? Uh ... yes," she stuttered. "Thank you. Edward – could you take him, please?"

Hild gave the sleeping child to Lord Godwine and he guided us carefully but swiftly down to Greenwich. We met with no more trouble and once he had delivered us to Lord Valgar, he slipped away. Perhaps that was the last thing he would ever do for the children of his previous master, but, then, who knew what the future held and whether we might meet again?

We made ourselves as comfortable as we could. Lord Valgar's boat had shelter for the women, a space enclosed by canvas, but there was none for me, though what did I care? I had done it! I had succeeded in delivering Lady Frida and her sons into the care of this kind man and now they were his responsibility. I was grateful to be there, for I had secretly dreaded he would turn me away at the last minute as being an unwanted passenger. But, no, I had no shelter, but here I was among his oarsmen.

His men loosed the ropes that held the two boats to the quay and used oars to push firmly away and into the main stream of the river. I guessed the other boat had supplies as well as some of his men. Our small party was all on one boat, with him.

Lord Valgar shouted no instructions. Everyone seemed to know exactly what to do. Strong Danish hands gripped the oars, bottoms shuffled into position on the benches and the sound of oars dipping into water began. We glided down the Thames, one boat leading the other.

They must have eyes like cats, I thought, to see in this gloom.

The high prows, with their fierce animal heads, pressed on into the current. I could barely see the stern, but knew that a skilled sailor was there, manning the rudder. I think the tide must have been with us, for I sensed we were travelling fast, every moment taking us away from the danger of Cnut's assassins, but also into an unknown world.

"They are safe and settled," a quiet voice informed me and I found Lord Valgar at my side. "You have done well, Vulfgar. Here are sheep skins for you to wrap yourself in and a pillow for your head."

"Thank you, my lord."

It was clear I was to curl up in the bottom of the boat just where I was and hope it did not rain. In fact, it was easier to sleep than I had expected. The sheep skins were warm and soft and the rhythmic movement of the boat rocked me quickly into oblivion.

I was woken by shouting. Some of the oarsmen were still rowing, but several were occupied in hoisting the sail, a huge piece of canvas, which needed strength and skill to raise into position.

I pulled myself up to view my surroundings. Ahead of me the sky held those first pale streaks of light that herald dawn. Behind there was only darkness and no sign of land. To our left, men on the other boat were also hoisting the sail.

As the wind seized the sails, so the rowers lifted their dripping oars clear of the water and pulled them onboard. They had earned a rest, the boat now being propelled forward by a strong westerly.

Food began to be handed out and passed from man to man. I was thrust a piece of bread to chew. Later, a skin of ale was shared. There was some friendly banter in Norse, at least I took it to be friendly, for the men were smiling and there was some laughter and no one looked in my direction, so I don't think I was the subject of any jokes.

After a while, Lord Valgar came to sit by me.

"Is all well?" I asked.

"They have slept," he informed me, "but one of the ladies, she is sick. The rocking of the boat," he explained. "Have you been on the sea before?"

"No," I replied, thankful I wasn't feeling ill.

"Sometimes people are sick. To start with."

"Is it a long way?" I wanted to know.

"More than a day, even with a good wind." He looked up at the lightening sky. "Pray, Vulfgar, there is no storm, or we shall all be sick."

Or worse, I thought. I knew boats could be lost at sea and I had never had any desire to be in one, but to escape from Cnut and stay with Lady Frida, I had no option. I had cast my lot with her, for better or worse.

I did pray. I prayed hard. There wasn't much else I could do. We were surrounded by water as far as the eye could see. I watched with fascination the great waves as we ploughed through them and the light dancing on the undulating surface of the ocean. Occasionally, a bird would screech and wheel overhead and once or twice I thought I saw creatures in the water, but couldn't see their size and shape. What I did *not* see, and was grateful not to see, were any other boats. I doubted Cnut could catch us in a chase, but what if we met with others on the water, men determined to raid and kill? That thought set me praying again.

That was probably what the occupants of the shelter were doing as well. The ladies did not come out at all, but I heard the cries of the children. Edmund's baby cry was soon quietened as, I presume, he nuzzled against a milk-filled breast. Edward's cry was more one of frustration. He could walk and was learning to explore and he was clearly unhappy about being confined in such a tiny space. It must have been very difficult for Lady Frida, with a sick servant and two troublesome children. I guessed we would all be very pleased when we reached land again, but of our new country, there was still no sight.

After a while, the wind dropped a little and the sail began to flap idly, so the men took up their oars again. I began to imagine I could see land, but it was only an illusion, born of my frustration. I had to admire these sailors who left dry land and set off into an empty seascape.

"How do you know the way?" I asked Lord Valgar, when next he came my way.

"The men have crossed this water many times," he explained. "They use the position of the sun, and at night they travel by the stars – if there are no clouds. You are not sick, Vulfgar, that is good. But the sea can be rougher than this. God is blessing us with good weather."

"What happens when we reach land?"

"We will anchor in a harbour and take on fresh supplies before we sail north along the coast of Denmark."

"Where is your land holding, my lord?"

"In the north. There is shelter for the boats in an inlet from the western shore. I will send a messenger to bring horses, and also a cart. There will still be some miles to travel."

He looked at me and smiled very slightly.

"Lady Frida will be glad of your service, for you knew her husband."

"I served him long before he was King," I said quietly.

"And loved him, that I can see." He paused. "I never met him. I only came to England after King Cnut ... came to power, but all speak well of him."

"Yet the King would kill his children?" I queried.

"King Cnut must needs make sure of the throne. Any who endanger him will ... will have to go." He frowned. "Some of your Saxon lords have already died and there may be others. Children grow into men. One day these aethelings could fight for the throne."

"Do you risk your life in helping them?"

A pair of blue eyes searched my face.

"What do you think?" was his quiet response, and he moved on to speak to the helmsman.

I knew I would never ask him why he took this risk, for the answer was clear, at least to me. Who could fail to risk *everything* to help Lady Frida?

I wondered what would happen when we reached his estates. He was much older than her, but would he marry her? I thought it likely. Who would not want to be her husband?! Then she would have a protector and her children would have an inheritance. That was surely what was in his mind. She would have no choice, of course. How could she refuse to wed her rescuer? Perhaps that's what she hoped for – because without a husband, she was vulnerable. Perhaps ... and I was shocked I had never thought of it before ... perhaps it was already agreed between them that they would marry once they were safely in Denmark and living under the rule of King Harald and not King Cnut. I had seen love in his eyes, but never noticed it in hers. What had I seen? I asked myself. Respect and gratitude, but that would be enough. She had had one great passion in her life, my Lord Edmund; was it possible she could have another? I doubted that.

I looked across the water and suddenly my mouth went dry. I could see something on the horizon.

CHAPTER 14

"Is that a boat?" I asked the nearest rower to me.

He stared where I pointed.

"Yes, a sail," he answered, and shouted something in Norse.

Our limp sail was pulled down, as was the one on our sister ship and I sensed we changed direction slightly. The boat I had spotted was a long way off, but we were taking no risks. It might be friendly, but equally, it might not. I kept my eyes fixed on that smudge on the horizon until I was sure I couldn't see it any more.

Sometimes, when the sail was up and the rowers could rest, the men started to sing. I noticed even Edward must have been entranced, for I couldn't hear him crying. I understood the occasional word and wondered if their songs were about the women in their lives. Perhaps they encouraged each other with tales of courage and exploits, which always ended in their claiming victory – goods and slaves and plenty of women. I knew the Danes had a reputation for selling prisoners as slaves, something our bishops had condemned.

That got me thinking about the bishop I knew best – Wulfstan of Worcester. I had gone to York with him at a time when Lord Edmund was in hiding and I had returned to my master with news of Swein's sudden death. In York, though, I had heard Bishop Wulfstan preach and I knew he was direct and fearless.

What is he doing now? I wondered.

It was rumoured he was drafting laws for King Cnut.

"Like Godwine," I muttered. "He's decided to back the winner."

Part of me despised these men for slipping so seamlessly into the enemy camp. Yet, another part of me said these enemies had conquered us and we were in no position to fight on.

Uncertain as I was about the future in a foreign land, masterless and almost friendless, I was still glad I did not have to live in England under Cnut's rule. In my heart, I longed to see Edward as King.

The dark was settling around us and, being unable to see any stars, I wondered how we could navigate. Our sister boat came alongside and there was some shouting across at each.

"We are lowering our anchors," Lord Valgar told me. "We will find land in the morning."

So I had another night in the open, a less pleasant one, for the drizzle set in and I slept badly. But as the dawn began to give the hope of a new day, I realised I could see land, far off admittedly, but definitely land and soon we were on the move towards it.

We travelled north up the coast a little; I think Lord Valgar was seeking a particular landmark, though to me it all looked the same – flat with sandy beaches and not a cliff in sight. Then we turned and headed east again and I could see there was a small inlet and a huddle of buildings above the shoreline. We had to stay onboard, but some of the men brought on more supplies. It wasn't long before we set sail again and travelled even further up the coast.

About midday, we came to a broad estuary up which we travelled until we came to a big harbour area where several boats were pulled up onto the sand and I guessed this was where Lord Valgar would leave his ships. There was also a jetty to which men tied the boats, one each side of the wooden walkway.

I was very stiff from sitting cramped for so long and I had difficulty scrambling out of the ship, but one of the rowers grabbed my arm and almost lifted me bodily onto the jetty.

"Need to eat more!" he laughed. "Get strong!"

I smiled and thanked him. I simply didn't have his physique and never would, for I had always been skinny, but I had got stronger because I practised hard archery and swordplay, so I could fight if called upon.

The jetty seemed to sway under my feet; then I realised it was I who was swaying – I was still on the water! So I staggered like a drunken man.

Lord Valgar, of course, was used to the sea and I could see he was standing tall and that he bent now to help Lady Frida and the rest of our party disembark. She looked as beautiful as ever, but Hild and especially Edith looked pale and ill. Perhaps both had been sick. Edmund was asleep and Edward was picked up by Lord Valgar, and our whole group steered onto dry land.

In one of the houses, we received some refreshment – a vegetable broth and bread fresh from the oven. I was glad of some hot food after more than a day eating only dry bread. There was a fire in the centre of the room, the smoke from which was struggling to find its way out through the reed thatch. Except for the language, we could have been in England. The language – ah! We were all going to have to learn it, if this was to be our home. A return to England was only going to happen, I thought, if Cnut and his sons Harold and Swein died, but now he was married to Queen Emma, there might be more sons. Edward and Edmund were the only survivors of Aethelred's first marriage and there were too many people backing the Danes for that return to be imminent.

"Wulfgar," Lady Frida's gentle voice broke into my thoughts. "We hope to travel to Lord Valgar's estate tomorrow. I don't need you at the moment, so if you want to explore, then you can." She paused and then smiled one of her sad smiles. "My lord always said you were good at being nosey and finding things out. I think I will need you to be my eyes and ears."

"My lady, I'll serve you in whatever way you want," I responded eagerly.

She touched my arm.

"Take some exercise for now," she instructed. "Come back in a while."

I was loath to leave her, but I could see she was in good hands, safe and warm, so I mooched around the small settlement, responding to any greetings with my limited Norse and breathing in the salty air. It was good to feel the breeze through my hair and get my legs working properly again.

Lord Valgar's boats had left the jetty and were drawn up on the shore. Perhaps they wouldn't be needed for quite a while.

Just for a moment I thought of Eric and his waking up to find us gone. How angry had King Cnut been? Or maybe he was pleased we had gone, for two small children couldn't really threaten him. In twenty years' time he could have a householdful of sons, just like King Aethelred had had, and two English aethelings in a far-off country would be no threat.

Among the buildings I found a small church made with rough stone foundations, wooden walls and a thatched roof. I paused in its silence to thank God for a safe crossing of the sea and to pray for my lady's new home.

The next day, a party arrived to help us travel. My lady chose to ride a horse, but Hild and Edith, with the children, were made as comfortable as possible in a wagon. I too had a horse, but stayed near the back of our group. Lady Frida, enveloped in a cloak of wool and fur designed to fend off the chill wind, was at Lord Valgar's side and I caught glimpses of them apparently in easy conversation. I became even more convinced that he would soon make her his wife.

The weather was dull and cold. We travelled along rough tracks, rutted and muddy, through a fairly flat landscape almost devoid of trees. Of which part of England did it remind me? Nowhere really, because I couldn't remember anywhere that was so empty. Perhaps the most similar was the east, where huge areas of the land were under water and the skies were more extensive than anywhere else I knew. The east wind here had a raw edge, such as I remembered in the Fens.

The light was beginning to fade as we approached our destination – a square which looked like a large animal pen and round it several houses and other buildings including an impressive hall house. I guessed it was a fairly self-sufficient settlement, with a smithy and a church, as well as houses for humans and shelter for stock.

"So this is it," I murmured to myself. "Our new home in a foreign land."

Servants came running from various directions, some taking charge of our horses, while others took our baggage (such as it was). Our party was brought into the hall and found there a blazing fire and an elderly lady waiting to greet us. I took her to be Lord Valgar's housekeeper, or perhaps his mother. She was certainly the lady of the house, for an impressive bunch of keys hung from her girdle.

"You are all welcome," she greeted us. "Such a long journey, but you are safe now."

"Lady Frida," Lord Valgar led her forward to meet our hostess. "This is my wife, Gunnhild."

Wife! That was the last thing I'd expected him to say!

"Dear lady, your husband has been our saviour. I cannot thank him enough."

Unlike me, Lady Frida showed no surprise. If she had hoped he would marry her, she was giving no sign of disappointment. I'm glad no one was looking in my direction or they might have seen how shocked I was.

Lord Valgar and his wife gave Lady Frida a room for herself, her women and her children. I was to sleep in the main hall with other servants.

So, here we are – in a new land with a new language to learn and new customs to get used to. But for how long, I wonder?

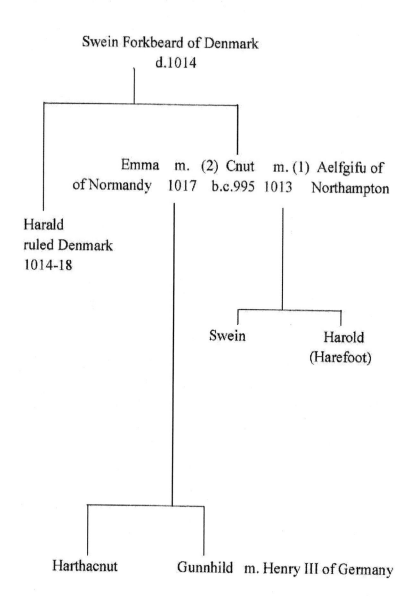

Swein Forkbeard of Denmark
d.1014

Emma   m. (2) Cnut   m. (1) Aelfgifu of
of Normandy   1017   b.c.995 1013   Northampton

Harald
ruled Denmark
1014-18

Swein   Harold
          (Harefoot)

Harthacnut   Gunnhild m. Henry III of Germany

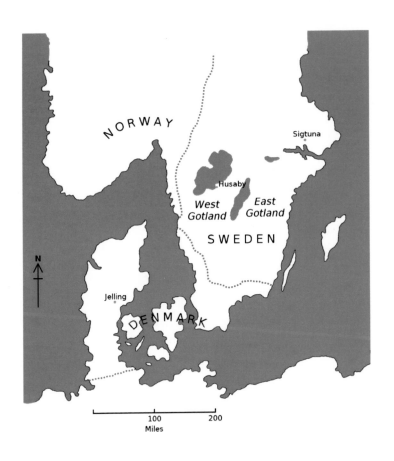

Scandinavia in the early 11th century
showing in particular Jelling and Sigtuna

PART II – DENMARK

CHAPTER 15

We slowly settled into the life of our new country. The landscape was not so very different from that of eastern England; there were wide open areas of flat land, some woods here and there and the occasional small hill.

"It is not dissimilar to the area around Lincoln," Lady Frida commented. "That's where I grew up," she added with a slightly sad smile, perhaps reflecting that much had happened in her life since her days as a child.

The food, too, was not unusual, except there was more bread made from rye than we were used to, but Lord Valgar and his household lived well. He traded across many miles, so we would sometimes have foodstuffs, especially spices, brought from far-off lands.

The language was our greatest challenge. Lord Valgar spoke perfect English and his wife did well, with his help, but his servants spoke Norse and we had to get to grips with this strange tongue. Edward was beginning to talk and he had a mixture of English and Norse in his limited vocabulary. Lady Frida insisted we spoke English to him and to Edmund.

"He must learn to speak English like a native," she asserted. "I will not abandon the hope that one day he will return to England and take his rightful place."

The servants spoke to him in Norse, so he quickly picked up both languages. He was proving to be a bright child, absorbing whatever was thrown at him and apparently unscarred by the disturbing events of his first eighteen months of life. I spent as much time as I could spare with him and I found him to be a happy little boy.

Edmund also was thriving. Lady Frida suckled him herself and kept him very close to her, even when he wasn't feeding. It was as though he was so precious she was afraid that, if she let go, she'd lose him. I noticed that he, like Edward, had his father's eyes. I think their resemblance to the late King was a comfort to his widow, as though she still had her husband with her.

I was far from idle. As soon as Lord Valgar discovered I could read and write and had some experience in managing an estate, I was employed by him in his work. He had lands in the central part of Denmark, quite extensive estates, which were managed by bailiffs. He also traded widely, and keeping tabs on all his goods, where they'd come from and where they were going, was quite a task. So, all in all, there was plenty for me to do. To begin with, I was only of use in dealing with his English trade, but he was very patient in teaching me and in encouraging my grasp of the language and I was a quick learner.

We had been there about a month when Lord Valgar made a proposition.

"I think it would be good if I took you all to meet the King."

"He is Cnut's brother, isn't he?" Lady Frida asked.

"Yes, his elder brother, Harald."

"Is it safe?" she queried.

"I think you will be safer if you meet him," Lord Valgar replied. "There is not a good relationship between the brothers. When King Swein died (he was the one they called Forkbeard), Harald became King of Denmark. When Cnut wanted a kingdom, he had to look abroad and his eyes naturally fell on England. He asked Harald to help, but Harald refused."

"But Cnut managed to conquer England anyway," she commented sadly.

Lord Valgar shrugged his shoulders.

"Cnut has no power here," he told us. "King Harald will, I think, have sympathy for you and your children."

"Where does he live?"

"Mainly at Jelling, that is our capital. It is to the south, a day or so's journey. I have horses. Vulfgar, I know you can ride. Can you manage Edward?"

"I think so, my lord. He may wriggle, but there'll be distractions to keep him amused."

That proved to be the biggest challenge of the journey, as Edward kept wanting to get off the horse and walk. Lord Valgar had provided us all with warm clothes. Lady Frida had a cloak of the softest pale golden fur, while I had one, I think, made from wolf skins. Even Edward had a fur wrapped round him, but he still wriggled. When we stopped for refreshment, I tried to wear him out and then he might sleep for a while, lulled by the motion of the horse. I was glad when we finally reached Jelling.

We had passed through a largely flat landscape to reach the Danish capital, which had access to the sea, not to the west into the North Sea, but to the east. It was nothing like the size of London and many of the buildings were made of timber, but it struck me as cleaner and less huddled. There was a fresher smell to it as well; perhaps the east wind blew away the unpleasant smells, but I had already discovered the Danish people washed more frequently than we English were used to doing.

Lord Valgar knew people here and we were comfortably housed with a wealthy trader.

"We are rivals," Lord Valgar joked, "but also work together to make good deals."

Our host laughed in agreement.

The next day Lord Valgar took us to meet the King. His hall was timber, but impressive, with its walls hung with many skins from wild animals, especially bear skins from the east (so I was told). They helped to keep the chilly autumn breeze from finding its way through the cracks.

King Harald didn't look much like his brother. He had darker hair and his eyes were light brown, which gave his face a warmer and more friendly look. He was clearly older, as there was no trace of Cnut's boyish appearance.

"Valgar!" he exclaimed. "You bring me visitors."

"Sire," Lord Valgar began, bowing deeply, "I bring you people from England, who seek refuge in our country."

"England? Ah! Running from my brother Cnut, I presume."

"Lady Frida is the widow of King Edmund, the son of Aethelred."

Lady Frida curtseyed and I watched Harald's face. His eyes twinkled and he could not suppress a smile.

"I did not know King Edmund had such a beautiful wife," he commented. "My brother took his throne, but did he take his life?"

"No, sire, my husband died of a sickness."

"And you have his children? You hold one to your breast."

"He was only born at the end of July."

"He is named Edmund after his father, who, of course, never saw him," Lord Valgar interposed, "but there is an older boy, whom the King did see and whom he named Edward."

I now had to bring Edward forward. He was somewhat overawed by all that was happening, so he clung to me and stared at the new people he was meeting.

"Ah, you make me wish I were blessed with sons," King Harald commented, wistfully.

We shared a meal with the King and Edward lost his shyness and caused great amusement with his toddler antics.

Before we left, the King took Lady Frida's hand.

"You are welcome in my kingdom. For as long as I am King of Denmark this country is your home and a safe haven. I am honoured that you are here." He lifted her hand to his lips, before releasing it. "Valgar, you are to take good care of these precious people."

Lord Valgar had been right to bring us because he knew that the King could not help but be charmed by Lady Frida and her two helpless boys. We could live without fear in Denmark.

As we left the hall, I asked Lord Valgar about the mounds and stones I had seen on my way in.

"You notice much, Vulfgar. We have a saying:

The cautious guest
who comes to the table
speaks sparingly.
Listens with ears
learns with eyes.
Such is the seeker of knowledge.

You are one such person. Here are things maybe you do not have in England. These mounds of earth were once places of burial in the time when Danes were pagans, but there are no bodies there now. The bones were moved into the church."

He indicated a wooden church.

"This was built about fifty years ago by another Harald, the one we call Bluetooth. He made the people Christians. He also had these stones erected."

Lord Valgar moved to show me the two huge stones that stood between the mounds.

"This one is the oldest, put here by Harald's father, Gorm, in memory of his wife. But, Vulfgar, look at this one."

I stared at the brightly painted picture on the other stone.

"It looks like a man with a snake wrapped round him," I said.

"It is the image of Jesus Christ, who conquered the devil. See on the back is an inscription."

I stared at the letters and couldn't make out what they said.

Lord Valgar laughed.

"It is not easy, even for us. I'll tell you. It says, 'King Harald ordered this monument made in memory of Gorm his father and in memory of Thyrve his mother that Harald who won for himself all of Denmark and Norway and made the Danes Christian.'"

"So what is the relationship between the present King Harald and this one, Harald Bluetooth?" I asked.

"The Harald who put up this monument was the father of Swein, the one nicknamed Forkbeard, the one who conquered your country in 1013."

"Ah, that is the man who was the father of Cnut and also this present King Harald," I added.

I enjoyed the visit despite the travelling and having to cope with a fidgety child. I felt I had a better understanding of Denmark, its leaders and its people.

We settled into our quiet life back on Lord Valgar's estate.

Christmas came and had, for us, far more peace and joy than we had experienced the previous year. Lord Valgar's children were there for the celebrations; normally they lived with their spouses on other parts of his estates. So the hall was crowded and filled with laughter and singing.

Then halfway through January news came that made me want to leap with pleasure.

CHAPTER 16

"Vulfgar, ask Lady Frida to come into the hall, please," Lord Valgar summoned me. "There is news from England."

We gathered by the fire, where a Dane was warming himself with a bowl of broth.

"Hakon is come from London this day," Lord Valgar told us. "You will find what he says of great interest."

"King Cnut has tightened his grip on England," Hakon reported. "There have been some deaths of men he feared would cause him trouble, including Northman son of Leofwine of Mercia and Aethelweard son of Aethelmaer the Stout."

Lady Frida looked grave.

"Earl Leofwine was a good friend to my late husband, especially when Swein was King."

That jogged my memory.

"I remember meeting him when Lord Edmund and I were in hiding at Evesham," I said. "His grandson was one of the hostages Cnut mutilated."

"Well, now he's lost his son," Hakon commented.

"I think there is more, isn't there?" Lord Valgar prompted the messenger.

"Yes. At Christmas there was a big feast with everyone there and Earl Eadric made a speech."

I frowned, simply at the image of that traitor preening himself in front of all the Danes.

"He said what a good servant he had been to Cnut and how he thought he should receive a bigger reward."

"The rat!" I exclaimed.

"Ah, I did not think he was your friend," Hakon responded and suddenly grinned. "You will like what happened next."

The hall was silent except for the slight sound of the wind outside and the occasional crackle of the wood on the fire.

"King Cnut looked at him and said, 'You wish your head to be raised high?' Earl Eadric stood proud and straight and said, 'Yes, sire.' 'I agree,' cried the King, and the Earl smiled."

Hakon looked round at us. All our eyes were fixed on him.

"Then the King called to one of his bodyguards, 'Come here. Cut off Eadric's head and raise it up!'"

We gasped.

"And did he?" I breathed.

"Yes! Eadric had no time even to move. The man slashed his head off with a single blow of his sword."

"Oh, that's terrible!" Lady Frida exclaimed. "He had no opportunity to be shrived. He died without confessing his sin."

"It's what he deserved!" I whooped with glee.

"The King said that he respected loyalty," Hakon continued, "and that Eadric had shown no loyalty to the late King Edmund and he did not trust he would show any to the present King."

"He could have made that decision a year ago," I objected.

"He has waited," Lord Valgar interposed. "I think he made sure Mercia was under control before he removed its Earl."

"Eadric had no burial," Hakon added. "His body was thrown in the river."

"More deaths," groaned Lady Frida.

"There may be even more," Lord Valgar said sadly. "Cnut will not let men have power unless he trusts them – and he does not trust many Englishmen."

"One man he trusts is Lord Godwine," said Hakon.

"He is another man who was a good friend to my late husband," Lady Frida responded, and then added quietly, "and to me."

She didn't catch my eye, but I reckoned she was remembering the night of our escape from London.

"Men must find their way in a new world," she said, more loudly. "I do not blame Godwine for aligning himself with a strong ruler who has no rivals."

I found it hard to sleep that night. Every time I closed my eyes, I saw Eadric being slain and my face creased with a smile. The traitor had, at last, met a fitting end, although I have to admit, a part of me wished he'd been hung, thus delaying the moment when death came, but then he might have been able to confess his sins to God Almighty before meeting him.

We felt safe on Lord Valgar's estates and were settled and happy. Lady Frida might wonder about the future, but I hardly gave it a thought, and the children were blissfully unaware that they were foreigners living on the charity of a generous man. I was more than paying my way, for I worked hard and Lord Valgar was warm in his praise of my work, so I was content with my lot.

One day I happened to be in the hall and noticed Lady Frida was teaching Lady Gunnhild how to do English embroidery.

"Is good my husband is here more," Lady Gunnhild commented. "Very often he is away, travelling the world."

But while we've been here, I thought, he hasn't left Denmark.

I watched the ladies as they worked, wondering if Lady Gunnhild knew her husband was in love with my mistress, but there seemed to be no edge to her comment and nothing in her behaviour which suggested jealousy.

I was glad of that, for she could have been a real bitch towards this young, beautiful woman to whom her husband had given a home.

Maybe she doesn't know, I thought, and reflected that Lord Valgar was very careful in his behaviour. His admiration was less obvious here than it had been in

London. Perhaps he hid it better, for I was sure Lady Frida still held his heart.

I wondered if he might establish us on one of his estates and in that way he could be in Lady Frida's company without his wife being there to see the look in his eyes. I thought it might be difficult for us all to get on well in the same household indefinitely. I couldn't see our future being anywhere except here, unless something dramatic happened back in England, like Cnut dying young.

As it happened, the situation was resolved, but in a totally unexpected way, one that none of us could have anticipated.

In the meantime, however, the days were lengthening, the grass was growing and the ewes were having their lambs.

Edward enjoyed running free. I doubt if he remembered how restricted his life had been during our months in London. Here, everyone was his friend. All the servants adored him, which was hardly surprising, because he had an infectious smile and a delightful way of putting his head on one side and staring at you with wide, innocent eyes. I spent as much time as I could with him.

Lady Frida was almost totally engrossed with Edmund, who was also thriving and had smiles for everyone. She was very possessive with regard to her second son; I think it was the fact that she had borne him after King Edmund's death. She was also very indulgent.

Edward she corrected if he was naughty, but Edmund was rarely disciplined and I feared he could grow up spoiled.

Spring had slipped into summer when everything changed. I was working on the accounts, when a servant interrupted me to say I was wanted in the hall. Lady Frida was already there and I could see by Lord Valgar's face that something was wrong.

"We have news," he said, gravely. "Sad news."

We hung on his words.

"Our King has died." He looked at us intently. "You know what that means?"

CHAPTER 17

"King Harald is dead," Lord Valgar reported, as we stared at him, speechless. "Who will claim the throne of Denmark now?"

Who indeed? I wondered.

"He has no children," Lord Valgar reminded us. "His brother will be king."

"Cnut!" I gasped.

"Oh, no!" cried Lady Frida, clasping her hands together. "My children!"

"I thought we were safe," I said, "but you think ... you think we aren't?"

"I am sure you are not safe," Lord Valgar replied. "King Harald was your protector, but once Cnut is King of Denmark, he will ... he will not want the aethelings to be free."

"What are we going to do?" Lady Frida had begun to cry.

Lord Valgar took her hand and enfolded it in his grasp.

"Do not fear, dear lady. I will find a way. I cannot let your children die."

It was hard to concentrate on my work. We had only a few weeks perhaps. Once the news reached England, we thought Cnut would act fast, Queen Emma keeping England secure for him, while he came here to claim the throne.

Lord Valgar caught me staring out of the unshuttered window.

"Vulfgar."

I pretended I hadn't been daydreaming, but noticed his face was serious.

"You are a good worker."

That was a relief! I thought he was about to scold me.

"There is work for you here. You could stay. I do not think your life would be in danger."

"Stay? Not go with Lady Frida?"

I was horrified. Was he saying I had to remain in Denmark? He had become like my master, so maybe I didn't have any choice.

Suddenly, he smiled.

"Ah, I see you want to be with your lady."

"Y ... yes," I admitted.

"I am thinking that Sweden might be a good place," he continued. "I have a house there and I do much trade. Perhaps I find you work there too."

"I am happy to work for you," I told him, "but I am my lady's servant and wish to do all I can to help her."

He needed to know where my loyalty lay, though I didn't want to sound ungrateful. I tried to read his face, but couldn't and he now left me to my work.

When we next gathered to eat, I could see he was pursuing the idea of Sweden.

"It is not too far to travel," Lord Valgar said. "We can be there quickly. My house is in Sigtuna and I have many friends there, for I trade much."

"Who is the King?" I asked.

"His name is Olof Skötkonung. He has been King for about eighteen years."

"Is he a man of faith?" Lady Frida wanted to know.

"He was baptised as a Christian a few years ago," Lord Valgar replied. "So the country has not been Christian as long as Denmark, but there is peace there and he is a good ruler. I believe he will welcome you." He paused and then added, "He has a son called Edmund, a man about your age, my lady."

Edmund! I thought. What a coincidence!

I had no real idea where Sweden was, except that I thought it lay east of Denmark. Much of Lord Valgar's trade was in the east, in the countries that bordered a great sea. For me these countries were names on cargo payments, but I would soon discover one for real.

Lord Valgar had me write letters to his contacts in Sigtuna to alert them to our arrival, but he would not be waiting for any replies, as he was anxious to be gone. Packing our few belongings was not time-consuming; our delay in leaving was simply the result of his needing to work out our best route.

"The waters of the Skagerrak are sometimes bad," he told us.

When we looked puzzled, he added, "That is the sea to the north, the one that separates Denmark from Norway."

"I think we shall go overland to the east coast where I have other boats."

"Then we go by sea?" Lady Frida asked.

"Yes." Lord Valgar looked at the sleeping Edmund and then at Edward, who was playing a game with me, one involving wooden counters. "It will take several days. Vulfgar will need to play many games with Edward."

He clearly thought Edward would prove restless, but, of course, Edmund was also an active child, who crawled everywhere and was close to learning to walk. He was not the tiny baby who had been happy to nestle close to his mother on the voyage from England. I foresaw a fraught journey.

We had horses to get us to the east coast. We travelled through fields which had been harvested. In places, the smell of drying hay made our noses prickle and took me back to a hot summer in England. Perhaps the weather would be kind to us.

The first part of our sea journey was through the islands of Denmark, so land was very near at all times. I marvelled at the skill of the helmsman, who steered us through narrow channels at times. There was plenty to see, so I managed to keep Edward occupied by pointing out the birds which flew over us and the fish of which we caught glimpses.

Unlike our journey from England, Lord Valgar moored up each night and found us a place on dry land to sleep. These were often very basic huts, but the owners were friendly and helpful, especially towards the two boys.

In this way, we edged our way along the coast of what Lord Valgar told me was Gotaland.

"A people called the Goths live here," he explained. "Sweden has been made by drawing the Goths and the Svear together into a single kingdom. They are stronger together."

"It isn't an ancient kingdom then?"

"No, less than twenty years, but Olof is a good king."

For many miles we sailed up a stretch of water with land on both sides, but the land to our right eventually turned out to be an island. As we left it behind, Lord Valgar told me about an even bigger island further east.

"It has *raukar*," he said. "Those are pieces of rock bigger than your churches, which rise from the water and they are strange shapes. The sailors tell stories of them, how they are people who upset the gods and were turned to stones as they fled. It is a beautiful island," he added, "with many flowers in the early summer, but we are going north."

We continued to hug the coastline, but even so, the wind whipped up waves, and Edith was seasick. I had to hang on tightly to Edward. In the end, I tied a rope round his waist and secured the other end to a bench. He revelled in the spray which drenched us and laughed at the great waves, unaware of the danger we were in.

I think Lady Frida had more trouble controlling Edmund than I had in controlling Edward. He was not used to the word "No" and wriggled and sometimes kicked, when he was restrained. Hild helped her, but I'm sure there was great relief each time we landed for the night.

"Today, we reach Sigtuna," Lord Valgar announced, as we settled ourselves onboard after, I think, our fourth night. To be honest, the days had merged and I wasn't sure how long we had been at sea.

Edith even managed a smile. She wasn't so sick now, but clearly didn't like water travel. None of the rest of us were ill.

The boats still hugged the coast until Lord Valgar pointed out an estuary and here we left the big sea behind and sailed between small islands for several hours before reaching Sigtuna.

The town was a busy port, with many ships moored up and others either coming (like us) or leaving. The long quayside was piled with timber and other goods and, from a distance, looked overrun by ants. As we grew closer, the ants turned into people, actively loading and unloading cargoes.

This was Sweden's equivalent of London, but it looked very different, for the buildings were wooden and, on closer inspection, not very old.

"Birka was the main town," Lord Valgar told me, "but that has gone now and Sigtuna is more important."

"You do much trade here?" I asked.

"Oh, yes. Many goods come here from the east, from Russia and beyond. I think you will be surprised."

I sensed our life here would be very different from what we had known for the last year. We had enjoyed a quiet time on a country estate in Denmark, but now we would be living in a busy town. I prayed it would still be good – and that we would be safe here.

My letters had reached Sigtuna and the old lady who kept house for Lord Valgar had prepared rooms for us and soon had food on the table.

"Where is Jakob?" Lord Valgar enquired.

"I've sent word to him that you're here," his housekeeper replied. "He'll come when he wants to," she added, shrugging her shoulders.

We had finished our meal of fish and bread by the time Jakob arrived.

"Ah, this is my steward," Lord Valgar announced. "He deals with my trade here in Sigtuna."

Jakob looked to be in his thirties, with light brown hair and a beard. I thought he eyed me with suspicion.

"Jakob, this is Lady Frida and her two children Edward and Edmund, her ladies Hild and Edith, and her manservant Vulfgar. They will live here. They are from England."

"England?!"

"That is not a good place for them to live now," Lord Valgar explained, but didn't say any more.

Jakob acknowledged us by a brief nod of his head.

"They have been with me in Denmark for nearly a year," Lord Valgar continued, "and Vulfgar is good with writing and figures. He can help you."

A pair of brown eyes stared at me and I wasn't sure why, but I felt uncomfortable under Jakob's gaze. I suddenly thought of the Jakob in the Bible and how he was a cunning cheat.

"I am happy to help in whatever way I can," I said, but saw no warmth in those eyes.

Time will tell, I thought. Don't judge him till you know him.

So we are here, in Sigtuna, which is somewhere in Sweden and we have to try and make this our home.

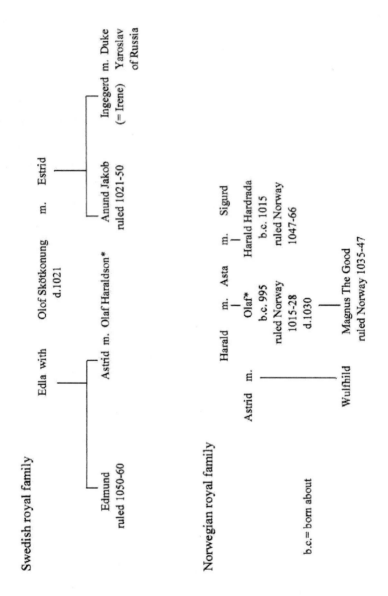

Swedish royal family

Edla with — Astrid m. Olaf Haraldson*   Olof Skötkonung   m.   Estrid
                                          d.1021

Edmund   Anund Jakob   Ingegerd m. Duke
ruled 1050-60   ruled 1021-50   (= Irene)   Yaroslav
                                                                         of Russia

Norwegian royal family

Astrid m. ——————   Harald   m.   Asta   m.   Sigurd

                    Olaf*   Harald Hardrada
                    b.c. 995   b.c. 1015
                    ruled Norway   ruled Norway
                    1015-28   1047-66
                    d.1030

Wulfhild   Magnus The Good
                    ruled Norway 1035-47

b.c.= born about

124

PART III – SWEDEN

CHAPTER 18

As I thought, our life was different in Sweden. For a start we lived in a town house, which was not as spacious as the country house in Denmark. It had a hall where we ate together and where I slept and there were some small rooms on two floors. I think Lord Valgar must have given up his usual room for Lady Frida, Hild, Edith and the children, because they shared a large room on the upper floor, while Lord Valgar had a small one. At ground level were service rooms with supplies and a place where Jakob came and worked. The cooking was done in a separate building. A housekeeper lived elsewhere with her husband and came in each day.

The houses were very close together and in that sense Sigtuna was like London, somewhat crowded and cramped and with the constant smell of water and a dampness in the air, especially when the sun wasn't shining. Nowhere was very far from the quays and the busyness of trade on which the town thrived.

"I am taking you to meet the King," Lord Valgar announced after a couple of days. "As in Denmark, it is important he knows you."

The King had his court in Sigtuna, so we didn't have far to go. He inhabited a large complex of buildings, some of which were of stone, but many were wooden. I had been told Sweden was rich in trees, so it was natural to build with timber.

As we entered the main hall, we could see someone sitting in a carved wooden chair on a dais.

"Sire," said Lord Valgar, bowing deeply. "I bring you visitors from England."

"Valgar, you usually bring me silk or silver from the east, not people from the west!"

"I have brought you silk as well," quipped the Dane and presented the King with a roll of blue material.

"England does not have silk, I believe," the King said.

"No, it does not, but England has the finest wool for cloth," Lord Valgar replied.

"And people running from that young bully boy, Cnut," the King added. "I take it, Valgar, your visitors have come to live here."

I think this was friendly banter between two men who knew and respected each other. I certainly hoped the King was going to be kind to us.

"Lady Frida is the widow of King Edmund, the son of Aethelred."

He took her hand and presented her to the King. She curtseyed and bowed her head.

"She has two sons by the King – Edward and Edmund. Their lives were in danger in England."

The King nodded.

"And her household, Hild, Edith and Vulfgar."

We also acknowledged the King in our different ways. We had charge of the children, who were remarkably quiet, perhaps a bit overawed, as well they might be, for this man had a presence.

King Olof, I guessed, was well into his forties. He wore his white hair long and had a thick moustache and beard, making him look what I thought a Viking would look like. England had been harassed by these fearsome warriors for more than two hundred years and we had finally been conquered by a young Dane, who had never looked to me like much of a Viking. But this man did. He wore a simple tunic, as the weather was mild, and thus showed the muscles in his powerful arms. He had several silver armbands and his hands were wrinkled and scarred.

He's fought a few battles, I thought.

King Olof had glanced at us servants, but let his eyes linger on Lady Frida.

"So young and so beautiful to be a widow," he said softly, as though for her ears alone. "These are hard times for you."

"Lord Valgar has been very kind," she said sweetly, "and has given us the hope that my children may live."

"Ah, yes, it is not you who threatens the throne of England, but your two cubs," commented the King. "They are too young to fight yet, but we can teach them."

"God has been merciful to us," Lady Frida said. "We are grateful for your hospitality."

"You must join me tomorrow. My son is returning from the country. Valgar, you must bring Lady Frida to meet him."

Thus it was that later the next day I found myself again in that hall. Hild and Edith stayed with the boys, but, as in London, I was allowed to be near Lady Frida as her servant, even though she was in the care of Lord Valgar.

The hall was filled with tables and benches. A fire burned in the centre to offset the cool of the day, and candles gave us light by which to eat and drink. Again, I could have been in London except that King Olof looked so different from King Cnut.

Lord Valgar took Lady Frida up to sit near the King, while I made myself at home with some of the retainers. I saw that she was introduced to a man I took to be the King's son. He too looked like a Viking with his long fair hair and full beard. His arm bracelets glistened in the candlelight. He had a woman at his side, whose gown shimmered and made me think it must be made of silk, perhaps one of Lord Valgar's presents to the family. Unlike Lady Frida, whose head was modestly covered, this woman had no headdress and seemed to flaunt her braided blonde hair. She too wore bracelets on her bare arms.

We ate well. There were several different kinds of fish, as well as roast meat and some vegetables. There was plenty of wine for all of us and that helped to loosen shy tongues.

When most of us had finished eating, the hall went quiet and a man began to play a small harp and to sing. Then another man began to tell a story. I think it was in praise of the King, recounting his exploits, his fearless deeds, the overcoming of his enemies and his reign of peace. At the end, the storyteller was given a silver plate as his reward.

The evening was a pleasant one and seemed to be a positive sign that Sweden would be a good place to live. Or so I thought. Something soon happened to unsettle me.

A few days later, Lord Valgar asked for my help.

"Jakob is busy with the accounts, so, Vulfgar, could you go down to the quay and collect an assignment of amber I am expecting?"

He gave me detailed instructions on how to find the right ship and with these I soon made contact with the relevant sea captain.

"Amber for Valgar? Ya, we have amber for him," the sailor said. "Here." He handed me a small parcel wrapped in hessian and cord. "And here is the bill."

I took the parcel and the piece of parchment. Curious, I tried to read the bill. I could see the word "amber" and the name of the ship. The price appeared to be 23, though I couldn't understand the currency. Was it 23 pieces of silver or what? I didn't think it could be silver. I had yet to get my head round how the Swedes did business.

Jakob wasn't pleased to see me.

"Why did Lord Valgar ask you to go for the amber?" he demanded.

"He said you were busy and he could see I wasn't."

He snatched the parcel and the bill from me and I made my exit. I went off to find Edward and take him for a walk.

The next day Jakob wasn't in the counting room (as I called it) so I decided it was a good opportunity to look at some of the bills to see if I could make sense of them, because I knew Lord Valgar wanted me to help him.

So I looked at the pile of parchments and was amazed at the variety of goods Lord Valgar was buying. Furs, spices, honey, beeswax, silk, amber – all these! I saw the bill for the amber and stopped. I found my hand was shaking slightly. The bill no longer read 23, but 28, the three having very cleverly been altered to an 8. Was I witnessing fraud or was there a very simple explanation? And what should I do, if anything?

Later, I had the opportunity of talking to Lord Valgar.

"I really want you to help me, Vulfgar. I sometimes wonder if Jakob is very efficient."

"The accounting is very different from what I'm used to," I confessed, "and Jakob is a bit ... possessive." I paused. "There is something that's puzzling me."

Lord Valgar looked at me intently.

"The bill for the amber I collected for you was 23, but it now reads 28. Does Jakob have a commission?"

He was silent, holding my gaze.

"I pay him a wage," he said slowly. "You say the bill has been changed?"

"I ... I think so. I was sure it said 23 when I collected the goods, but maybe I was wrong."

"If you are right, I have a thief working for me."

CHAPTER 19

I was horrified!

"I may be wrong," I spluttered.

"I fear you are right," Lord Valgar sighed. "I have thought for a long time that he is cheating me, but I have no proof."

He looked straight at me.

"There is your task, Vulfgar. I would like you to get me the proof."

My insides went cold.

"It will not be easy and you will have to be very careful, but I know I can trust you. If there is evidence, you will find it."

"He ... he doesn't like me," I countered.

"A man who is doing wrong does not like to work with a man who is honest. Take your time. There is no hurry. I want to be sure before I act."

He looked at my furrowed brow.

"We have a saying:

Better weight
than wisdom
a traveller cannot carry.
The poor man's strength
in a strange place,
worth more than wealth."

I stared at him, puzzled.

"It means the best thing to carry in your baggage is wisdom rather than expensive goods. A man with no money can still have wisdom. You are not a rich man, Vulfgar, but I think you have some wisdom and will get more."

That didn't really cheer me up and my heart was heavy. There are some kinds of spying I enjoy, like my time in York with Bishop Wulfstan; all I had to do was keep my ears and eyes open – no one was my enemy. This kind of spying was different. If I found evidence that Jakob was a thief, I would make an enemy of him – and perhaps of his friends. This was not York – I was a foreigner in a strange land and more vulnerable than in England. But I was in no position to argue. Lord Valgar had saved the lives of the two aethelings and he was keeping all of us at his expense. I really had no option but to do as he asked.

I said nothing of all this to Lady Frida, for she too was adjusting to life in a very different place. At least the language was no real barrier now. Edward spoke English and Norse with perfect ease and Edmund was busy copying him. Lady Frida insisted their English must be perfect, because, in her heart, she hoped one day they would return to the land of their birth.

"You will find Sweden is much colder than you are used to," Lord Valgar told us. "Sometimes the rivers freeze and we use sledges to move our goods to and from the coast."

He provided us with warm clothes and soft fur cloaks for when we ventured out. He gave Lady Frida some exquisite leather gloves and also some tiny woollen mittens for the children, as well as fur hats for us all.

"The clothes are a sign of our friendship," he told us. "We have a saying:

Give each other
good clothes
as friends for all to see.
To give and take
is a guarantee
of lasting love."

He had given us clothes and, in return, I would be his spy.

He had told Jakob I was to help him.

"Vulfgar is English so he can read and write in that language. He is still learning our Norse, but you can help him there. And he can help with adding figures and running errands."

When we were alone, Jakob said, "Is Lord Valgar paying you?"

"No. I am Lady Frida's servant and he provides for her and her household. This is a way in which I can repay his kindness."

I did my best not to antagonise him and also not to make him think I was spying. I meekly did as he asked me and made no attempt to pry. When he wasn't in the counting room, I did look through some of the bills, but found nothing odd. If he was cheating Lord Valgar, he was probably holding back for the moment. Part of my task was to be patient and allow him to relax and, perhaps, lower his guard.

I did not spend all my time in the counting house. I would often go down to the quays and sometimes took Edward with me. I would talk to the sailors, asking where they had come from and getting them to describe their homeland. I learned some traders took boats up a great river in Russia, and pulled them overland to the next river, another great one, that took them down to Byzantium.

"Byzantium?" I asked. "I've never heard of that."

"Its capital is Constantinople, a place where two seas meet," a sailor called Swen told me. "There is a very beautiful church there, the Church of St. Sophia. The ruler has soldiers who are Norsemen."

"Really?"

"Ah, we Norse travel everywhere," he added proudly. "We trade with many lands, even east of Byzantium, journeys which take months."

"The world is much bigger than I thought."

"Ah, and then there is the land in the west," he added.

"England, my home, and beyond that, Ireland."

"We go north to Scotland, to many islands and through rough seas," Swen said. "A dangerous voyage takes us to a big island with fire in its mountains. Many Norse now live there. We call it Iceland. It is in the far north and very dark in winter."

"When we left England, we couldn't see Denmark and it took us days to reach land," I commented. "But the sailors knew it was there."

"We are very brave sailors," Swen boasted. "We go in our ships even when we cannot see land and we do not know if it is there. That way we find lands no one has seen before." He smiled broadly. "I have heard that beyond Iceland there is a green land and even land beyond that."

I began to think he was telling me stories, for I knew the Norse loved their sagas and some of them were full of imagination, strange places and strange beasts.

Edward was always very interested in the boats and what the sailors were doing. I had to keep tight hold of him, for he had little sense of danger and had a habit of getting very close to the quayside. Also, there were so many people around and most of them busy moving goods that he could easily have been hit by men hurrying with their loads.

When on my own, I had to watch my step because there were mooring ropes ready to trip up the unwary walker, as well as piles of shipments and wicker baskets with fish flapping in them, caught that day and still alive.

There were a couple of other lads about my age and we would play a game of racing each other along the busy quayside, leaping over obstacles, dodging round people and arriving at the so-called finishing line. This was a place where there was a break in the quay, created by a stream, which poured its water into the main river at this point. Wooden walls had been built both sides of this inlet in order to channel the water.

The game got more serious when one of the lads reckoned he could jump across the gap made by the stream. We egged each other on until we all decided we had to try. We knew we had to get across, because failure would result in getting very wet!

I may be skinny, but I have long legs, so when it came to my turn, I took a good run at it and easily leaped across the gap. The others made it too and from then on the finishing line became the other side of the stream.

I was glad of the exercise. I didn't want to sit in the counting room all day. In fact, Lord Valgar gave me plenty of opportunities to practise my fighting skills too. As he was on good terms with the King, he got me access to the swordplay of the royal retainers. There was also the opportunity to use the butts. Sweden was at peace, but no one took that for granted, so every able-bodied man was meant to prepare himself for combat. I was improving both with the sword and with the bow.

Lord Valgar was right about the cold, but we still went out, though wrapped up well. One day, we all went down to the quay. I had charge of Edward and behind us came Lady Frida, Hild and Edith, their progress being slightly slower as Edmund insisted on walking.

We discovered the river was frozen.

"Will you use sledges?" I asked Swen, who happened to be repairing his fish baskets.

"No, the ice is too thin. It may look solid, but it will not even take the weight of a man."

"Look, Edward, at how he weaves the twigs to make the basket."

We were engrossed by Swen's dexterity, when we heard a scream.

"Edmund's out on the ice!" cried Lady Frida.

CHAPTER 20

I looked out at the white surface and saw little Edmund waddling further from the quay. Somehow he had escaped the ladies, got down some steps and out onto the ice.

I raced to the quayside.

"Take care of Edward!" I yelled, as I leaped down the steps.

"It won't take your weight!" Swen shouted.

I hesitated on the edge of the ice. I had to rescue Edmund, but how? I lay flat on the ice and pulled myself along. That way my weight was spread out and not directed on one patch. Even so, I felt very insecure, but what else could I do?

"Edmund!" I heard Lady Frida calling loudly. "Come back here! Now!"

The child took no notice, as usual.

"Edmund," I called him more softly. "Look at me. I'm swimming on the top of the river."

He stopped and turned to look at me. He was still beyond my reach, but I was edging closer.

"Aren't I clever? Can you swim on the river?"

I had his attention. He was curious now about the ice and bent down to touch it with his mittened hand.

"It's hard, isn't it?"

I realised I would have to remove my glove in order to grab him and get a firm grip.

"Let's feel the ice," I tempted, as I slid off my glove and saw he was beginning to fiddle with his mitten. Then I had him! My hand caught his cloak and I dragged him closer, so that I could get my hand through the belt on his tunic. He didn't like it and began to kick.

The return journey was a nightmare. I only had my feet and one free hand to use to propel us both back to the quay and he was fighting me all the way. I feared his little boots would break the ice. I was pleading with God for our safety.

Just as we reached the steps, there was a creaking sound and the ice began to break up, but we had made it. Swen grabbed me and hauled me free of the icy water. I was soaked from the waist down, but we were safe and Edmund was not wet at all.

Lady Frida took charge of Edmund, who was now having a tantrum.

"There, there, it's alright, you're safe." She tried to calm him, but made no attempt to discipline him.

Swen helped me up the steps and onto the quayside.

"Go home and get dry," he advised.

"Thanks for your help," I said warmly and slapped him on the back.

He rewarded me with a grin showing his few teeth.

Back home, we all gathered round the brazier to get warm. Edmund had been given a toy and something to eat and had calmed down. Edward was very quiet; I think he sensed there had been some danger. He came to sit by me.

"Wulfgar, you are brave," he whispered, tipping his head to one side as he looked at me.

I smiled at him. I was getting very fond of him, for he was like a baby brother I had never had. I hoped he would grow up to be like his father. King Edmund's eyes gazed at me.

"Your father was very brave," I said. "He had the nickname Ironside, because men admired his valour."

"I want to be brave," he said solemnly and I knew it would fall to me to teach him to fight.

Later, when everyone had gone to bed and I was about to settle down on my mattress, Lady Frida crept into the room. She had a cloak wrapped round her, but her hair was loose. I had never seen her hair and was struck by how it shimmered like gold in the firelight. I'm sure my heart missed a beat.

"Wulfgar," she said softly, as she approached me.

I stared at her and didn't move as she came close.

"Wulfgar, dear boy."

She wound her arms round my neck and pressed her cheek against mine.

"You saved the life of my little boy," she murmured. "I will never forget."

I would never forget what it felt like for her to be so close. I could feel my face beginning to burn. Then she released me, gave me a smile that would melt any man and drifted back to her room, leaving me incapable of sleep for at least an hour.

We had no more mishaps with the ice, because the children were never given the opportunity to get into danger when we walked by the quayside. Edmund would try to escape the clutches of the women, but he never succeeded. Edward, on the other hand, was happy to hold onto me.

Christmas arrived and there were celebrations in Sigtuna's wooden church and feasts with the King and his court. There was always plenty of fish for these feasts, some I had never eaten before, but what I particularly loved was the singing, the music and the story-telling. The Swedes knew how to do all those very well and I would be lost in the atmosphere they created.

January and February were lean times for trade, as travel was more difficult despite the alleged use of sledges on frozen rivers. Furs were the main commodity that came into Sigtuna, many of them from Russia. The tales I heard about that place intrigued me, but it also sounded like a place of battles, with many warring factions.

I continued to help in the counting house, but had never found Jakob cheating, so had begun to think I was wrong about him. Then life changed.

"I am going on a journey," Lord Valgar announced.

"Back to Denmark?" I asked.

"No."

"Are you not needed there?"

"No, my son can look after my interests there." He looked me in the eye. "I do not want to meet the new King."

I nodded in understanding.

"I will be away for perhaps two months." He paused. "Jakob has done nothing wrong?"

"I don't think so," I answered.

"While I am away, I think he may try," warned Lord Valgar. "Be very careful. We have a saying:

When passing
a door-post,
watch as you walk on,
inspect as you enter.
It is uncertain
where enemies lurk
or crouch in a dark corner.

Do not let him suspect you watch him."

I did not like this task, but I knew I had to do it. When Jakob wasn't in the counting house, I would look at the bills, but couldn't see anything suspicious. Then, one day, Jakob asked me to go down to the quay with some money to pay the ship's master. I say "money"; I still wasn't sure whether it was real currency such as we had in England or some kind of token system. What I had learned, however, was that if the bill said "twenty", then twenty "tokens" were handed over.

As I walked down to the quayside, I suddenly decided to stop and count the tokens. There were 31 of them. I thought about the bill for the commodity. Was it not a bundle of furs? And what was the price? I had a feeling I had seen a bill for 34.

My hand shook slightly as I replaced the tokens in the pouch. At the quayside, I found the right ship.

"I've come from Lord Valgar with payment for the furs," I called, and the captain came across to me.

"Ya," he acknowledged.

"I'm not sure I've got the right amount," I continued. "I don't have the bill."

"It was 31."

"Ah, luckily that's what I have. May I have a receipt, please?"

The captain raised his eyebrows.

"I'm new to this," I said, "and I've got in a bit of a mess."

He smiled, obviously taking me for a stupid boy, and graciously counted the money and gave me a receipt, which I hid inside my tunic.

When I had the opportunity, I looked again at the bills and found the one for the furs. It read 34 and yet the captain had said it was 31. The figure must have been changed, but it was very cleverly done.

I hid the receipt under my mattress. I had the first piece of evidence, but I would need far more than this to prove Jakob was a thief.

CHAPTER 21

I was determined to be as casual and pleasant as possible with Jakob, for I had to give him no reason to suspect. The plan worked well. I did as I was told and never made any attempt to look over his shoulder or query anything. I ran errands for him; in fact, that seemed to be the main way he used me, for that meant he could be alone in the counting room. He didn't know that I was often in there in his absence, carefully going through the bills, but trying not to give away the fact that I had done so.

Over the next few weeks, my patience was rewarded and by the time Lord Valgar returned, I had evidence of four transactions where Jakob had cheated his master.

"You have something to report, Vulfgar?" Lord Valgar asked.

"Yes."

I laid out my evidence and explained what I had done. Lord Valgar looked at everything very carefully and slowly.

"He alters the bills in a clever way," he concluded. "A one can be made into a four and a three into an eight. It is impossible to see the change. It is only because you have receipts from the ships' captains that we can see he is doing it."

He looked up at me and there was a real sadness in his face.

"This is not good," he remarked. "I do not like to tell a man I do not trust him."

He shook his head.

"What will you do?" I asked.

"First, I need to catch him," he explained. "I believe you. You have done well to give me this evidence, but I need to catch him for myself. So I will say nothing. We pretend we do not suspect him. You continue to help him as he asks and do not check the bills. We pretend all is well."

I didn't ask him how he intended to catch him, as I thought it best I didn't know. My role was to act as though he was still a trusted servant and do whatever he asked.

The late spring and early summer was a busy time for trade, but often I took Lady Frida to court and then spent time honing my swordplay and archery, while she mingled with the courtiers. Lord Valgar encouraged this and I suspected it gave him the excuse to keep a closer eye on Jakob, for he did not often come with us. Lady Frida knew enough people now not to be dependent on his company and I often saw her talking to the wife of the man I presumed was the King's son, Edmund. The King himself liked talking to her and sometimes she would comment on their conversations.

"Today the King asked how the English Witan works," she said.

Another time I heard the King was interested in how we punished criminals in England. Such conversations led us to reminisce about England and wonder how life was there now, under a Danish king. News came occasionally. We knew therefore that Cnut was in Denmark, and that his men ruled England. We knew that life was hard, for the English had had to raise £72,000, an enormous amount of money; this was for paying his Danish army. Londoners alone had had to pay Cnut £11,000. Danes occupied all the positions of power and many English thegns had lost their lives.

We grieved to hear such news, but were thankful we felt safe in our new homeland.

One day, as I was about to leave with Lady Frida, Lord Valgar stopped me.

"I have the evidence," he said quietly. "I am going to confront him today."

"Alone?"

"No, I have asked a fellow merchant, a good friend of mine, to be there."

I nodded in understanding and left for court. When we returned, there was no sign of Jakob. Lord Valgar wasn't around either, but he came in later.

"It is done," he said. "I will need you to help me more."

"Of course," I responded.

I didn't like to ask how the meeting had gone. I could imagine it would have been very tense, with Jakob protesting his innocence, until all the incriminating evidence gave him no option. Perhaps there had been no need to use the information I had supplied, but, even so, I doubted Jakob would be pleased to see me if he met me in the street. How right I was about that!

Over the next few days, I combined my two roles, that of helping Lord Valgar with his business and that of being Lady Frida's escort to court. On one occasion, Lady Frida told me about a conversation with the King.

"He is related to Cnut," she said.

"Really, my lady?"

"Yes, it is by marriage and does not mean he supports him," she began. "Swein Forkbeard, the father of Cnut, married Olof's mother. It was a political match."

"But that makes them sort of brothers, yet we are here – and safe."

"Olof and Swein were allies in the past," she continued. "They joined forces against Olaf Tryggvasson of Norway and defeated him. That's nearly twenty years ago, for a different Olaf is King there now."

"Swein Forkbeard died in England," I remarked. "I remember that well. It was at the end of Christmas in the first year of my service to Lord Edmund, some five years ago. Olof did not continue the alliance with Cnut?"

"It seems not. Also, Olof is now a Christian and does not wish to pursue war. In the past, he was very keen to conquer other lands, but is now content to draw together the Goths and the Svear and make Sweden a great nation."

"He has a fine band of soldiers, my lady. I suspect they would like to fight for real rather than simply practise fighting each other."

"I think there are some tensions," she admitted. "Some people wish he would go to war again. I believe that lands in the east used to pay him tribute, but do not do so now."

"He doesn't fight to get back their tribute?"

"No, and that disappoints some. Also he is treading a difficult path with his faith. There are many who still hold to the old pagan ways and do not like it that he is a Christian."

I was disturbed by this information and wondered how safe we really were.

"He has the support of his son," Lady Frida broke into my thoughts. "I think that in effect they rule together."

She smiled at me.

"Don't look so worried, Wulfgar. The Lord delivered us from Cnut. Surely he will keep us safe? He has a special place in his heart for the widows and the fatherless."

I wished I shared her confidence. I still struggled with why God had let Cnut defeat us and why King Edmund had died so young, but I would not share such dismal thoughts with my mistress.

The days were long now, longer than I remembered in England, but I had also noticed the days became very short in the winter. There were plenty of boats coming and going in Sigtuna, sometimes quite late, so I was not totally surprised when a message came to the house just as I was preparing to sleep that there was a consignment for Lord Valgar. He was not around and would have sent me anyway, so I went out into the half-light dressed only in my tunic for the night was not cold. A slight breeze ruffled the hair on my bare arms.

When I arrived at the quayside, there were no signs of unloading a boat and I was puzzled. Then I heard a slight rustle and a figure launched itself at me from the shadows.

CHAPTER 22

I felt the blade before I saw my attacker. His blow to my right arm made me scream and I struggled and failed to find the handle of my seax.

"Spy!" hissed the shadow. "You cost me my job. Now you die!"

Jakob came at me with his seax. I wanted to fight back, but the pain was too great, so I turned and ran – ran for my life. Over the bales of goods, over the mooring ropes – I had done this in fun, but now it was in earnest. I knew he was chasing me. One false move, one trip over some hazard, and I was a dead man.

"Englishman dies!" Jakob cried, but he wasn't close enough to get me again with his seax.

I prayed he wasn't as fit as I was, even with my wounded arm. I could see the end of the quay and the inlet I leaped over with my friends. I forced myself to run faster – I had to get across.

I landed on the far side and kept running. Somehow I had to get away from him.

Then I heard a sound that thrilled me – a cry and a splash. Jakob hadn't made it across the gap and was in the water. I was safe. Even so, I still ran all the way back to the house and locked the door.

I sat on a chair and got back my breath, before I looked at my arm. The blood was everywhere – the whole of my forearm and hand were red and sticky. I found a cloth and some water and began to clean it, but it was awkward trying to do it with my left hand. I was shaking anyway.

Then I heard someone trying the door and I began to shake even more.

"Vulfgar!"

I recognised the voice outside the door.

"Lord Valgar, just a moment."

I hurried to let him in.

"Good God, Vulfgar, whatever has happened?"

"Jakob ... he tried to kill me."

"Sit down," he ordered.

With real gentleness and dexterity, he cleaned the wound and bound it. As he did so, he heard my tale of the attack.

"I am very sorry," he said. "I tried to keep you out of trouble, but Jakob must have guessed you had helped me to find the evidence. This is not good. He will be a dangerous enemy."

I found it difficult to sleep that night, partly due to the pain from the cut and partly I kept reliving the attack. It is one thing to fight men in a straight fight, but quite another to have an assassin come out of the shadows. I kept telling myself I should have guessed it was a trick, being lured to the quay at such a quiet time. I hadn't been on my guard and had only myself to blame for my wound. But at least I had got away. Now I was alert to the danger and prayed he wouldn't catch me unawares again.

Lady Frida was very concerned when she discovered what had happened.

"He could have killed you!" she cried.

Edward sat with his head on one side, staring at my bandaged arm.

"You were brave again," he said solemnly.

"Not brave enough to fight him," I replied.

"That would have been foolish, Wulfgar," Lady Frida reproved me. "You couldn't have wielded your seax effectively with a wound like this. You were wise to flee. And now, you are not going anywhere. Jakob may be lurking just outside the house. Maybe Lord Valgar will bring us news."

Apparently, he had gone out early and Lady Frida was making sure no one left the house until his return. When he did come back, his news took us all by surprise.

"It is good to see that you are more calm now, Vulfgar," he said. "You did not sleep well, I suspect."

I shrugged my shoulders.

"There is quite a stir," he told us. "The wife of Jakob is making a complaint."

"Wife?!" I exclaimed.

"She says you have killed her husband."

"But I never touched him! I never drew my seax. I simply ran for it." I paused. "Killed? Do you mean he's dead?"

"His body was found in the water. She says you pushed him in and he drowned."

I stared at him, horrified. I had heard the cry and the splash, and been relieved. It had never crossed my mind that Jakob wouldn't make it back on to dry land.

"We have a man who deals with the law and he is demanding you come and give evidence."

In England, when there is a dispute, each man brings his supporters to testify that he tells the truth. I wasn't sure how the system worked here, but I was horribly aware of the fact I was a foreigner and had no one to speak for me – except Lord Valgar and he was a Dane.

There was quite a crowd in the hall where the justice met, for news had spread quickly that a man had died and foul play was suspected.

Jakob's widow made her case.

"He took my husband's job and now he takes his life," she cried. "He hit him on the head and pushed him in the water."

I had my turn then.

"Jakob attacked me. It was unprovoked. He slashed my arm with his seax and then I decided to run for it. I leaped over the gap in the quayside, but I don't think he made it, for I heard a cry and a splash."

"You didn't go back to help him?" the justice asked.

"He was trying to kill me! I ran for the safety of the house and locked the door."

"He hit him!" the widow screamed.

"There is bruising on the forehead," the justice admitted.

"That could have happened when he fell," Lord Valgar intervened.

"Why do you speak?" the justice asked.

"I employed Jakob, but I found he was stealing from me, so he lost his job."

"It was his fault he lost his job!" the widow shouted, pointing at me. "Jakob said he made up bad evidence."

"No, Vulfgar was not involved. I found evidence of stealing for myself," Lord Valgar asserted.

"But he worked for you for many years," she countered. "Only since this Englishman is here is there trouble."

"I haven't spent much time here in the past, but I have been here now for many months and I have seen his cheating for myself. When I was away, I suspected him. Now here, I know for certain."

"What we have," the justice intervened, "is the word of the Englishman that he did not kill Jakob and the word of Jakob's wife that he did."

"But she wasn't there," I objected.

"Silence!" ordered the justice.

My heart sank and I feared they would doubt my word because I was a foreigner.

CHAPTER 23

Lord Valgar was frowning. He too was a foreigner and I guessed he was thinking like I was, that they would say I was lying.

"Was anyone there?" The justice looked at the crowd.

The quayside had been empty. There was no one to verify my story.

"Yes, I was."

The silence was profound. Swen pushed his way to the front. I stared at him in disbelief. I didn't think anyone had witnessed the attack.

"What did you see?" the justice asked.

"First, I heard something," Swen told him. "I was settling down to sleep on my boat when I heard voices."

"Whose voices?"

"I didn't immediately recognise them, but then I saw Wulfgar being chased by Jakob, who was shouting 'Englishman dies!'"

A gasp came from the crowd.

"You know these men?" the justice asked.

"Yes, they work for Lord Valgar and are often down here dealing with his merchandise."

"Go on."

"I started to get out of the boat to try and stop Wulfgar being killed," Swen continued, "but I could see him running well. These lads often race along the quay and I knew he could outrun his attacker. He did. He got across the gap – I saw that – and then I saw Jakob fail. He tried to jump over, but he didn't make it and fell in the water."

"You didn't go to his aid?" the justice asked.

"No! Serve him right, I thought. He was wielding a knife and intent on murder. If I'd fished him out, he might have tried to kill me instead. I'd seen him earlier in the evening and I'd thought he was drunk. He was acting like a mad man. I reckoned Wulfgar was safe, so I settled down to sleep."

A hush had settled over everyone, as though we had been stunned into silence. I couldn't believe my ears! Swen had seen what happened! He knew I hadn't killed Jakob! Surely that would settle it?

The widow broke down in tears and people started talking all at once, and in the general hubbub I saw Lord Valgar speak to the justice, who nodded.

"Case dismissed!" he shouted over the noise.

Lord Valgar hustled me out. Later I went down to the quayside to thank Swen.

"It was good for you that I saw what happened," he said. "There isn't always justice for foreigners."

I thanked him again and as I walked back to the house, I wondered if I would ever be in England again. Perhaps I would be forever a stranger in a foreign land. If so, I had to make the best of it. It was no good dwelling on the past or speculating about a gloomy future. I was the servant of a beautiful woman, and had the challenging task of helping Edward to grow up to be worthy of the English throne.

That evening, as we ate together, Lord Valgar gave us some news.

"I have been to see Jakob's widow and I have given her some money. She has no right to it and I made that clear, but I am very sorry about what has happened and I wanted to help her."

"How generous you are!" Lady Frida exclaimed. "It must be terrible for her. Perhaps she didn't know he was cheating you."

"I think she did not, so she has much to deal with – his thieving and his death. But, Vulfgar, I think you are safe. Jakob has no friends I believe who will hurt you."

"I hope not! But it has taught me to be more on my guard."

"Your arm does not hurt too much to write?" he asked.

I assured him I could still do his work, and I was glad that the wound did not fester, but healed well.

We now entered a quiet time in Sweden with no major events to trouble us. We heard little of what was happening in England, but we did know that Cnut now had a son by Emma, whom he had named Harthacnut. That meant that Edward's chances of being King of England were getting slimmer, as Cnut had three sons (by two different women) who could succeed him. We never spoke of going home, but Lady Frida was making sure the

158

boys' English was perfect, so I knew she had not given up hope entirely.

Edward was thriving and eager to have his first sword, but he had to wait until the spring of 1021 when he turned five. Edmund copied everything his older brother did and, of course, he wanted a sword too. I thought Lady Frida would indulge him, for she usually denied him nothing, but, on this occasion, she heeded my advice to wait another year.

I was doing well in my work and was now as skilled in bargaining as Lord Valgar himself. The advantage he had, at least in my eyes, was that he had travelled to many of the places with which we traded. The exotic lands in the east were a mystery to me. While I had lived in England, I'd had no urge to travel, but now I had seen something of the world beyond our English shores, I was intrigued to see more.

I was getting some experience in another area too – that of girls. A group of them, about five in number, began to follow me around. I guessed they were all a few years younger than me and one or two were quite pretty. I would simply laugh at them.

Then, one day, I was going down an alleyway in the town and found two of them blocking my way. As I turned to retreat, there were two behind me. I was trapped! They closed in and the leader advanced right up to me.

"We think it's time, Wulfgar, that you learned how to kiss properly," she said, and gave me a seductive smile.

What should I do? Push them away and run for it? Or stay? I had kissed the occasional serving girl – a swift, passing kiss in a corridor – but I reckoned these girls were offering far more. I decided to stay.

"You first then," I said, as boldly as I could, for my knees felt very weak.

She put her arms round my neck and pressed her lips to mine. I was beginning to enjoy it, when another girl pushed in.

"My turn now," she demanded, and the experience was repeated.

I kissed all four of them in turn and while engrossed in the fourth, I heard a squeal and they all scattered. An older man walked past me and raised his eyebrows at my behaviour. I felt a little foolish – for having been caught in the act, but I had no regrets and decided this lingering kind of kissing was rather nice.

The next day, I was returning from the quayside and as I passed an entrance, I heard my name.

"Wulfgar," a soft, female voice spoke.

I naturally turned to see who wanted me. There was a girl in the shadows of a small storeroom and she reached out to grab my arm and pull me in.

"I missed yesterday," she said.

I found I was very close to the least attractive of the group. She had a long, hooked nose and her eyes were too

160

close together. She was also much fatter than most of them.

"Kiss me, Wulfgar," she urged.

There wasn't much else I could do, but I hadn't expected what happened next. She had one hand firmly round my neck, but with her free hand, she clasped one of mine and forced it onto her breast. Then she let go and began to grope under my tunic.

I ended the kiss, but she nuzzled against me.

"I've got plenty, haven't I?" she whispered. "You can have me any time."

I didn't want her and somehow managed to extricate myself, mutter some thanks and hurry home, my face burning with embarrassment and my body feeling it was on fire.

I was very glad when Lord Valgar gave me some unsolicited advice.

"It is best, Vulfgar, not to get physically involved with a girl unless you are serious about marrying her."

He had obviously been told something! I thanked him, took his advice and made sure I was never alone or in a situation where any of the girls could get me. But, sometimes, when I was lying awake at night, I would relive the parts of the experience that had been pleasant.

I was kept so busy that I hardly noticed autumn slipping into winter.

"I think the King is dying," Lady Frida told me as Christmas 1021 approached. "He fought very many battles when he was young and has now enjoyed several years of peace, but I think the end may be coming."

The King had continued to enjoy talking to her when she was at court, but I had noticed he wasn't always there and his son seemed to be taking on more of his father's work.

"I shall miss him," she said quietly. "He was always a good listener. It is good that in these final years he has come to a faith in Christ and found true peace."

We were all at the main Christmas feast, but even I could see how frail the King was. He seemed to have shrunk and no one was surprised by the news, soon after, of his death.

I didn't expect his passing to make much difference to our lives, but there I was wrong.

CHAPTER 24

The funeral for Olof was very unusual for these people. Of course, for those of us from Christian England it was natural to have a service in the church accompanied by singing and a multitude of candles. However, for the Swedes, it was strange, for Olof was a Christian king, not a pagan, having undergone baptism only fourteen years earlier.

Edmund stayed with Hild and Edith, but Lady Frida thought it would be good if Edward attended the funeral.

"He needs to see what happens when a king dies," she told me, "because one day he may be a king."

I'm sure he would have behaved himself, for he was a serious child, unlike his younger brother, but he was put in my care, which meant I too went to the funeral. Lord Valgar, naturally, looked after Lady Frida.

The service was solemn, but very different from the last funeral of a king that I'd attended. Nearly six years earlier, my master had died young and we had been struck down with grief even as he had been struck down with illness. On this occasion, we were remembering an old man and a long reign. He had drawn the Goths and the Svear together more than twenty years before and he had held them together as a nation, proud and respected.

The service was in Sigtuna, but the coffin was then taken many miles southwest for burial at Husaby.

Apparently the King had asked to be buried there, as it was the place where he had been baptised.

Thus it was several days before we were invited to eat with the court. Neither of the boys came, but I went as usual, though I sat well away from the important people.

The old King's son, the one I took to be Edmund, presided at the feast, with his wife at his side. Lord Valgar and Lady Frida were welcomed as honoured guests and I noticed she was sitting next to a man I didn't recognise, someone about her age, with the long blonde hair that so many of these men had. It became clear that Edmund was succeeding his father without any opposition, so any unease I may have had about our still being welcome and protected in Sweden melted away. Olof had been sharing power with his son and thus the transition was easy.

Afterwards, I commented on this to Lord Valgar.

"Yes, there is no problem over the succession," he agreed, "but you are wrong about the new king's name. He is Anund."

"Oh, I thought his name was Edmund, like my late King."

"Edmund is the name of his brother," he explained. "He has been in Gotaland, looking after that area for his father, while Anund has been here, alongside the King."

I must have looked puzzled.

"Edmund was at the feast. He talked much to your lady."

Ah, I thought, the man with the blonde hair.

164

The next time we went to court, there was no sign of Prince Edmund and I presumed he had returned to Gotaland, but at Easter I realised he had returned.

Shortly after Easter, Lord Valgar left us for a few weeks, as he had business in the east. We continued to receive invitations to be at court, so I would take Lady Frida there. I noticed that she would be sought out by Prince Edmund and he would be very attentive. I was reminded of Lord Valgar's behaviour when we had been in London. Edmund was very much younger than the Dane and I began to wonder if Lady Frida was enjoying the company of this Swedish prince, a handsome man of her own age. I frequently saw her smile at him and laugh at his jokes. I was pleased for her, as it seemed to breathe new life into her.

I also took Edward to court, so that he could watch the royal retainers practising their swordplay. Sometimes we joined in and I had the opportunity of improving my fighting skills and Edward had the opportunity of having his first lessons from men who knew how to fight. They enjoyed teaching the "little prince" as they called him; I don't think they understood the word "aetheling", but they knew his father had been a king.

We were all happy and settled – at least, I thought we were. Lady Frida smiled far more and even looked younger, as though the strain of exile had slipped away. Edward was enjoying his lessons in swordplay and I was teaching him to use a bow and arrows. Edmund wasn't far behind, but he didn't yet have the strength and balance to learn to fight with these hardened soldiers.

One day, we had gone to court, Lady Frida, Edward and I. She was with Prince Edmund and others, while Edward and I mingled with the fighting men. The day was warm and pleasant, so we were only wearing tunics, our arms and legs bare to the sunshine. The smell of sweat was strong as we jostled with each other and honed our swordplay, our damp hands struggling to grip our weapons.

A cry from Edward stopped me and I turned to see his arm was bleeding.

"I'm sorry," a man said. "I didn't mean to cut him."

The lad was being very brave in the face of the accident and someone quickly bound the wound to stop the flow of blood.

"I'll take him home," I said. "I'll go and find his mother first. Look after him for me."

I went into the hall in search of Lady Frida and although there were several people there, she was not among them. Puzzled, I began to look in other areas of the court complex. Where could she be? She was unlikely to have gone home without Edward.

I was now in a less frequented part and trying to find my way back to the fighting area, when I ran round a corner and saw her. She was in the arms of Prince Edmund, no light between their bodies, their mouths devouring each other.

I gasped and stopped suddenly. They heard me and pulled apart.

"Wulfgar!" she spluttered.

"Edward's been hurt, my lady." The words tumbled out.

"Oh, no! Where is he?"

She followed me quickly, as I worked my way back to the boy. We took him home and she bathed his wound, which proved not to be too deep.

"Will I have a scar?" Edward asked.

"I don't think so," Lady Frida replied, "but we must be careful that it is kept clean."

Edward tipped his head to one side and looked at me.

"I hope I have a scar," he said solemnly.

I couldn't help but smile. He is a warrior in the making, I thought.

Nothing, of course, was said by Lady Frida about what I had seen. It was none of my business if she and Edmund kissed. She had clearly been enjoying the experience, so had no need to be rescued from unwanted attentions. If she had been resisting him, it would have been a different matter, for part of my role was to protect her.

As I lay on my mattress that night, I found sleep eluded me. I was not troubled by Edward's wound, as I reckoned he should recover quite well from that. Rather I kept seeing Lady Frida in Edmund's embrace.

I had no right to be upset, I told myself. But to be honest, I was upset. I didn't know of anyone who had kissed her like that since the death of her husband.

But you have often thought she could remarry, I argued in my head. She is still young and you are not the only one who admires her beauty.

Of course, I knew she had admirers. I had seen Lord Valgar's face and had even expected him to marry her, until I found he already had a wife. So why was I so upset?

You're jealous, a little voice said.

I dug my face into my pillow and tried to blot out the internal whispers, but I couldn't because it was the truth. I was jealous. In my heart, *I* wanted to hold her like that and kiss her. I knew I never could, but that didn't stop me from wanting to. I had watched her in the arms of my late master and felt no pangs of jealousy, but at that time I had been young and still learning the ways of adults. Now I was an adult and I could feel the passion stirring in me that must have stirred in him and led to our race across England to rescue her from Malmesbury Abbey.

It made no difference that I told myself I was a fool and would have to get used to her being with someone else. I pummelled my pillow and prayed to God to help me.

CHAPTER 25

As expected, Edward's wound quickly healed and he was anxious to return to the fighting arena. So the three of us became frequent visitors to court. I always stayed with Edward, while Lady Frida, I was sure, was somewhere with Prince Edmund. I tried not to think about them together. While I was concentrating on the fighting practice, it was easy to forget, but when we walked back to our house and she was bright-faced and talkative, I felt a pain within.

This routine continued even after Lord Valgar returned. He must have noticed their relationship, but he said nothing to me. I felt sorry for him, for Edmund had supplanted him, and Lady Frida certainly spoke less to Lord Valgar when the prince was around.

I wondered how long it would be before the marriage was announced, but nothing was said, which puzzled me. There was obviously something going on between them; I was sure even the King must have noticed and yet no one spoke of their future together. I was soon to learn why.

Christmas 1022 was approaching and it would be Anund's first Christmas as King. I didn't expect any changes, as he had seemed happy to continue with the pattern set by his father.

One day in early December I did, however, catch an encounter which made me wonder. I was at court and had left Edward at the butts while I relieved myself. The other side of the midden fence, I heard two voices I recognised. I hadn't intended to eavesdrop, but I was in no position to move quickly away.

"Edmund, I'm warning you," I heard Anund say.

"I'll do what I like," his brother responded.

"No, you will not. I am not just your brother, I am your King and I'm ordering you to sort this out before we reach Christmas. Or ... or I will sort it out and you won't like that."

That was all I heard, for I think Edmund stomped off, perhaps with Anund in pursuit.

A few days later, I noticed Lady Frida was unusually quiet. I was busy putting wood on our fire to stave off the cold and could see she was huddled in a chair with a solemn expression. She had sent Hild and Edith out with the boys, so we were alone in the hall.

"Wulfgar, bring a stool here and sit beside me," she said.

I obeyed and was surprised when she slipped her hand through my arm and held it tight. Then she leaned her forehead on my shoulder and I could feel my heart racing.

"My lady, is something wrong?" I managed to whisper.

"Yes," was the barely audible response.

I waited, wondering what I should say next.

"You know about Prince Edmund for you saw us. He has the same name as ... He seemed like a godsend. He made me feel alive again. He made me feel like a woman.

I had forgotten what a kiss was like, what passions a man can stir."

She paused. I couldn't have said anything if I had tried.

"He is not free to marry. He ... he has a wife in Gotaland. He didn't tell me until yesterday."

"Oh, my lady!" I was genuinely horrified. He had taken advantage of a vulnerable woman and treated her abominably. I wanted to hit him!

"I have thought much since then," she continued, "and I realise now that I did not love him. I was flattered by him, while his youth and physique attracted me. I have been very foolish."

"No, my lady, not foolish," I argued. "You have a tender heart and ... and life has been hard since your husband's death."

She was quiet. I wondered if she was crying. I remembered the conversation I had overheard and wondered if Anund had forced his brother to confess he was already married.

She continued to hold my arm.

"Thank you for listening," she whispered. "Pray for me."

"I do, my lady."

Then she squeezed my arm before she withdrew her hand, saying, "Ever my faithful servant. God bless you."

I got up to put more wood on the fire and hide my embarrassment.

"How old are you now, Wulfgar?"

"Nearly twenty, my lady," I said, busy with the logs.

"Old enough to marry. I would not stop you," she asserted. "There are many pretty girls in Sigtuna."

"I am happy to serve *you*, my lady."

I could feel my face burning and it wasn't just the heat of the fire.

Prince Edmund had left Sigtuna by the time we next went to court. I presume he had gone back to his wife and the whole court could issue a sigh of relief. Lady Frida put on a brave face and I could see from my place elsewhere in the hall that she was trying to be friendly and cheerful, even though she was probably weeping inside. I also noticed that other men now began to pay attention to her. It looked as though they had been waiting for Prince Edmund to leave the way clear, but none of them had his youth and good looks. Indeed, one particularly attentive man was even older than Lord Valgar.

In February, I passed twenty and was surprised by what happened.

"Vulfgar," Lord Valgar hailed me, "come here. I have something for you."

Puzzled, I obeyed.

"I have known you for more than five years," Lord Valgar began, "and you have worked well for me. You understand the trade and sometimes you even give me good advice. I value you."

I glowed at his praise.

"You are no longer a boy, but a man," he continued, "and now you should dress like a merchant."

I realised there were some clothes draped over the chair. He now picked up a splendid tunic made of fine cloth, far superior to the rough cloth one I usually wore.

"Here is a new tunic," he said, handing it to me, "and also a new cloak."

He indicated the fur-edged, thick woollen garment still on the chair.

"Oh, my lord, these are wonderful. And they are for me?"

"Of course, you deserve them."

Dressed in my new clothes, I felt like a new man. I genuinely felt I had changed into someone different.

"Now the captains of the ships, when they see you, they will respect you as a merchant, not just as a servant," he told me.

I was thrilled and loved my new clothes and the confidence they gave me when I went along the quayside. Lady Frida noticed the change.

"Wulfgar, you look splendid. Lord Valgar has dressed you well."

She was standing in front of me in admiration of my new attire and now put her hands on my arms.

"You are indeed a man now," she said proudly and gave me one of her heart-thumping smiles.

The days were lengthening, the boys were thriving and all seemed well. Edmund was now determined to learn to fight like his brother, and Edward encouraged him. Even Lady Frida seemed more at peace, as though her brief liaison with the Swedish prince was but a faint memory. I had no idea a huge change was on the horizon and I was taken completely by surprise.

I can still remember the day. It was early April, the spring sunshine had some warmth to it and I heard birdsong breaking the silence of winter. I had come into the hall and put my cloak on a chair. I was warming my hands and whistling softly to myself when I was interrupted.

"Wulfgar."

Lady Frida strode towards me. I backed slightly out of politeness, but she continued to close in on me. I kept backing, until I felt the wall behind me, and still she came forward.

"Wulfgar." She put her hands on my shoulders and I felt my mouth go dry. "You have been such a rock for me."

I hardly heard her words, for now her body was pressed against mine and I couldn't escape.

"You mean so much to me."

Her voice was soft, enticing, yes, seductive. She lifted her face. I could not take my eyes from her lips as they parted slightly. The battle lasted but a brief time and I clasped her to me and kissed her with hunger.

The bliss was short-lived. What was I doing? I let go of her as though her body burned my hands, and forced my head back.

"My lady ... I'm sorry. I couldn't help myself."

My apology was feeble, but she did not move. Instead she put her hands round my neck and pulled my head so that our lips met again.

The second kiss was sweeter than the first, for it was hers, not mine. It was madness, but it was *her* madness, and I savoured it. My hands felt the tingling muscles in her back.

When our lips parted, she leaned herself close against my face.

"Wulfgar, I need you," she whispered.

"I am your servant, my lady." My voice was low and hoarse, for I had difficulty forming the words.

"Come into my bed," she urged.

"I can't do that, my lady!"

I'm sure she felt my recoil, but she was not about to let me go.

"But you love me," she responded. "I'm sure you do."

How could I deny that? I worshipped the ground she walked on.

"Y ... yes," I stuttered. "But my love means I cannot violate you. The sharing of a bed is only for those who are married."

She moved to look me full in the face. Those beautiful blue eyes seemed to gaze into my soul. Her golden eyelashes flickered slightly.

"Then marry me."

CHAPTER 26

Lord Valgar was in the counting room and barely glanced up when I walked in.

"I'm not checking up on you, Vulfgar," he quipped. "I wanted to find that bundle of furs and see if there are enough for a consignment to Normandy."

I stood quietly waiting, but I think I must have been fiddling with my belt because he looked up.

"Something is wrong?" he asked. "You look worried."

"I'd like to talk to you."

He indicated I should sit down, but I found it hard to meet his gaze. I noticed I was flexing my fingers and clasping and unclasping my hands.

"Have you done something wrong and you need to tell me?" he enquired.

"I've done nothing wrong. Well, no, that's not true. But I couldn't help myself. She was so close."

"She? Are you talking about Lady Frida?"

I nodded.

"She ... she wants me to marry her."

The silence was profound. It seemed neither of us was breathing.

"What did you do?"

"I kissed her." I now looked at him and saw no anger in his face, just puzzlement. "She came right up to me. She pressed herself against me. I ... I ..."

Suddenly, he smiled.

"Vulfgar, if she had done that to me, I too would have kissed her. You are a lucky man."

I stared at him. He leaned back and his face creased into a laugh.

"I ... I feel so confused," I muttered.

"Women, they are not like us. She has been a widow for more than six years. She has done well. A man would marry again quickly, but she has missed being with a man. You thought she could live for the rest of her life without one, but she has found she cannot."

"Prince Edmund ..."

"Ah, yes, Edmund was a bad man. He desired her, but he did not tell her he was married. He reminded her of what she was missing. He roused her passion, but could not satisfy it. Now she wants someone to do that, so she looks around. There are old men who look at her with longing, me included. Some are free to marry her, but she does not want an old man. She prefers a young one and, more than that, she wants a man she can trust, and she knows, Vulfgar, that she can trust you, for you have loved her deep and long."

I stared at his wrinkled, handsome face. I had recognised all those years ago that he was in love with Lady Frida because ... because I was, and now he was saying he recognised I loved her too.

"We both love her," I acknowledged, "and therefore want the best for her."

"I cannot offer her marriage, but I have done what I can. I have been a provider and protector. If she marries you, I will still be that. You are a good man, Vulfgar. You have proved your loyalty and your love. But I think perhaps you feel unworthy of her."

"She is the widow of a king and who am I? A free-born Englishman, yes, but not of noble blood."

"Does that matter?"

"In England, it would be unthinkable."

"If you were still in England, she would not be making this proposal?"

"No," I asserted. "She would be looking to marry a nobleman."

"But the only people of her status here in Sweden are already married or ... somewhat old, as they are widowers, whose wives have already died. And if she wishes to marry an Englishman, then there is no choice, for there is only you." He paused and then frowned slightly. "I do not mean that unkindly. As I say, you are a good man and one she can trust and one who has the same longing, namely that of seeing her sons restored to their homeland. You have a bond she does not share with anyone else – and cannot share, for no one else knew her husband, the father of her precious children."

I didn't really know what to say.

"She wants you, Vulfgar. You would never have asked her, but come now, would you not like to be her husband?"

"Oh, yes, but I have never been that, even in my dreams."

"You are sure this is not a dream?"

"Kissing her was no dream, though it felt like heaven."

"You have not given her an answer?"

"Not yet," I admitted. "I can't really get my head round the idea."

He nodded and smiled again.

"You will. Take a little time to think about it. Do not let her hurry you. She has waited six years, so she can wait a little longer." He paused. "You need her. We have a saying:

A lone fir
in an open field
withers away.
A lone man
loved by none
how can he live long?"

He slapped me on the knee.

"I think it will be good, but I will be jealous as hell!"

I was so glad of this older man's advice and, frankly, surprised by his encouragement, but Lord Valgar was known for his generous spirit and he was showing that now. Of course, he wanted to be Lady Frida's husband, but he couldn't. However, he was not going to stop me, rather he pressed me to accept.

I did take his advice to take my time. I had always been her servant and to become her lord instead was a big change. But I could see it was not a whim on her part and that she had thought seriously about it.

"I saw you had become a man," she told me one day, "and I will admit I wanted to feel your body close to mine. But you are such an honourable person that you would not take advantage of me and I respect you for that. I always want you in my life, Wulfgar, and if you are my husband, then you can never leave me."

"I would never leave you anyway," I protested.

"Marriage will make us closer," she countered. "We will be there for each other, whatever happens, and there for my sons. I do hope you will say yes."

She had reached over to hold my hand and the look on her face was not that of a seductress, but of a friend, an equal.

"We have been through much together already," I said. "I want to be with you. Just give me a little time."

I still wrestled with my unworthiness, but it was irrelevant to her, and here in Sweden I was now regarded as a merchant rather than a servant. I began to sit with the courtiers on our visits to court and no one treated me badly. Rather they accepted me as one of them and that helped to make up my mind.

Lord Valgar, as generous as ever, offered us his room as our own and actually found lodgings in another house.

We married in early September. In the bed we now shared, she proved to be a good and gentle teacher and we were soon satisfying each other's passion. Sometimes I would wake in the night to find her caressing my body. Until then, I had only guessed at the joys of marriage; now I knew them.

Edward and Edmund took the change in their stride. I was still their friend rather than their father and that was how I wanted it to be. I had begun to tell them tales of King Edmund and the battles we had fought, because they needed to know their heritage.

It was about this time that Lord Valgar brought us news of another marriage.

"You know, Vulfgar, that there has been trouble for Cnut in Denmark."

"Thorkell, wasn't it? I remember him. He was called 'The Tall', and he was ... very tall."

"Cnut sent him to govern Denmark, but he rebelled and tried to govern the country for himself, so Cnut came, with English forces, to conquer him. Can you guess who fought for Cnut and led the English?"

I looked at him, and by his slight smile knew it would be a man with whom I was familiar.

"Godwine?"

"Yes. He did well for Cnut and now has the reward of a wife."

"Someone important, I presume."

"Thorkell had allies, two brothers, Ulf and Eilaf, who are earls. They have now submitted to Cnut, and Cnut secures their loyalty with marriages. He has married his sister Estrith to Ulf, and their sister Gytha he has married to ..."

"Godwine!" I thought for a moment. "So through these women, he is now related to the King of England."

"Indeed. It is an honour."

"I hope she's pretty," I remarked.

"No one is as pretty as your wife," laughed Lord Valgar, and I smiled in response.

I thought of Godwine and his political marriage. Perhaps his wife was pretty, but her looks would be irrelevant. His ambition would be the main factor and I thanked God that I had been able to marry for love.

The days were shortening and Christmas was fast approaching. The nights were sometimes cold as well as long. What a blessing to share a bed and feel the warmth of Frida's body close to mine.

"Wulfgar," she whispered, bringing me back from the edge of sleep. "There is something I should tell you."

CHAPTER 27

I flickered open my eyes and tried to see Frida's face, but it was too dark. Was she about to divulge some terrible secret and ruin my happiness?

"Wulfgar, I think I am with child."

"What?"

I was taken completely by surprise! I don't know why. Frida had proved to be very fertile while married to King Edmund, and our relationship was equally as passionate.

"With child!" I gasped. "Are you sure?"

"Almost sure. The signs are there and I feel as I did with both Edward and Edmund." She paused. "You are pleased, I hope."

"Of course, my love," I said, stroking her hair. "Just surprised."

She laughed softly, but I stopped her by kissing her.

It took me several days to get used to the idea of being a father, of having my own Edward or Edmund. Or maybe it would be a girl and grow up to be as beautiful as her mother. Frida was certainly very happy at the prospect of another child. A young husband and a baby were making her feel young.

"I am not so very much older than you," she complained, when I teased her.

"Not like Queen Emma and Cnut?" I laughed. "I think you despised her for marrying a man ten or more years her junior."

"I despised her for abandoning her children," she chided. "There are great advantages in having a younger husband."

She winked at me and I had to laugh. I certainly had no complaints.

We didn't say anything to the boys until Frida began to show. She had worked out the baby should arrive about the end of June and we didn't see much point in telling them too far in advance. She was a bit sick, but nothing that gave cause for concern.

"You are filling my house," joked Lord Valgar. "Soon there will not be room for you!"

Frida looked so well and happy that I was taken by surprise one night, as we lay quietly together.

"Wulfgar, I think this child is different."

"Different? What do you mean?"

"It kicks too much."

I laid my hand over her stomach, but the child wasn't kicking then.

"You are worried, my love?"

"A little. It is not the same."

"We will pray that all is well."

We did, and I also took to slipping into the small church in Sigtuna whenever I could. There was a statue of the Virgin Mary and I would kneel there and ask for her help.

"You know what it's like to be pregnant, and you know what it's like to give birth in a foreign land. Please, please, help my wife. Keep her well. Give us a safe delivery."

Her anxiety was affecting me. Sometimes she would laugh and say it was nothing, but, at other times, I picked up her tension.

Then, one day, she casually announced, "Hild thinks it may be twins."

My mouth fell open and I must have looked like a landed fish. She glanced across at me.

"Two children, Wulfgar, not merely one."

I was still speechless, my mind spinning. Twins! Childbirth was dangerous enough and two children doubled the danger. And would they live? They would be tiny. I remembered what Edmund had looked like and I couldn't imagine two that size inside my wife.

My instinct was to go to her and enfold her in my arms.

"Wulfgar, we must trust the Lord," she said. "He has brought us safely thus far. The boys need their mother as well as you."

"He does not always answer prayer," I countered.

"I know, you're thinking of my dear Edmund. But think too, that out of that sadness has come some joy. We have made good friends and found a safe place here in Sigtuna. And we have each other."

"I couldn't bear to lose you," I whispered.

That fear began to dog me and I was assailed with regrets. If I hadn't married her, she would not be pregnant and her life would not be in danger. Why could I not have remained her admirer, but kept my distance? Then I would feel her close to me and I would know why I had married her. But the dark cloud of childbirth would not go away and it grew darker as it grew nearer and she was beginning to struggle with her movements. The twins were obvious for she was very large and Hild had only the double birth as an explanation. I prayed she was right and I kept praying all would be well.

I was often sent out with the boys.

"Go and do some fighting," Frida ordered. "You are making me nervous."

So the three of us would go to court and get some fighting practice. Edward was now eight and Edmund nearly seven and both were learning well, as they seemed to have their father's natural talent. The King's soldiers remarked on their aptitude.

"I hope I fight a battle one day," Edward said.

"They are cruel and bloody affairs," I replied. "Men die or are so maimed they die."

"Have you ever killed a man, Wulfgar?"

"At the Battle of Assandun, the priest was attacked by a Dane and I had to kill the man to save the priest's life." I paused. "I didn't really enjoy it, but it was him or me."

"That's how it is, I suppose," Edward pondered. "Kill or be killed."

"In England, we didn't kill women and children, but not everyone holds back like that," I told him, for I knew the Danes would massacre anyone in their way. "Practise, practise, practise and be always ready," I advised the aetheling.

The warm weather was making Frida very lethargic and I continued to worry. One day, I took Hild on one side.

"Yes, of course, it is dangerous," she agreed, "and Lady Frida is not as young as she was when she had Edward and Edmund. But she is healthy and strong and loved."

"Loved? What difference does that make?" I cried.

"Her will to live is strong. She will fight to stay alive – for all of you."

I was still concerned and was glad of Lord Valgar's presence, for he too tried to keep me calm. I had difficulty concentrating on the work and he was remarkably patient with me.

Then, on the first day of July, it happened – Frida cried in pain and I was told to take the boys out of the house. I took them with me to find Lord Valgar and he agreed that he and his housekeeper would look after them for the time being.

Edward's huge eyes looked up at me, as he tipped his head to one side.

"Will mother be alright?" he asked.

"We pray so," I muttered, but he could read the creases in my forehead.

I returned to our house, determined to be as close as I could be. I paced the hall, I sat down, I stood up, I fiddled with my belt, I flexed my fingers, I wandered round in circles. The hours passed. I tried to have some food, but I wasn't hungry and soon pushed the platter away.

I began to relive the birth of Edmund, as I heard cries from above, only this time I was scared. I wondered about going upstairs and standing outside the door, but decided to stay where I was. I began to feel sick and got stomach cramps, but my darling wife was going through something far worse.

Then Edith came hurrying down and she wasn't smiling.

"There is a little girl," she told me, "but we are sure there is another child. Keep praying," she urged.

A girl! I had a daughter, but I also had a wife in danger of dying.

I continued to cry out to God for a safe delivery. My head began to spin and I sat down to stop fainting completely. In fact, I think I must have passed out, for I was suddenly aware of a hand on my shoulder and of being gently shaken.

"You have a son as well," Edith spoke through the blur.

"And Frida?" I gasped.

"Very tired and there is some bleeding, but we are hopeful."

CHAPTER 28

I sat in the hall, staring at the empty brazier. I had a son and a daughter; Hild had been right about the twins. But these next few hours were crucial. If they could not stop the bleeding, Frida would die.

I couldn't stand it any longer. I hurried up the stairs and knocked on the door. Edith opened it and let me in. Frida lay on our bed, dishevelled, her hair soaked in sweat, her face bright with exhaustion. I knelt by the bed and took her hand.

"Dearest," I whispered.

Her eyes opened and slowly focussed on me.

"Wulfgar." Her voice was tiny.

"A girl and a boy, dearest."

She closed her eyes again and smiled.

Don't die! I shouted in my head.

"I'm so proud of you," was what I actually said.

"You'll need two names."

"*We'll* need two names," I countered. "You are not to leave me."

Suddenly, she opened her eyes wide and looked at me.

"You will live," I urged, "and you will suckle them."

I think my words registered and it was as though she was wide awake and fighting to survive.

"Are they alright?" she asked.

In my concern for her, I'd failed to ask if the babies were alright.

"Come and look," Edith said, and pulled me over to a makeshift cot, where two tiny bundles lay, their eyes tightly shut. Red and wrinkled, they had no beauty, but they were mine.

"They're very small," she continued, "but have good lungs."

To prove that, one of them began crying and that set off the other.

"Here, hold your son."

One of the bundles was put in my arms and I rocked him gently. The little girl was picked up too and taken to Frida, who cradled it and whispered words of love.

So began the life of our two children. Frida did not die and made a full, but slow, recovery. We named the boy Wulfsige (but always called him Wulf) and the girl Edith (after Frida's sister-in-law), but as there was already an Edith in the household, our daughter almost immediately took on the name Edie.

Edward and Edmund were thrilled, especially by their little brother.

"We'll teach him to fight," Edward said. "I'm sure he will be brave, just like you, Wulfgar."

Frida had our room for her and the babies, and I was back to sleeping in the hall. Whenever I asked if I could return to our room, she always said, "Not yet".

I was beginning to get frustrated and cross, so, one night, I went in uninvited. She didn't throw me out, but she wouldn't let me touch her. The following morning, I demanded an explanation.

"Dearest Wulfgar, I am afraid," she said. "I don't want any more children. The twins' birth was really hard. If I have another child, I think I'll die."

"Can we not still be close sometimes?" I asked.

She let me put my arms round her and then she began to weep. When she had calmed down, she nestled against me.

"I do want you so much," she whispered, "but we must curb our passion."

"I understand and will let you guide me."

So we entered a new phase in our marriage when we often had to control our longing for each other. I had to respect her desire not to get pregnant. But we had two adorable children. They were very small and I feared that one or both might die, but God answered our prayers for their good health, and both began to thrive. It was a happy time in our lives. Edward and Edmund showed no jealousy, simply impatience, for they wanted Wulf to grow up quickly. I took them to court and their fighting skills were improving, as were mine.

The twins were nearing their second birthday when an opportunity arose for me to be tested in a real battle.

"You know, Vulfgar, there are rumours of war," Lord Valgar told me.

"What exactly is going on?" I asked. "I've heard snippets of stories."

"Olof, the late King, would not fight Cnut, as they were, in a sense, brothers, but neither would he help him by killing Edward and Edmund. Anund is different. He feels no such bond. He too would not kill the aethelings and that is why they are still safe here, but he feels there is nothing to stop him fighting Cnut."

"But why would he fight Cnut?"

"The King of Norway and our King fear Cnut grows too strong. He holds England and he holds Denmark. His father once ruled Norway and Cnut would like to do the same. They plan to fight against him together and curb his power."

"Those men who practise each day will soon be fighting for real then," I commented.

"The King will need others besides these."

"I could fight with them!" I exclaimed.

I hadn't been old enough to fight Cnut in England, but I was old enough now. At 23 I was strong and skilful, a match for any Dane.

The next day, Lord Valgar and I were at court and the talk was all of the impending war.

"Our spies say Cnut is planning to invade Norway in the south, very near our border," King Anund told a group of us. "We plan to join the men of Norway and teach the Dane a lesson."

"Can I come and fight with you?" I asked. "You and your father have given us protection and this would be a way of repaying you."

"Wulfgar! You are a brave and generous man!" Anund exclaimed. "I will need people like you."

"Wait!" Lord Valgar intervened. "We know Cnut has Englishmen in his troops. They have fought for him before, when there was trouble in Denmark."

"What difference does that make?" I asked.

Lord Valgar looked me in the eye.

"If you were face to face with Godwine, could you kill him?"

I hesitated.

"Sire, Vulfgar could be fighting Englishmen he knows and that would not be good. Not if, one day, Edward returns to be King of England."

Anund was nodding.

"I really appreciate your offer, Wulfgar, but Valgar is right. It is not good for you to fight the English, but we Swedes will have no qualms about killing anyone who fights for Cnut."

I was bitterly disappointed, but could see the logic of their arguments. In my heart I knew I could not kill Godwine, for he had been my late King's true friend and had also helped us escape from England.

Frida, of course, was delighted that my offer had been refused.

"I could not bear to lose you," she said, clinging to me. "I've lost two husbands and I do not want to see you die in battle."

"I may well have to fight one day," I argued, "but it doesn't look as though it will be just yet."

I heard later that there had indeed been Englishmen among Cnut's forces. There was a big battle at Holy River and Cnut was defeated.

"He has gone back to England with his tail between his legs," was the verdict.

"But he is not a man who takes defeat," Anund countered.

I thought of how persistent he had been in his invasion of England; he simply wouldn't leave us alone, even when harried out of Kent.

"I fear he will return," the King added.

He was right and Cnut's new expedition had a profound effect on our little family.

CHAPTER 29

The year of our Lord 1027 was a quiet one and we did well with trade, so much so that Lord Valgar took on a new clerk. He was a round-faced lad in his late teens, from a family Lord Valgar knew well, and he was keen and quick to learn. I was reminded of the youth I had been when I arrived in Sweden. Seven years on and I was now a man, a merchant and the father of two children. I could never have imagined how my life would change and I thanked God daily for his blessing.

The trouble began in the spring of 1028, when we had news Cnut had brought fifty ships from England and was preparing, from his base in Denmark, a fresh invasion.

"If he tries to fight on land, I think we can stop him," Anund declared, "but I suspect he's learned his lesson. All those ships suggest a sea-based invasion and that could be too far away for us to help the Norwegians."

The King was right and news filtered through that Cnut had sailed up the western coast. He had bribed some leading men to change sides and the combination of Cnut's formidable army and the traitors in the Norwegian camp meant Olaf Haraldson was fleeing for his life, and Cnut became the King. Olaf had a brief stay in Sigtuna before fleeing further east, where we understood his wife had a relative who would give him sanctuary.

Refugees flooded into Sweden and some joined us in Sigtuna. Anund welcomed them, and those who were warriors joined his own men in the practice area.

Edward and Edmund were growing in confidence in their fighting skills. Edward was now twelve and Edmund close to eleven.

One day, Edmund had stayed at home while Edward and I went to court and joined the fighters. As I rested for a moment, I became aware of Edward and his opponent, a man I didn't know and presumed was a Norwegian. They were fighting well, too well.

Suddenly, I knew something was wrong – Edward was fighting for his life!

"Stop now!" I shouted, and ran over to where they were battling.

The stranger reluctantly put up his sword and I sensed his displeasure.

"Edward, it's time we left," I commanded.

I said nothing, but later in the day Edward took me on one side.

"Do you think that man was trying to kill me?" he said quietly.

I looked at his serious face, the eyes of his father made huge by his fear.

"Maybe," I breathed. "If he was, he was trying to make it look like an accident."

"So perhaps I have an enemy?"

"I suppose it's possible that Cnut sent him to ... to reduce the opposition."

We were now on high alert. I warned Frida. She was

terrified, but she had to know. We were sure that if the man was truly an assassin, then he would try again, so Edmund was kept in the house and Edward never left my sight, which was just as well, for a fresh attack came.

The killer tried to do the deed when he thought Edward was alone, but I was close by. Edward had drawn his seax in response to a slight movement he'd sensed and had found himself facing his attacker. On his own and caught unawares, I think he would have succumbed, but I was near enough to come to his aid and, between us, we soon had the man on the ground, disarmed and pleading for mercy.

By then, others had gathered and it was an easy matter to bind his hands and take him to Anund.

"Leave him with me," the King told us. "He will soon tell us everything."

The man had abused the refuge given him at the Swedish court and was now in their hands. I didn't ask how the prisoner would be made to tell, and took Edward home.

The next day, a message came from Anund summoning me and Lord Valgar to court.

"I am very sad that I have harboured an assassin," the King told us. "The man pretended to be fleeing from Cnut, but he was not."

"Did Cnut send him?"

"I do not think so," Anund responded. "He appears to have acted alone. He hoped to kill the princes and return to Cnut to be rewarded."

"Why now?" Lord Valgar asked. "The boys have been here several years and there has been no hint Cnut wanted them dead."

"Cnut has a queen, ja?"

We nodded.

"She wants them dead. It is claimed there was a plot to restore the sons of Edmund to the throne."

"We know of no such plot!" I protested.

"She may have lied," Anund said. "But she stirred up fear, enough fear to put the princes' lives in danger."

I could feel myself going cold all through.

"Wulfgar, I cannot promise to protect them," the King added. "You see how it is. They are not safe, but I have an idea."

He turned to Lord Valgar.

"You have many contacts in the east. I think you should take them to Russia." He turned back to me. "My sister, Ingegerd, is married to Yaroslav, who holds court in Novgorod. You will be a long way away from Cnut there. He is powerful now he holds England, Denmark and Norway and even threatens my kingdom, but he holds no sway in Russia."

Russia! I'd heard so many tales of this place, but thought I'd never see it. Now I looked at Lord Valgar.

"The King's idea is a good one, Vulfgar. I can get you all to Russia."

We had made many friends in Sigtuna, but the attack

on Edward had shaken us. Frida was so frightened that she could not sleep well, and even the boys had become nervous. I worked with Lord Valgar to organise our escape.

Thus it was that, within a few weeks, we were again at sea, sailing east into, at least for us, the unknown. Lord Valgar came out with one of his sayings,

"Moderately wise
a man should be
not too crafty and clever.
A man's fate
should be firmly hidden
to preserve his peace of mind.

It means it is good that you do not know what lies ahead. If we knew the future, we would worry. Does not Job in the Bible say, 'My times are in your hands, Lord'? We can trust God."

This was a long journey, across the great sea. Edward and Edmund loved the sense of adventure and were now old enough to be responsible passengers and acute observers of our surroundings. Wulf and Edie were a bit more of a handful, being only four years old, but the older boys proved to be excellent at keeping them amused, especially Wulf, while Hild and Edith did their best between bouts of sickness. Edie often sat with me, sometimes nestling under my cloak and smiling up at me. She was the image of her mother and I adored her, but I was careful not to spoil her, for I didn't want to breed a wilful daughter. Five days at sea brought us to the mainland and from there we continued to sail up a wide river.

"This river is called the Neva," Lord Valgar told me. "Russia has many rivers and many lakes."

"I once heard tell that Vikings took their boats up waterways to their source, then dragged them overland to the next river," I commented.

"It's true," he confirmed. "It can be done. But trade has been difficult for a while and we have not been able to go far south." He raised his eyebrows. "Everywhere there is war and men wanting power. Vladimir held the whole land, but on his death his sons divided it. Yaroslav holds the north and there is peace, for the present. We pray it will be a good and safe place for you."

We sailed into a large lake called Ladoga, well known for its sudden storms, but we were blessed with calm weather. On the sixth day of our journey, we travelled up another river Lord Valgar called the Volkhov to the city of Novgorod, where Yaroslav and his Swedish wife Ingegerd held their court.

The east! We were in the east, far, far away from England, and the possibility of Edward ever becoming king seemed as far away too. But, surely, here, we were beyond the hatred of Queen Emma and her influence on her ambitious husband.

So, we are here, in Novgorod, in the land of the Rus and we now have to try and make this our new home.

Russian ruling family

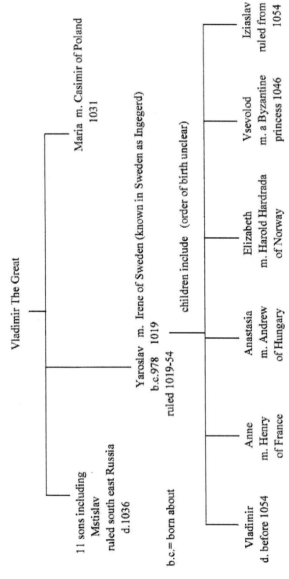

Vladimir The Great

Yaroslav m. Irene of Sweden (known in Sweden as Inggegerd)
b.c.978   1019
ruled 1019-54

Maria m. Casimir of Poland
1031

11 sons including
Mstislav
ruled south east Russia
d.1036

b.c.= born about

children include (order of birth unclear)

Vladimir
d. before 1054

Anne
m. Henry
of France

Anastasia
m. Andrew
of Hungary

Elizabeth
m. Harold Hardrada
of Norway

Vsevolod
m. a Byzantine
princess 1046

Iziaslav
ruled from
1054

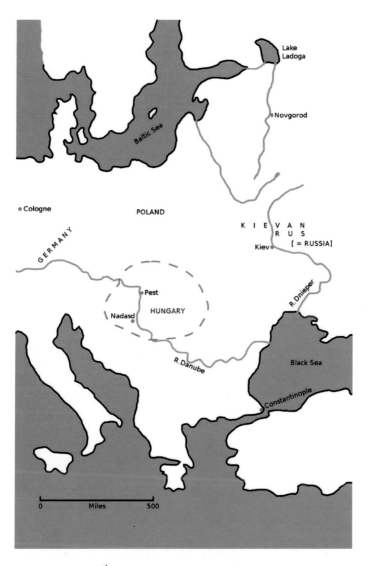

Europe in the 11th century, the red broken line showing the
approximate boundary of Hungary

PART IV – RUSSIA

CHAPTER 30

Novgorod was an amazing city, its magnificent buildings making Sigtuna seem a poor town by comparison. There were stone churches and other grand buildings. Also the streets were wide, giving the city a sense of space and importance. We were all in awe of our new surroundings.

Lord Valgar had connections here and found us somewhere to stay, at least for the present.

"I need to deliver a letter I have for King Anund's sister," he told us. "It may be that Duke Yaroslav will offer you a home at court."

Within a few days, we presented ourselves to the Russian ruler and his Swedish-born wife. They greeted us warmly.

"Our brother Anund writes of your plight," the Duke said. "He is sad to see you go, but fears he cannot ensure your protection."

"Cnut grows in power," Lord Valgar responded. "He now has control of Norway and threatens Sweden."

"And the little princes are put in danger," Yaroslav added. "Come here, boys."

Edward and Edmund approached the Duke. He was about fifty, rather stocky and short with a huge moustache and a beard. His presence and the splendour of his court and capital had tied all our tongues. The language being used was Norse, which helped to make us feel more at home.

"What are your names?"

"I am Edward." As he spoke, he tipped his head to one side, as though studying this ruler. "And I am the son of King Edmund of England."

"And I am Edmund." He stood shoulder to shoulder with his brother like warriors in a shieldwall. "I'm his brother."

Yaroslav smiled.

"Yes, I can see the likeness. And you are their mother," the Duke addressed Frida.

She curtseyed.

"And how old are you, Edward and Edmund?"

"I'm twelve."

"And I'm eleven."

"Nearly old enough to fight."

"Oh, yes," they chorused.

"We both fight well," Edward added.

"And who has taught you to fight?" The Duke looked at me.

"We've had the privilege, sire, of learning our craft with the best fighters in Sweden."

"So you are Lord Wulfgar, Lady Frida's husband?"

I bowed.

"Anund talks about you all, even the little ones."

I had a child in each hand.

"Our children, Wulf and Edie," I said.

Wulf bowed and Edie curtseyed, but neither managed even a smile, as I think they were overawed.

The Duke ordered some food and we were soon gathered informally round a table. I noticed the Duke had a marked limp and suspected this was a war wound. His wife had watched our audience in silence, but she now came alongside Frida and fussed our children in a warm and motherly way. She was much younger than her husband, but as this meant the two women were not too far apart in age, I hoped this could be the beginning of a real friendship. The Duke also had a sister, Maria, who was much younger than him.

"Lord Wulfgar, what do you think of my city?" the Duke asked, as he dug his teeth into a piece of roast meat.

"It's wonderful," I replied. "Such beautiful buildings. Your residence here appears to be extensive."

"Ah yes, the people of Novgorod call it Yaroslav's Court. At present, it is the grandest building in the city, but there will be more." He paused. "I need a large court for all the royal refugees."

He pretended to be serious, but his face broke into a broad smile.

"There is room for you all. You are very welcome. But you are not the only ones fleeing from Cnut."

"Olaf is here?" asked Lord Valgar.

"Indeed, and his wife, son and daughter. You will meet them soon."

Before we completed our move into the royal residence, I got Lord Valgar to explain something of Yaroslav's history.

"His father was Vladimir. He styled himself a Grand Prince or Grand Duke, though he was like a king. There were so many sons that they fought against each other for power and to control every part, for Vladimir had left different parts of the land to different sons."

"A recipe for war?"

"Often and yes, in this case. Yaroslav had Novgorod and the north. His main rival held Kiev to the south. Many of the brothers were murdered and Yaroslav battled his brother, Svyatopolk, until he finally defeated him about nine years ago. But only four years ago another brother, Mstislav, wrestled back the area near Kiev and now there is a somewhat uneasy peace."

"More wars then?"

"I think Edward and Edmund will get an opportunity to fight," he sighed. "It is part of their responsibility as aethelings to be warriors and leaders of men. We have a saying:

A king's son should be thoughtful
thorough and silent
brave in battle.
A man should be happy
and in good humour
to his dying day."

207

Yaroslav generously provided us with rooms in the court complex and we very soon met his family and his other "guests". Irene was his second wife (her name had been changed from Ingegerd on her arrival in Russia from Sweden) and they had several small children. Olaf of Norway and his wife Astrid were refugees, as we were, and had with them a boy, Magnus, who was the same age as Wulf and Edie, and a girl called Wulfhild, who was a little older. Edward and Edmund were therefore older than all the other children at court, but they didn't mind as they were beginning to see themselves as too grown-up for the childish games played by the younger ones. They had plenty of opportunities to continue honing their fighting skills and this was greatly encouraged by the Duke.

I didn't worry too much about who was who, as I was busy finding my way round Novgorod and being introduced to essential contacts.

"I plan to return to Sigtuna," Lord Valgar told me. "I am needed there, but you can do me great service by your presence here."

The plan was that I would build up our trade in Russia and, living here permanently, I could do that better than Lord Valgar could do with his fleeting visits. We would both benefit and as long as there were no major wars, we would continue to make good money through our trade.

Frida spent her time, naturally, at court with the women and the children. She would chatter away to me about the goings on and I would listen with half an ear,

208

usually. One night, she demanded my full attention, as we lay close in our bed.

"There are tensions here," she told me, "and I am beginning to understand them."

"Like what?"

"Irene was betrothed to Olaf, but without her father's approval," she continued. "The Swedish King decided to marry her to Yaroslav and, of course, she had no choice in the matter."

"When was that?"

"1019. We were in Sweden then, but not living in the court as we do here, so I don't remember anything about it."

"We hadn't been there very long at that time," I commented.

"Irene's father then had Astrid married to Olaf instead."

"Why did it matter which daughter married which ruler?"

"I'm not sure, except that I think Astrid is not legitimate. I remember Prince Edmund telling me about his family. Astrid is his sister and Irene is the sister of Anund. Edmund and Anund are half-brothers."

I was trying hard to follow all this.

"So when Olaf had to flee from Norway," I said, "he came east with Astrid to the place where Astrid's half-sister is."

"Yes, you've got it, Wulfgar."

"In theory, the two women should get on because they are sisters, well, half-sisters, but, I think you are hinting all is not well."

"Because Olaf and Irene wanted to marry, but she was forced to marry Yaroslav."

"And now he is here, in her court, and they are in each other's company every day," I concluded.

I could see this could be causing difficulties if Olaf and Irene still had feelings for each other, but nearly ten years had passed. Perhaps Olaf was satisfied with Astrid. When I suggested this, Frida had more to add.

"I don't think Magnus is Astrid's son, but Wulfhild is her child."

"What do you mean?" I asked.

"Magnus is Olaf's son by another woman, but he is being brought up as Olaf's heir. Maybe Astrid couldn't have any more children after the birth of her daughter."

The picture was getting clearer.

"Olaf is here with a wife he didn't want, and who has borne him only a daughter," I summarised, "and he is constantly with Irene, whom he desired to marry and who is proving to be a very fruitful wife."

This sounded like an impending storm! Would it blow over or rip the court apart?

CHAPTER 31

The next time we all dined together, I found I was sitting next to Olaf and so had the opportunity of talking to him.

"I remember you were at the siege of London," I began.

"London?"

"When you pulled down the bridge."

He laughed; he had a deep laugh which made you want to join in.

"That was a long time ago," he replied, eventually. "1014 I think. I was only a lad – in the eyes of some."

"A lad?" I was puzzled. "I remember you and Thorkell the Tall in deep discussion. I don't think he was too keen on your idea."

"I'd known Thorkell a while. I left Norway to go raiding when I was ... about Edward's age. I had command of ships and men. Thorkell and I teamed up, but he was sometimes wary of my more outlandish ideas."

"Your plan to pull down the bridge was brilliant," I commented. "I watched the whole event from the riverbank and was cheering you on to success."

"I remember the cheering crowds," he grinned.

"It was a significant moment, because King Aethelred was able to take London and then move north to confront Cnut."

Olaf pulled a face.

"He got you in the end though," he muttered. "And now he's got my kingdom too."

"Is there any news?"

"Not much. I believe he's put Hakon, one of the lords of Lade, in charge." He lowered his voice. "There were traitors in my camp."

I nodded in sympathy. We'd had the same problem in England.

"Perhaps they won't like being ruled by the Danish," I suggested.

"That's what I hope for – and pray for."

From my conversation, I realised he wasn't as old as I'd thought. Back in 1014, he had seemed a mature warrior, short, stout and very muscular, but he had probably only been about twenty then, his harsh lifestyle having contributed to the strong muscles and rough appearance. I guessed he had always been shaped more like a barrel than a single lath and that's how he had earned the nickname "Olaf the Stout". He was good company and very easy to talk to. I never saw him looking in Irene's direction, so wondered if, perhaps, there was nothing there now. After all, they had both been married to their spouses for quite a while.

I didn't dismiss Frida's words as gossip, but I didn't dwell on them. For one thing, I was too busy with the trade, because Lord Valgar had returned to Sweden and left me to look after our business interests in Russia. I revelled in my work. There was only one aspect of the trade in this new country which bothered me and that was the selling of slaves. Lord Valgar and I had agreed we would not traffic in people, but it was hard to see the gangs of (usually) foreigners being herded as though they were cattle. Other traders tried to make me buy, but I knew that if I bought any, I would simply have set them free without contemplating selling them on. At present, I didn't have enough money for that kind of generosity and anyway, these people were so far from their homeland that I feared being released would only make their lives even more uncertain. Perhaps, one day, I would find a way to help.

I was therefore taken by surprise when Edward sought me out and asked that we find a quiet place to talk. He looked even more serious than usual.

"What is it?" I asked, when we were alone.

"I saw King Olaf kissing Irene," he said in a low voice.

"They are like brother and sister," I responded.

"They were not kissing like brother and sister," he persisted. "They ... they were ... you know."

I felt a tremor go through me.

"Have you been spying?" I demanded.

"No!" he cried. "I was sitting, polishing my sword after all the men had finished fighting. Everyone had gone except King Olaf. I was in the shadow of a wall and I don't think he knew I was there."

My eyes were fixed on his face. I had no doubt he was telling the truth.

"The Duchess came into the area. She didn't see me either. I saw her go over to him and they both moved into an archway, out of the sight of anyone who might come into the area, but I could still see."

He paused and swallowed hard.

"Then he put his arms round her and began to kiss her. She didn't stop him. She ... she let him touch her ... her breasts."

I sighed deeply and looked down at my feet. What should I say?

"A long time ago," I began, "they were betrothed, but then her father had her marry Yaroslav and gave Olaf Astrid as a wife."

"You think they still love each other?" he asked.

"I don't know."

"But even if they do, they shouldn't be ... be kissing like that, should they?"

I looked at his solemn face.

"No, Edward, they should not. They are both married."

"They might be doing more and that would be wrong too, wouldn't it?"

"Very wrong. Sharing a bed is only for those who are married to each other. There is a word for that."

"I think I know it. Adultery." He looked at me intently. "If Duke Yaroslav knew, he ... he might kill King Olaf."

Our eyes were locked.

"So what should I do?" he whispered.

"Say nothing. Pretend you have not seen them. I will not say a word either. Sometimes the wisest thing is to keep our mouths shut. You can choose to be silent."

I thought it best to say nothing even to Frida, though I was sorely tempted.

"Irene is with child," Frida told me one night in the privacy of our room.

I made no comment as my mind was whirling.

"Do you think ...?" I managed to mutter.

"You have the same thoughts as me," she replied. "Who is the father?"

"I pray that it's Yaroslav."

"I think it is. I asked her some questions, discreetly, of course, and have worked out the child was almost certainly conceived before Olaf arrived here. He hadn't been here long when we came and she is a few months into her term."

"That's a relief."

Frida was quiet.

"Is there something more?" I enquired.

"Because she is pregnant, she can share a bed with him without worrying about conceiving his child."

"I hope they are curbing their passions. But ..." I wrapped my arms more tightly round her. "Do we have to curb ours tonight?"

Her answer was to cover my mouth with kisses.

As Edward and Edmund were older than the many other children who inhabited the court, they attracted Yaroslav's attention and I would often see him talking to them or showing them things or explaining what new buildings he was planning for Novgorod. Edward, in particular, was singled out; I think the Duke noticed he showed more interest than Edmund, who didn't have as much patience with adults.

I happened to be there when Yaroslav suddenly asked Edward, "If you saw something that you thought was wrong, what would you do?"

I held my breath.

CHAPTER 32

Edward studied the Duke's face.

"It depends what it was," he said solemnly. "If I saw a man beating his slave, I might try to stop him and find out if the slave deserved the beating. But I know slaves are thought of as property. They have little value in England compared to a free man."

The Duke was watching his face.

"What if ... what if it was a moral issue? What if you saw a married man kissing a woman who was another man's wife?"

"I can choose to stay silent," Edward answered, without even glancing in my direction.

The Duke continued to study the lad's face, but Edward stared back at him in such a cool way that I was proud of him.

"You have the beginnings of wisdom," the Russian said at length. "You will make a fine king. I hope, one day, the throne is yours."

"I must prepare as best I can for such a great responsibility," Edward replied, "but I must not let that hope stop me from living in the present."

Yaroslav looked across at me.

"He is remarkable!" he exclaimed. "You tutor him well."

"He has a natural aptitude for gaining knowledge and wisdom," I commented. "He will learn from any who will teach him well."

"Edward, they call me by a number of names and one of them is Yaroslav the Wise. I will do what I can to teach you how to rule wisely."

Later, when Edward and I were alone, he asked me, "Do you think the Duke knew?"

"About seeing something? I don't know. It was an odd question." I paused. "I've been thinking about it. Perhaps the Duke hoped to make you a spy and get evidence of his wife's behaviour. If so, he failed because you made it clear you wouldn't always say what you'd seen."

"Wulfgar, did my father marry for love?"

"Oh, yes. It's quite a story."

"Tell me."

"Frida was the wife of Earl Siferth and when he was murdered, she was imprisoned in Malmesbury Abbey. King Aethelred intended to confiscate all her lands, but your father rode across England and rescued her. Then he married her and stopped the confiscation."

"Did he marry her for love or for the property?"

"That's a good question," I responded, admiring his shrewdness. "I was there at the time and though some may have accused him of wanting the property for his own purposes, I know he married her for love. They were devoted to each other."

"Can I marry for love?" he asked.

I was quiet for a moment.

"Not necessarily," I said slowly. "If, for instance, you met a girl in a street here in Novgorod and liked her and got to know her, you couldn't marry her. As an aetheling, you have to marry someone of royal or, at least, noble blood."

"It may not even be someone I've met," he commented. "That's what happens sometimes, isn't it? Marriage for people like me is about political alliances." He paused. "I hope that I like her – and that she likes me. It must be dreadful to be married if you don't even like being together."

I was stunned by the maturity of his thinking. He had seemed still a boy in Sweden, but here in Russia, he had become a man even before his thirteenth birthday.

He looked at me and suddenly grinned.

"But there's no hurry, is there?"

"None at all," I agreed. "And, anyway, I hope your mother wouldn't force you to marry a girl you really didn't like."

Christmas was fast approaching and Irene tried to explain to us what differences we would find.

"It was Yaroslav's father who decided Russia should be Christian."

"That's not very long ago then," I commented. "England has been Christian for about seven hundred years."

"My homeland was pagan until my father was baptised and even now there are still many pagans in Sweden. And in Norway too," she added.

"The Duke's father was Vladimir. Have I got that right?" I asked her.

"Yes. We tell the story that he was unhappy with paganism, so he sent envoys to investigate other faiths. Some went to Arabia to bring back news of Allah, some to seek out the faith of the Jews. Others went to Rome and yet others to Constantinople."

I was intrigued, as, I think, was Frida.

"All returned and laid their information before Vladimir," Irene continued. "He could see Allah was not the true God. Also he became convinced Jesus was the Son of God, so we could not be Jews."

"Ah, that left Christianity," I concluded. "Isn't that the faith common to both Rome and Constantinople? Did he have a further choice to make?"

"There isn't such a big difference as with the two he rejected," she agreed, "but the East does worship in a way the West does not. Also we look to the Patriarch who is in Constantinople, rather than the Pope who is in Rome. It is the Patriarch who has provided us with a bishop."

"But you talk of differences," I said. "All we have noticed so far is the language. Your services are not in Latin."

"No, they are in our own language, which means that *everyone*, even the peasants, can understand. Also ..."

She smiled broadly. "At Christmas you will see the church at its best, because our worship is very beautiful. I was overwhelmed when I first came here from Sweden – the singing, the bells, the incense. Oh, I thought I was in heaven! And that is why Vladimir chose the East because his envoys worshipped in a great church in Constantinople and told him they could not tell whether they were on earth or in heaven."

"I have heard it is a grand city," I responded. "Traders tell me of its magnificent buildings, including the huge church."

"It is dedicated to St. Sophia," Irene said. "Yaroslav hopes one day to build a similar church, perhaps ...," she lowered her voice, "... perhaps when he has control of all Russia and can build it at Kiev. That is his dream."

"It is a good dream to have," Frida confirmed. "With Christ at the heart of a country, there will be less war."

I made no comment, as I was wondering how he could take control of all the area around Kiev without fighting some battles.

So we had our first Christmas in Russia and the worship, as the Duchess had promised, was very moving and we, too, wondered if we were in heaven, but the harsh Russian winter reminded us that we were not.

Edward did not mention Olaf again and even though I did keep my eyes and ears alert, I noticed nothing to concern me. If he was intimate with Irene, he was being very discreet. She, meanwhile, was beginning to show she was with child.

A new princess came into the world in the late spring and joined the numerous other youngsters who filled the court. Thankfully, she bore no resemblance to Olaf. Wulf and Edie had settled in well and now had plenty of playmates. They had made a special friend of Magnus, Olaf's son; he was almost exactly the same age and something of an outsider, like them. We had no qualms for their well-being. Edward continued to spend some time with the Duke, who had taken a liking to him and was determined to teach him all he could. My only concern there was that I knew Yaroslav had won his status by the murder of many of his brothers. If Edward was ever to be King of England, I hoped it would be by a peaceful accession.

So the year of our Lord 1029 slipped by. Our family was settled, Frida was healthy and happy, and I was beginning to grow rich through my hard work. The only person ill at ease was Olaf, who often seemed like a caged wolf who wanted to be free to hunt down and devour its prey. I wondered if he would ever be able to return to Norway, because Cnut was a real power with which to be reckoned. But, that winter, an unexpected storm in the North Sea rocked Cnut's boat.

CHAPTER 33

"There's news from Norway!"

Olaf grasped me by the arm. His eyes were bright with excitement and his cheeks red with exertion, for I think he had been running.

"A storm and a drowning!" he crowed.

"Cnut?" I gasped.

"No, sadly not the man himself, but the next best thing. Hakon. He's dead."

"Hakon?"

"The Lord of Lade who's been governing Norway for the Dane," Olaf replied. "He's out of the way. Now's my chance."

"But how does that really change things?" I queried.

"They are leaderless. I can step into the breach."

He clapped me on the shoulder and hurried on to share the news with others.

When, later, I joined the rest of the court, I found everyone was talking about the news and, as I listened, I was surprised that most were so positive about Olaf's return to power. I didn't say anything, as I assumed I didn't know enough about the situation, but I was interested in Edward's reaction, when we spoke of the news a couple of days later.

"Olaf's going back," Edward told me, "but I don't understand why. The Norwegians didn't want him as king and that was why he fled in the first place. How does Hakon's death change that?"

"I've been thinking the same, but assumed Olaf had received news of a change of heart, if not a specific invitation to return."

"That's what he needs – an invitation," Edward agreed. "Otherwise there will be fighting and he could be fighting fellow Norwegians."

I wondered how much of this was his own assessment and how much Yaroslav had influenced his thinking. I soon discovered.

"The Duke is encouraging him to go," Edward said. "Do you ... do you think he hopes Olaf will get killed?"

I looked at his solemn face and troubled eyes.

"The Duke hasn't asked the questions you're asking?" I queried.

"No. He seems very positive that this is a good time to go back and claim the throne."

"You don't agree?"

He was quiet for a moment.

"He is Yaroslav the Wise, but I think Olaf's return is a mistake. I would not go back to England simply because someone important had died. Even if Cnut died, he is likely to be succeeded by one of his sons. I would need to be sure the English wanted me."

His eyes seemed to grow bigger.

"If Olaf goes back," he whispered, "and is killed, he can't be Irene's ... lover."

Edward had sensed a cynical ploy on the part of the Russian Duke, a way of removing his rival for Irene.

"I hope he isn't killed," I said. "He's very likable, but perhaps a bit impulsive. His mad idea to bring down London bridge worked, but maybe this is a mad idea which won't work."

We said goodbye to Olaf and wished him well. Astrid and the children cried and hoped to hear of his success, which would then prompt their return as well. If Irene shed some tears and Yaroslav heaved a huge sigh of relief, I never knew, but I missed his lively chatter and the occasional sparring match. He was a good fighter, but he would need some support to win back his crown.

"And now we go to war," Yaroslav announced. "The spring has come, the snows have melted. Let us hope the rivers are not too full and that they are fordable. I'm off to ring the bell."

He limped out of the hall with us foreigners looking totally mystified. Before long, we heard one of the church bells ringing out across the city. One of the children ran past me shouting,

"The veche bell! The veche bell!"

We simply followed the crowd out into the market square. What followed was some sort of meeting, but the talking was too fast and furious for me to understand. I think Yaroslav was saying he wanted to go to war and asking for their support. In England, a king ordered his shire reeves to raise the fyrd in each county, but things were clearly different here. I got the impression Yaroslav won the day.

Later I caught up with Edward, as I was sure he'd be able to explain it all.

"The veche is the gathering of all the townspeople; well, there aren't any women or slaves. The other Russians all have a voice. Novgorod has a special bell that is rung and which calls people to the market square. In other towns, they ring the ordinary church bells."

"So Yaroslav called a gathering of the townspeople to call them to war?" I asked.

"To get their consent really," Edward responded. "The Duke has only his *druzhina*."

"That's the group of fighters we practise with?"

"Yes, and that's not enough. He needs more men. There is something called the *opolchenie* – that's like an urban militia, but they have to agree to go to war with him."

"Do I gather they did agree?"

"Yes."

"So where is this war to be?"

"Somewhere in the south. The Duke wants to retake land that used to belong to Russia. I want to go with him. He says we will be fighting on horses."

When Edmund heard of the plan, he too wanted to join the fighting force, but Frida said no, and for once, her will prevailed. Edmund went around scowling, but she wouldn't back down.

"I can't let them both go," she told me. "I might lose both my sons and I couldn't bear that. You will go with Edward, I trust."

"Yes and I'll do what I can to bring him back alive, perhaps unscathed, but war is a dangerous business."

It would be my first experience of actually fighting rather than being an observer. Edward and I intensified our practice of fighting while on horseback. It seemed the Russian way of doing battle wouldn't be like the English. There would be foot troops, but no one mentioned a shieldwall.

We were soon on the move. Yaroslav wanted to surprise his enemy. We still didn't know who that was. We were moving south, so was the plan to capture the area around Kiev from his brother? I thought that for several days, as we slowly moved through the Russian countryside. As in England, moving an army is a slow business, the privileged among us had horses, but the ordinary fighters, who'd been drafted in for the campaign, were all on foot and therefore we had to go at their pace.

Yaroslav must have been planning this venture for some time because there were supplies provided at various points along our route. We had makeshift tents for overnight shelter and a band of cooks who kept everyone well fed. Yaroslav would limp through the camp every so often to encourage his men and keep up their morale. He usually took Edward with him, the younger man acting as a physical support. Yaroslav was a superb horseman, but

227

his old injury meant he couldn't fight on foot. However, he had a presence which inspired. All the time I guessed Edward was watching and learning – and I was praying both he and I would survive the trip.

After nearly a month and several hundred miles, we reached our destination – not Kiev, but the western border country.

"Ruthenia," glowed Yaroslav. "I want to wrestle it from the Poles; they've had it too long."

So this was the land that had been Russian and Yaroslav felt he was only taking back what rightfully belonged to him.

We met little opposition at first, because the farmers had no intention of fighting, but two days into our invasion, we heard a Polish force was coming to confront us. The clash, when it came, was real enough, but the fight was unequal, for our forces were superior. However, it gave us a good experience of what a true battle was like.

Wielding a sword and a shield, as well as keeping control of a frisky horse, was a major test, but I kept close to Edward and could see he had risen well to the challenge. At one point, I was too busy fending off arrows and clashing with armed riders to see if he was alright, but then I caught a glimpse of his helmet and could see he was still in his saddle.

The day was ours and we were exultant. Yes, we'd had losses, but both Edward and I had no serious wounds.

The Poles soon sued for peace and Yaroslav took Edward with him in his delegation to meet their leader.

"The King is Casimir," he told me later. "I didn't understand all that was said, but a deal has been done. Ruthenia is Russian again and the treaty is to be sealed through marriage."

He looked at me, and, for a moment, my heart sank. Surely not Edward? He was only fourteen!

"Casimir is to marry Maria, the Duke's sister." He paused. "They've never met."

"She is pleasant enough," I remarked, "but she will go to live in a foreign land. Such is the lot of princesses."

We made the slow journey back to Novgorod, where Maria would learn of her future.

Our campaign had been a great success, but what of Olaf? Had he fared as well? We found there was still no news. In fact, it was August before we heard what had happened in his campaign to retake Norway.

CHAPTER 34

Olaf had reached Sweden safely and had met up there with other Norwegians, who had sought refuge two years earlier. Anund apparently gave him some warriors too, men who were spoiling for a fight with the Danish. But there was no invitation and there had been no change of heart, so that, when Olaf sought to invade Norway, he met with resistance from both Danish troops and Norwegians. The cause was lost and, at a battle in July, Olaf had been killed.

Everyone in the Russian court mourned; even Yaroslav appeared to grieve, but, privately, I suspect he smiled with satisfaction. Edward told me they had not talked about it. If Yaroslav had had any sense, he'd have guessed Edward had seen through him. I was proud of this intelligent, serious, deep-thinking young man.

"You remind me," I told him one day, "of your father's brother, Athelstan."

Edward smiled.

"Mother says Edmund is more like my father than I am."

"I'd agree. Edmund has your father's ... impulsiveness. He doesn't much care what people think. But Athelstan was more serious. Your father felt he would make a better king and was devastated when he died. Your father then realised the burden of kingship was likely to fall on his shoulders."

"It is a burden," Edward agreed, "but also an honour and a calling. If God makes me King of England, he will help me to be a good and wise ruler."

Frida tried her best to comfort Astrid. They had both lost a husband who had been a king and both knew what it was like to be alone and vulnerable. Astrid, with Wulfhild and Magnus, remained in Novgorod; there was no suggestion they should leave – after all, where would they go? Magnus appeared to take his father's death in his stride, but he may have shared his grief with Wulf and Edie and put on a brave face in public. At the age of six, he was old enough to understand the significance of what had happened.

The successful campaign in Ruthenia seemed to have inspired Yaroslav and he now got support for an invasion of other lands. He gave us no details, but I gathered from Edward that Yaroslav was trying to extend his power in the north as a counterbalance to the power of Byzantium far away to the south.

"He is always thinking and planning," Edward said. "I have learned that a leader cannot sit back and be content. When he is not considering war, he is working on new laws. The other day, he was asking me about the system of wergild in England, as he would like something similar in Russia to stop the blood feuding and killing."

This time, Frida gave way to Edmund's demand to fight, but she did insist on Edward staying behind in Novgorod. I was meant to ensure Edmund didn't die and I guessed that would be harder to achieve than in Edward's case.

The assembled force set off in early autumn and travelled due west. Within a week, we were in the border country and, to begin with, found no opposition. I wasn't sure where we were or who ruled this land, as I was too busy keeping close to Edmund, who didn't think he needed a protector.

When the clashes came, I discovered Edmund too was a natural warrior, young though he was. He had skill and agility and managed to keep out of trouble. He was not as reckless as I expected him to be, but he certainly showed little fear.

"Son of Ironside," I muttered, as I watched him wield his sword, but then I was fighting for my life and lost sight of him.

At the end of the day, I needed treatment for a slash to my arm. Where was the aetheling? I couldn't immediately go looking and when I did, I found him with a group of soldiers, who were swapping stories of their heroism. He had no wounds at all!

Again, Yaroslav did some sort of deal with the leader of the area, a province called Ugaunnia, which had access to the great sea across which we had sailed two years earlier. As Edward had suggested, the Russian Duke was strengthening his position in the north.

We returned triumphant to Novgorod and discovered there was more news from Norway, news which surprised us.

"My husband is buried at Stiklestad in the far north of Norway," Astrid told us, "but strange things are happening there."

"What things?" Frida asked.

"There is a fresh spring of water which has appeared and there are healing powers in the water."

"Miracles?" I queried.

"That is what people are saying," Astrid confirmed. "Many are going there on pilgrimage and hoping to be healed."

It certainly was a strange tale, though we knew of places in England where healings associated with a saint took place, but Olaf wasn't a saint.

Over the next few months, we got more snippets of information on life in Norway.

"Cnut has put his son Swein in charge," Yaroslav informed us. "He's there with his English mother. Perhaps you knew her, Wulfgar. She is named Aelfgifu."

"I knew *of* her," I acknowledged, "but I've never met her. I remember Cnut married her back in 1013. She has borne him two sons, I believe."

"Swein is the eldest, Harold is the other. It's Swein he's put into Norway. He won't be very old then, about sixteen." Yaroslav paused. "We hear that mother and son are making themselves unpopular, by demanding new taxes, when the Norwegians are already finding life hard."

"They might wish they hadn't killed Olaf!" I joked.

"You say that in jest, but it could be true," Yaroslav commented. "These so-called miracles taking place at Olaf's grave, well, they may be real or simply stories, but there's one man who is taking full advantage of them. He's an English bishop called Grimkell."

Astrid told us Olaf had taken Bishop Grimkell with him when he had sailed from England in 1014 and conquered Norway. Olaf had been zealous in making his country Christian and the Bishop had played an important part in the process.

"I hear he is saying Olaf was a saint," Astrid said. "He points to the miracles at Stiklestad, where he has had a chapel built, and he is urging my husband's body to be re-interred."

It took a year, but the Bishop succeeded and Norway began to revere its dead King as a saint.

I was amazed. To me, Olaf was no saint. He had a background of raiding and pillaging and even after his conversion to Christianity, he'd been known to use force to get his Norwegian subjects to follow his lead. But I couldn't deny what had happened.

"Every king needs a Grimkell," I remarked to Frida. "What Olaf couldn't achieve in life, he's achieved in death through a very clever bishop."

"Don't be so cynical, Wulfgar!" she scolded, but I simply smiled.

Magnus, naturally, took a great interest in what was happening back in his homeland and I think Astrid must have been sending letters to friends and allies. Swein, young though he was, remained in charge, but I had a feeling that opposition to his rule was growing.

It was about this time that Harald arrived at court. He and Olaf had the same mother, so that made him a half-brother of the dead King. He was in his teens, perhaps slightly older than Edward, but not much. He had certainly suffered.

"I fought with Olaf at Stiklestad," he told us. "It was a cruel battle because no one likes to fight his fellow countrymen. We thought they'd welcome Olaf, but they didn't."

He had only narrowly escaped with his life and had been in Sweden for the last year, recovering his strength and building up his own fighting force.

"King Anund thought they might see some action if I brought them here," Harald admitted. "I hope Duke Yaroslav can find us something to do."

We didn't get sight of his men for they were stationed at Gardorika on Lake Ladoga, north of Novgorod, but we got the impression it was a big group.

Yaroslav was busy following up the most recent campaign, not with a marriage, but by beginning to build a town.

"He is going to call it Yuryev," Edward explained. "He is naming it after his patron saint Yury. It's all part of his plan to keep control of the area. Ugaunnia is paying him tribute each year."

I could see Edward was fascinated by how the Russian Duke maintained sovereignty over newly conquered or reconquered lands. He was fascinated too by Yaroslav's role as a lawgiver.

"If he ever becomes King of England, he'll have had a good preparation," I concluded.

Yaroslav decided to use Harald and his men in a campaign to the north. Neither Edward nor Edmund were involved, so we didn't hear much about it, except that Yaroslav was very pleased with Harald's skills as a warrior and as a leader of warriors. I think the success encouraged Harald to try and make an impression elsewhere; I doubt Yaroslav paid him very highly. So after a couple of years, Harald took his men south in the hope of becoming part of the Varangian guard in Constantinople at the heart of the Byzantine Empire.

Harald had gone south by the time we received wonderful news from Norway. In the year of our Lord 1034, an invitation came for Magnus to become its King.

"I'll believe it when it happens," Astrid declared. "We are going back to Sweden and hope that we can get more definite information there. Magnus is only ten. He can't fight wars and I won't have him do that anyway. We must be absolutely sure that all of Norway wants him before we enter the country."

Magnus was very excited and his good fortune was praised by everyone. Even Wulf and Edie were pleased, though sorry to lose his presence.

"We will never forget you," they declared.

What we didn't realise was that this was only the beginning of some huge changes in all our lives.

CHAPTER 35

Early in the year of our Lord 1035, the welcome news came that Cnut's son Swein and his English mother had been driven out by the Norwegians and that Magnus had been made their King. It was the cause of a great feast in Yaroslav's court.

"You see what can happen, Edward," the Duke exclaimed. "Who would have thought when Olaf was killed that Magnus, his son, would be King of Norway? There is hope for you."

"What England needs is an unpopular ruler," Edward wisely remarked. "But we do not hear that Cnut is disliked that much."

Yaroslav nodded.

"There are even Englishmen among his closest advisers," he commented. "Godwine and Leofric are names I've heard."

"I knew Godwine," I intervened. "He was very close to Edward's father, but Leofric has come to prominence in more recent times, I believe."

"Don't give up hope," the Duke advised.

I don't think Edward had, but he did have his feet firmly on the ground and knew his chances of being King of England were slim.

More good news reached us in the late summer. Swein had joined his half-brother Harthacnut in Denmark, but hadn't lived long in exile. There was speculation that

Harthacnut didn't want a rival, as he had been governing Denmark for a while and Swein was his senior by a few years, but more reliable sources said Swein had died a natural death.

"I remember his grandfather, also called Swein, the one they nicknamed Forkbeard, dying unexpectedly," I remarked. "He had conquered England, but he didn't live long enough to consolidate his power and we forced Cnut out. Perhaps this family makes a habit of dying young."

My words were almost prophetic, for by Christmas fresh news had reached us that astounded everyone.

"Cnut is dead!" Yaroslav announced. "A messenger has just brought the news."

We had been summoned to hear of this astonishing event.

"Killed?" several of us all asked at once.

"No. He made some preparations for the welfare of his soul," the Duke explained, "so it seems he knew he was dying. But what he has *not* done, as far as we know, is name his successor."

We looked at each other.

"Harthacnut," said one.

"Harold," said another.

"Harthacnut has been in Denmark for several years," Yaroslav responded, "but Harold is in England. Harold, the one they call Harefoot, is older and his mother is a formidable woman, as she showed in Norway. We all know who was really in charge there and she's back in

England now. On the other hand, Harthacnut also has a formidable mother, who is the Queen of England, a status Harold's mother was never given."

"It could be a battle between two ambitious mothers," I concluded.

Alone with Edward, I asked him what he thought.

"There are six aethelings," he said, "but only two will be considered."

When he saw my puzzled expression, he explained what he meant.

"Edmund and I will not be considered because we are far away and perhaps forgotten by most people. Some may even think we are dead. There are two other aethelings also in exile, Edward and Alfred, but Queen Emma sent them away. She will want her son by Cnut to be king and will not press the case of her sons by King Aethelred."

"So it's between Harold Harefoot and Harthacnut, you think."

He nodded.

"And who will win?" I asked.

"Harthacnut needs to go to England quickly or he will find Harold has taken the crown."

We were powerless to influence events and news took a long time to reach us and could sometimes be garbled, but over the next few months we gradually heard what happened.

A council was called in Oxford, where the champions of Cnut's two sons were heard. Godwine, loyal to the Queen, spoke for Harthacnut, while Leofric, Earl of Mercia, spoke for Harold Harefoot. What they decided was really interesting – the country was to be divided between the two of them, Harold to have the north and Harthacnut to have Wessex. There were echoes of the treaty Cnut had made with King Edmund in 1016 after we'd lost at Assandun.

Everything seemed settled, but there was a problem. Harthacnut was still in Denmark. We heard rumours that Magnus was causing him trouble, well, not Magnus himself, as he was only twelve, but the men who advised and backed him. The Norwegians had the Danes worried, and while they remained a threat, Harthacnut wouldn't leave.

The initiative therefore passed to Harold and he succeeded in being made regent of the whole country, including Wessex. I noted he hadn't actually been crowned king, so there was obviously still some uncertainty.

Events in England were not affecting us though because, as Edward had rightly surmised, he and his brother were not considered, and remained exiled from their homeland.

A far more relevant event for the Russian court was another death. Again we were summoned to hear the news. Yaroslav was sitting on his dais with Irene at his side. His numerous children had gathered, as well as those of us who made up the extended court.

"I have news of great importance," the Duke declared. "Something I have been waiting for – eagerly, but patiently."

The hall was completely silent; there was not even a murmur from one of the youngsters.

"My brother, Mstislav, has died," he announced.

He paused to cast his eyes round all those gathered. I'm sure every eye was fixed on his face.

"He has ruled the south for twelve years, but his death means I can now rule a united Russia. We will, of course, have a period of mourning, but ..." (and here he smiled broadly) "... but then we will rejoice."

Yaroslav was fond of Novgorod, for the city had been good to him in his struggle for power, but Kiev held the key to the whole nation. His court would have to move to that city, which, I understood, was more than five hundred miles to the south.

He and his druzhina (his warriors) left, but his wife and children and our family all stayed in Novgorod for the time being, as there were rumours of trouble.

"The Pechenegs have taken the opportunity of Mstislav's death to try and capture Kiev," Irene told us.

Edward and Edmund got no opportunity to fight this time. The Duke had a considerable force at his disposal and had to act fast. It wasn't long before news came that he had had a decisive victory over these invaders from the east.

Other news, and of a tragic nature, came to us from the north, just before Christmas. It gave us information of events in England in the late autumn, events which shocked us all.

"Lord Valgar has written to me," I told Frida, Edward and Edmund.

I had made sure Wulf and Edie were elsewhere in the court complex.

"He does not know all the facts," I continued, "but assures me that the essential part of the story is true."

I had their attention.

"We know Harthacnut is in Denmark and it appears he's made no move to return to England. This has put the proposed settlement in jeopardy. There are rumours, and that's all they are, that Queen Emma was hiding in Winchester with some of the late King's treasure and, fearful that Harold Harefoot would take all England, she recalled her sons Edward and Alfred."

"Was that not dangerous for them?" gasped Edward. "Look at what happened to Olaf."

"If she had control of Wessex and had troops loyal to her, it might have been safe, but the truth is she had neither, it would seem."

"Did they go back to England?" Frida asked.

"Edward landed at Southampton and made it safely to Winchester," I reported. "But Alfred landed in Kent, where there was more support for Harold. However, and this part of the account is very strange, Alfred met Godwine, whose role was to escort him safely to Winchester."

"They're older than us, aren't they?" Edmund intervened.

"Yes, by more than ten years," I replied. "Edward I remember well, for he was with us at Penselwood and Sherston, and even Brentford. He must be past thirty now. Alfred was a few years younger."

"Was?" Edward queried. "Something has happened to him."

"Something terrible," I said.

CHAPTER 36

"Edward has returned to Normandy, Lord Valgar writes, but Alfred met with treachery," I told my audience.

"Godwine?" asked Frida.

"Godwine was meant to give him a safe escort, but as they all rested for the night at Guildford, men came and seized Alfred and killed most of his supporters."

"So where was Godwine?" she cried.

"No one knows. It does look as though Godwine had given up supporting the Queen and had decided to back Harold Harefoot and therefore let Alfred be captured."

I paused.

"Something terrible you said then happened," Edward said quietly.

"Alfred was taken away, taken right away, in fact, taken to the outskirts of Ely."

"Ely? But that's miles away, in the middle of the Fens," Frida exclaimed.

"Lord Valgar doesn't explain why he was taken to Ely, but what happened next has become the talk of England."

Everyone was quiet, hanging on my words.

"On the edge of the waterway, some distance from the settlement, Alfred's captors dealt with him cruelly. They gouged out his eyes and left him to die."

Edward went pale and even Edmund looked troubled. Frida began to weep.

"The monks had heard something and came to investigate," I added. "They found Alfred and took him back to the monastery, but he didn't survive such an ordeal. They had no idea at first who he was, but eventually men from Queen Emma, who had tracked the kidnappers, arrived and then the truth emerged. He has been buried as befits an aetheling."

We never spoke of Alfred again. Edward, in particular, knew the risks of being an aetheling because he'd had his own brush with death. Edmund was beginning to realise that with privilege went danger.

Our next news from England came several months later and confirmed what we had thought. Harold Harefoot had won and the Archbishop of Canterbury had finally crowned him as King. Emma had fled to Bruges, while Harthacnut still lingered in Denmark, having missed his opportunity.

By then we were all settled in Kiev and having to find our way round another great city. Yaroslav again accommodated us in his court complex, even though I was now rich enough to have kept a separate house. He was as determined as ever to school Edward, and also Edmund if he was willing to learn, in the way to rule.

We found, however, that the aethelings were not the only foreign exiles. Two young men had arrived from Poland and had helped Yaroslav in his fight against the Pechenegs.

Hungarian royal family

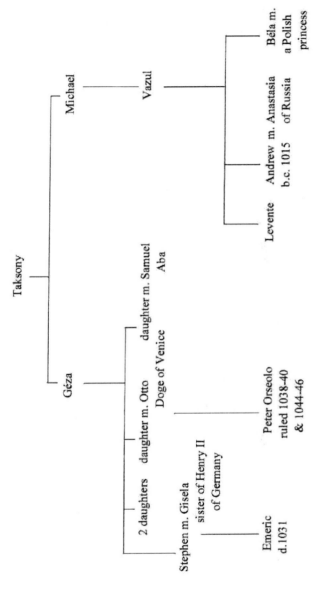

"Edward and Edmund, come and meet Levente and Andrew," Yaroslav said on our arrival at the Kievan court. "They have a similar story to yours."

The new arrivals appeared to mirror in age the aethelings and, after the formalities of introduction, we all sat down to a meal and the youngsters had a chance to talk. The language was something of a problem, but with the help of others and with the use of hand movements, we gradually learned their story.

They were the sons of a Hungarian prince called Vazul, who had been cousin to the reigning king, Stephen. When Stephen's only son died in 1031, Vazul should have become the heir, but there was opposition, especially from Stephen's wife, Gisela, who wanted Stephen's sister's son, Peter, to succeed. I didn't manage to grasp the reasons for this, but what followed was very clear. Vazul was accused of trying to kill the King and, I think maybe without any kind of trial, was mutilated by having his eyes gouged out and his ears filled with molten lead. I noticed Edward stopped eating at this point. Like me, he was probably remembering Alfred.

Vazul had three sons and they all fled from Hungary, fearful that they might suffer the same fate. They had found refuge in Bohemia, at the court of its duke. Here they had met King Mieszko, who had been forced out of Poland at about the same time. Within a year, that King was able to return to Poland and the brothers went with him, because they hoped to live a better life there. In

248

Bohemia, I gathered, they'd hardly been able to survive. Poland was a definite improvement. In fact, the brother called Béla had done so well as to marry Mieszko's daughter. That he was the youngest puzzled me because I thought the King would have married off his daughter to the eldest, who was Levente. I think religion came into his choice.

For a while, therefore, life in Poland was good, but once this brother was married, it seems things went downhill for the other two and they decided a fresh start somewhere else was needed. Now they had turned up in Kiev – and just in time to help Yaroslav defeat the Pechenegs, so they were welcomed with open arms.

"Is Stephen still King of Hungary?" I asked.

As far as they knew, he was still alive, though sick and frail and completely dominated by Gisela. They expected Peter to succeed, but after that, who knew what might happen?

The parallels with the aethelings were obvious. They all had a right to be considered as the next king, but there were forces working against them. However, none of them had lost hope.

Levente was about 23 and Andrew about 21, while Edward was now 20 and Edmund 19. It was hardly surprising that these young men began to spend much time together. Yaroslav encouraged this and continued to give them insight into how to rule a country, but he was also busy, for now that he had Kiev fully and had made it safe from its enemies, he began to build – stone fortifications with an entrance through a great gate, a huge church in imitation of St. Sophia at Constantinople, and a palatial court.

"The Duke is making a library," Edward told me.

"A library? You do surprise me."

"He is far more than a warrior," he assured me. "He is also a man of learning and he's keen that others should have access to the wisdom of the ancients."

"Where is he getting the books from?" I asked.

"Harald is a good source. You remember him? He came from Norway, then went south, where he now serves in the Varangian Guard. He has captured many places and is allowed to keep some of the booty. He sends the Duke books and paintings and beautiful metalwork."

I was impressed.

"He also sends the Duke gold to be kept safe here for when Harald returns one day." He paused. "Wulfgar, I have no treasure and I have no army."

"You would only need those if you planned to invade England and take the throne by force."

He smiled slightly.

"You are right. I only wish to be King of England if they want me. I wouldn't want to reach its throne over dead bodies."

From my point of view as a merchant, Kiev was a wonderful place to live, as the city was on the great caravan route from the east to the west and numerous goods came in from many parts. Kiev also had its own goods, the market for which could now flourish in these times of peace. These goods included jewellery, metalwork, glassware, ivory carving and the painting of ikons, which were religious paintings popular in the Orthodox church. We could live comfortably and not be totally reliant on the Duke's charity.

It was now that I was able to do something about the slaves. To be honest, I had often complained to Frida about the number of slaves for sale and then, one day, she told me to stop whining and do something. So I used some of my wealth to acquire a building with several rooms. It would be my counting house, but also a living place if necessary. I realised that any freed slaves could be vulnerable and lost, so I needed not only to pay for their manumission, but also supply them with a means of earning a living.

I talked to Frida and we agreed she could teach the women to sew and also to embroider, for there would be a market for such work, especially examples of "English" embroidery. Hild and Edith could also help with their teaching, though they were both growing frail. The men could be trained in metalwork or carpentry, if they did not already have a skill.

I tried to ensure I purchased slaves who were related and who could therefore offer support to each other, and this plan worked well, the house soon being fully occupied. The women were happy cooking and sewing and the men I managed to link to local craftsmen.

One day in the slave market, I spotted a youngish man with a shock of black hair, slightly dusky complexion and bright eyes which darted everywhere. He might have sold well, except he had a withered left arm and left leg. His future looked bleak.

"Buy him!"

I turned, but there was no one near enough to have spoken those words and, actually, I heard them in English! A tremor went through me. I thought I had heard the voice of God and if it was that, then I must obey.

I bought the slave and found his name was Boris and he was from the far south. I took him back to the house, puzzled as to what I could do with him.

All the rooms were full, so I decided he should bed down in my counting place. I left him while I went to find some food for him, and, on my return, discovered he was looking at my piles of parchments.

"You are a merchant?" he asked.

I nodded.

"Do you deal in silk?"

"Sometimes. It isn't always easy to get."

"It comes from the east, a very long way. What about silver, copper, tin? They come from the mountains called the Caucasus."

I stared at him, amazed.

"You know about trade?"

"My father was a merchant, but he died and my uncle sold us all as slaves." He paused and looked intently at me. "I may only have one arm, but I can read and write and add figures."

I couldn't help smiling. I had been wondering (and praying) about finding an assistant and, unwittingly, I had purchased a slave with perfect qualifications.

"I haven't purchased you to be my slave, so you are free to go back home, but would you like to stay and work for me?" I asked.

"Willingly." He smiled back. "The rest of my family were sold off further south. They have moved me from place to place, hoping someone would buy me. You have saved my life."

Thus Boris began a new chapter in his life and proved to be an excellent worker. His devotion to me was somewhat frightening, but I think I met many of his expectations, for he lived well and more than earned his keep.

I cannot say that every other aspect of our lives was so satisfying and harmonious. My "house of freed slaves" did produce some problems.

CHAPTER 37

It took me some time to appreciate just how vulnerable some of these freed slaves were. Quite a few had been captured as a result of war and were seen as legitimate booty by the victors, goods to be sold for profit. Others had been seized in border raids, much as in England where men living in the border regions sneak across to steal cattle. Occasionally, poverty had caused a family to offer itself for sale in order to survive.

In whatever way they had become slaves, the result was usually the same – they felt they were less than human. Often they had been treated like animals, herded, beaten, barely kept alive, with little or no respect being shown to them. Such kindness as Frida and I showed could result in weeping, as they faced the pain of their past.

I certainly did not understand how some of the women had been abused. Slowly their stories of violation emerged. Perhaps, then, I should not have been surprised at their behaviour.

One day, I came into the yard unexpectedly and saw Edmund with a house girl pushed up against the wall. I knew what he was doing!

"Edmund! Stop that!" I shouted, running towards him. "Let her go!"

I grabbed his shoulder and pulled him back. The girl looked briefly at me, her eyes huge, before pulling down her dress and running away.

"Why have you stopped me?" Edmund complained. "I was just getting stuck in."

"This is no way for an aetheling to behave," I countered.

"She didn't mind. I was going to pay her."

For a moment, I was speechless. Then, I marched him off to find Frida.

"Edmund, how could you?" she exclaimed, on hearing what had happened.

"It's quite easy. I'm sure Wulfgar could show you how it's done."

"This is no joking matter!" she responded. "I have told you that you are to respect women, not violate them."

"But some of them like it."

"It's irrelevant whether they like it. This kind of union is for marriage, and marriage only. It's not some casual act like ... like the shaking of hands. It's intimate, personal. You are exploring something hidden and private. For that you have to wait until you're married."

"I bet Wulfgar didn't wait," he argued.

"Yes, I did. Your mother was the first woman I lay with and I've not been with any other woman since. Your mother is right. This is for marriage. We men need to respect women, especially vulnerable ones like that girl, and not take advantage of them."

He was silent and sulky.

"Certain standards are expected of an aetheling," Frida continued. "You cannot act as men of lower status may act. They too should have higher moral standards, but have not always been taught well. You are meant to set a good example of Christian living. The Lord would not have you ... well, he would have you wait until marriage. This is his command and you'll regret it if you do not keep it." She paused. "Edmund, God does know what is best for us. Listen to him and not the urges of your body."

Edmund slunk off and I heard Frida sigh deeply.

"You have indulged him too much," I remarked.

"He's *my* son. Don't tell me how to bring him up!" she snapped.

I bit my tongue. I didn't want to argue with her, but I feared we hadn't seen the last of this kind of behaviour on Edmund's part.

"Edmund tells me you caught him at it," Edward said a few days later, when we were on our own.

"Yes," I sighed, "and I don't expect that was the first time."

Edward shrugged his shoulders.

"The daughters of Yaroslav ... he hasn't, has he?" I asked, alarmed.

"No, I don't think so. He prefers serving girls. They are more pliable. He is not so foolish as to risk a princess."

He was quiet for a moment.

"He's younger than the rest of us and he ... he tries to keep up."

"You mean you're all ... doing this?"

"No, but he needs something to boast about, so he boasts about his conquests."

"And you?"

"It's alright, Wulfgar," Edward smiled slightly. "I have no conquests. I am keeping myself for marriage, as I should."

I felt I needed to spend more time with the young men and so took every opportunity I could (when I wasn't engaged in business) to be part of their conversations. After all, I was less than ten years older than Levente, so near their generation. The language was no longer a difficulty, as we had learned some Hungarian and they had learned some Norse. So I gradually learned more about the princes' past.

"King Stephen was the first Christian king," Andrew explained, "and has done much to stabilise the country. He has founded monasteries and established areas for bishops. He has reduced the power of many nobles, abolished tribal divisions and set up provinces with governors he appoints."

"It must be said that he has made Hungary a single kingdom," Levente added, "but Christianity is not totally accepted."

"Our family were not Christians," Andrew added, "and that's why there was opposition to our father being named as heir."

"The King has been very harsh in his treatment of those following tribal beliefs," Levente muttered. "I ask you – would you regard blasphemy and adultery as crimes like theft and murder?"

No one answered.

"He also tried to make everyone marry," Levente continued. "Not priests, of course."

"Not priests?" I queried. "Does Hungary look then to the Pope in Rome?"

"Yes," Andrew answered. "I know it's different here. This is the first time I've experienced the Byzantine style of worship."

"You say your family wasn't Christian," Edward queried, "but you come with us to church."

"I do. You'll have noticed Levente doesn't."

Andrew glanced at his brother, who shrugged his shoulders.

"It was in Poland that I converted," Andrew continued. "Béla was the first to accept Christianity."

"The little sneak!" Levente interposed. "He wanted to ingratiate himself with the King – and it worked – he got the King's daughter."

I noted the bitter tone and remembered that Béla's marriage had been a major factor in their leaving Poland and coming to Kiev.

"Don't take any notice of Levente," Andrew said. "We continue to argue about Christ. I'm convinced now that he's God's son, but Levente still holds to the tribal beliefs."

One day we were polishing our swords together in the practice yard and taking a rest after our exertions, when the conversation took an interesting turn.

"You're very quiet today, Edward," Andrew commented.

Edward didn't look up, but remained intent on his task.

"What's up?" Andrew pressed.

"Just a bit low," was the murmured response.

"He needs a girl," Edmund commented. "I know one who's very willing. She's no great beauty, but you can close your eyes."

"He wouldn't know what to do," Andrew laughed.

"She'd teach him," Edmund asserted. "She knows how to please."

"I don't want a girl," Edward muttered.

"Cheer up, Edward, it'll probably never happen," Levente quipped.

"What?" asked Edmund, pausing in his puzzlement.

"That's the trouble," his brother responded, "it feels like it never will happen. I'll never return to England. You and Andrew seem to be able to keep up your spirits, to keep hoping, but I struggle."

"We think there's a real possibility of going home one day," Levente admitted. "That's why we keep practising with our swords."

"I don't think I'll ever be king," was Edward's despondent answer.

"Enjoy the moment," Andrew recommended. "You've no responsibilities at present. Live life to the full."

"Get some experience with the girls," Edmund said.

"My conscience won't let me do that," Edward answered. "I'm sorely tempted. My body screams sometimes, but it simply isn't right in the eyes of the Lord."

"You have to go with your conscience, Edward," Levente agreed. "But try to find some positives in the current situation."

"Positives like ... like you have us as friends," laughed Andrew. He leaned across to give Edward a mock punch on the arm. "There are other ways of having fun besides what Edmund suggests."

I was pleased to see a faint smile on Edward's face. I could feel his disappointment. Exile was harder for him than for me, as I had my work as a merchant and also I had the blessing of a beautiful wife. Too often Edward looked as though he was carrying the weight of the world on his shoulders.

On another occasion, the conversation turned to religion and the differences between the beliefs of the two Hungarian brothers were explored.

"It was good enough for our ancestors, so it's good enough for me," Levente declared.

"But if you discover something fresh and something that is true, then you have to think again," Andrew countered. "Being in Poland gave me the opportunity to rethink everything."

"Christianity is a load of 'Don't do this' and 'Don't do that'," Levente answered. "Where's our freedom?"

"It's a different kind of freedom," Edward said.

I noticed Edmund wasn't joining in.

"Christ has set us free from our past," Edward continued. "It's like going into battle with simply your weapons and not having to carry all your food and equipment for living. You can concentrate on what's really important."

"The tribal gods are too far away," Andrew said, "and they don't seem to care. The Christian God has actually become a man. He knows, really knows, what it's like to be human."

"And even to be a fugitive, with a price on his head," Edward added. "It's like he's at my side."

"And more," Andrew said. "He promised to come and live in us. That's a staggering truth, Levente."

"But there is a cost," Edward conceded. "Christ becomes our King and we are to obey him."

"That's what I mean," Levente responded. "I don't want to be bossed around."

I suspected Edmund felt the same way, but he wasn't saying anything.

"But Christ is a *good* king," Edward insisted. "He gives us guidelines, not laws. He shows us the best way. We may not like it, but we can be sure of his unselfish regard for us and for our well-being."

Levente shrugged his shoulders and smiled.

"I don't mind you all being Christians," he said, "but I'm sticking to my pagan ways, even if that means I won't ever be King of Hungary."

"Is that what could happen?" I asked. "If the opportunity comes to go back, would they only accept as king a man who is a Christian?"

"Probably," Andrew answered, "though much may depend on what Peter is like as a ruler. He's untried, unknown."

"Who is he, this king-in-waiting?" I enquired.

"Stephen's sister married the Doge of Venice and Peter is their son," Andrew told me. "So he's been brought up in Italy and is therefore Catholic, as is Gisela, Stephen's wife, for she is German and is determined the Catholic church should be supreme in Hungary."

"One reason our father was rejected," Levente added, "is because he had gone through a form of baptism in the Orthodox church, though I don't think he'd really changed his beliefs."

"Also, our parents were not married," his brother admitted.

"Now there's another reason not to be a Christian!" Levente exclaimed, grinning broadly. "You can lie with women outside marriage!"

They obviously had differences in their beliefs, but the brothers were at heart good friends and eager to help each other. Such discussions as I heard were all held in a good atmosphere and without rancour.

"From the news we're getting from England," I said to Edward later, "it sounds as though Harold Harefoot is acting more like a pagan than a Christian, but no one's rebelling at the moment."

"I wonder if I shall ever return, Wulfgar," he answered wistfully.

"Patience, Edward, have patience. And in the meantime, walk the path God has given you."

He suddenly banged his fist down on the table where we were sitting.

"I'm tired of being patient!" he shouted. "Why doesn't God at least give me a wife, even if he won't give me a kingdom?"

His anger took me by surprise and I didn't have an answer for him.

Later I wondered if his outburst was prompted by Yaroslav's announcement that Andrew was to marry Anastasia, one of his daughters.

"The Duke is taking a gamble," Edward commented to me when I expressed some surprise. "He thinks Andrew is likely to become King of Hungary."

"But Levente is older," I countered. "Why didn't he marry Anastasia to Levente?"

"He's not a Christian. There is no way the Duke will have a pagan as a son-in-law. Also, you've heard them talk. If they go back to Hungary and the people want a Christian king, then Andrew will be the choice, even though he's younger than Levente."

"But they might want a pagan king."

Edward shrugged his shoulders.

"As I said, it's a gamble."

CHAPTER 38

Over the next few years, we had news of changes in both England and Hungary.

The first event was the death of King Stephen, which finally happened in September in the year of our Lord 1038. As expected, Peter was crowned as the new king, but all was not well.

"Peter swore to Stephen that he would care for his widow, Gisela," Andrew reported, "but he has 'cared' for her by locking her up and confiscating her estates."

The brothers had contacts back in their homeland and were getting regular reports on what was happening.

"Peter seems determined to replace all Hungarian councillors, elders and magistrates with Germans," Andrew told us. "They say his German followers behave like wild beasts and are grabbing land and castles and causing great suffering."

"Perhaps you will be invited back," Edward suggested.

"There is real anger against the church," Andrew responded. "Peter and his administration is closely tied to the Christian church and therefore opposition is gathering around pagan leaders."

"The old Magyar customs are being pursued," Levente added. "The pagan leaders are said to be sacrificing white horses under oak trees in the once-sacred groves. We would not be welcomed back if they thought we would impose Christianity."

"You would be happy for Hungary to be pagan, brother," Andrew exclaimed, clapping him on the shoulder.

Levente smiled.

"Maybe," he said slowly, "but there are political advantages in Hungary being Christian. It gives Germany no excuse to invade and also enriches the culture of the country through contact with the west."

"Is Germany involved?" I asked.

"Their king has just died," Levente replied. "He has been succeeded by his son, Henry. The father was Holy Roman Emperor, so we can expect the son to take any opportunities he can to enhance his power. I've no doubt he has his eye on our homeland."

"Duke Yaroslav hopes to make a friend of Henry," Edward remarked. "Though Cnut is dead, there is still a fear the Danes are too powerful."

"Their power is split at present," I responded. "Harold Harefoot holds England and Harthacnut Denmark."

"But if something happened to one of them," Edward replied, "I think we can expect the two kingdoms to be reunited."

The news from Hungary continued to be bleak, but Edward's comment on the Danes proved prophetic. In the year of our Lord 1040, in the late spring, news reached us of the unexpected death of Harold Harefoot at Oxford.

The previous year, Harthacnut had joined his mother, Emma, in her exile in Bruges and they had quickly crossed over to England to claim the throne. Again, the other three aethelings were ignored.

Edward was also right about Yaroslav's concern to check Danish power. In the autumn, the Duke sent a delegation to Henry at Altstadt. I was not privy to any suggestions he made to the German monarch, but I knew Yaroslav was a wily politician, as well as a fearsome warlord, so I wondered what he might be plotting. He had many children, several of whom were now of an age to marry and could therefore be useful in furthering his network of alliances. He had already married off Anastasia to Andrew and she had borne him a daughter.

The news from England suggested that Harthacnut was proving as unpopular as Harold. He had barely arrived in the country before he was burdening its people with heavy taxation demands. We heard the price of wheat had increased greatly and many people, high-born and low-born, were suffering.

In May in the year of our Lord 1041, there had been some sort of rebellion in Worcestershire and two of Harthacnut's tax collectors had been killed. The English King waited a few months before taking revenge. His men apparently spent five days burning and looting Worcester itself and also ravaging the countryside around.

"Why don't the English recall an English prince?" Andrew cried in exasperation. "Edward, I can't imagine you acting like this tyrant."

"I hope I wouldn't," Edward replied. "There is so much suffering there in England. Both our homelands are places of grief and pain."

This time it was Andrew's words which seemed prophetic, for before the year was out, we had the strangest of news.

"Wulfgar, you knew Edward, the son of King Aethelred and Queen Emma," Edward said.

"Yes," I answered. "I remember him well, but, of course, I haven't seen him for many years. He must be in his thirties now. Is there some news of him? He's in Normandy, I believe."

"Indeed. He has returned to England."

"What?! Has something happened to Harthacnut?"

"No, it is Harthacnut who has invited him to come home and to live in his court," Edward reported.

I was stunned.

"But ... but why?" I stuttered.

"The rumour is, to keep the English quiet," Edward replied. "Harthacnut is very unpopular. The Danes may like him, but the English do not. You remember there was trouble in Worcester. Harthacnut is still King, but at his side, like a pet dog, he will have his English half-brother, and that may stop any further trouble, even if there is still much discontent."

There was stunning news from Hungary too, news that Peter had been deposed and forced to flee. He'd gone to the court of Henry in Germany and the Hungarians had made a man called Samuel Aba King in his place.

"Who is this man?" I asked.

"He is a relative – through marriage," Andrew confirmed. "King Stephen appointed him to head the royal court as his palatine, but Peter removed him from this post."

"Now Peter's gone," Levente added, "the Hungarians have grasped the man who is there, in the country, rather than asking us back."

This was a hard time for all these young men. Edward and Edmund had again been ignored and their father's half-brother was now in the English court and no doubt being encouraged by his mother, the powerful Emma, to see himself as a future king, as Harthacnut had shown no inclination to marry. Andrew and Levente had also been ignored, and a man, connected to the Hungarian royal family through marriage, had taken the throne at Peter's overthrow.

I could sense Edward's frustration, but Frida was puzzled by him.

"Edward lost his temper with me this morning," she complained. "He used to be such a placid child, but he has grown up to be very irritable."

"Edward has a strong sense of being an aetheling, of being called to be King of England and he's frustrated," I tried to explain.

"Edmund is also an aetheling and could be considered as King, yet he has such a sunny disposition," she countered. "Why can't Edward be like Edmund?"

I could have answered that Edmund didn't have his brother's sense of duty and was more intent on enjoying himself, but I didn't dare say anything against the favoured son.

The following year brought more news that got us all talking.

"Samuel Aba is as unpopular as Peter," Andrew told us. "Our contacts at home say he is promoting peasants and despising nobles. That won't please the people with power and money."

"He's in trouble with Bishop Gerard too," Levente added. "He is the bishop most people listen to. It doesn't bode well for Samuel that he's made an enemy of Gerard."

"He is said to have executed people who oppose him, so the Bishop had better watch his head," his brother commented.

Then news came from England.

CHAPTER 39

Edward rushed into my counting room, while I was deep in a discussion with Boris. We both looked up at his flushed face.

"Some news?" I asked.

"Amazing!" he gasped.

"Sit down and get your breath," I said.

He did, and I noticed he couldn't stop smiling.

"News from England," he breathed. "Harthacnut was at a wedding and no doubt stuffing himself as they say is his wont, when all of a sudden ... crash! He fell down in some sort of fit."

"And?"

Edward had paused to take a deep breath.

"He only lasted a few days," he reported. "Harthacnut's dead!"

His eyes were bright with excitement.

"That's the end of the Danes!" he cried.

"But who will be King?" I asked.

"No doubt about that – the pet dog, of course, though I expect he'll be his own man now and not do as the previous King told him."

"So Edward is finally King of England." I paused. "Do you know I remember his telling me, all those years ago, that he would be King one day? It was some sort of prophecy. It didn't make much sense to me. After all, your father was King and you'd been born, so I couldn't see how King Aethelred's Edward could ever be King."

"But we can't control the future and we have no idea what it holds," Edward replied. "You couldn't have known then that Cnut would triumph, my father would die young and I would be an exile."

"And who knows what will happen next?" Boris added. "The last two kings have had very short reigns and you're the next in line. The new King isn't married, is he?"

"No, but now he's King, he should," Edward responded. "It is one of the duties of a monarch to provide an heir."

"And Harold Harefoot and Harthacnut failed badly in that respect," I said, "as in many others. At least Edward is not following a highly popular king."

"The Danes might be anxious though," Edward replied. "You don't think someone else will try to invade?"

"Who is there?" I asked.

"Cnut's sister's son, Swein Estrithson, perhaps."

"But won't he try to claim Denmark? Don't forget Harthacnut was king there too, but Edward won't be," I warned.

I was proved right in believing no threat to England came from Denmark. Harthacnut's death left a gap there, which more than one person was trying to fill. We heard Magnus, well-established in Norway, was making a bid for it. There was also a son of Thorkell the Tall, who had some power, but no royal blood, as far as I knew. Then there was Swein, Cnut's nephew, perhaps the man most acceptable to the Danes. No one was bothering with England.

It was about this time that the marriage took place of another of Yaroslav's daughters.

Harald, who had miraculously survived the battle in which his half-brother Olaf had died, reappeared in Russia. He had been making a reputation – and a fortune! – in Byzantium. He had the young men on the edges of their seats with his tales. Some were so unlikely that I doubted they could be true, but he was not a man to argue with. He was now about 28.

"I am determined to recover Norway," he declared.

"But Magnus is king there," Edward told him, "and has been for the last eight years."

"Magnus! He's not even twenty. What kind of warrior is he? I doubt if he has much of a beard," he added, fingering his own very full one.

Magnus had left us as a child, but I thought he had probably grown into his role as King of Norway by now. We had heard he had gained the nickname Magnus the Good.

"Well, I shall go there anyway," Harald continued. "You say the throne of Denmark is vacant. I fancy being king somewhere." He paused. "And for that I need a suitable bride."

Yaroslav had just joined us and Harald stood to acknowledge the presence of the Russian Duke.

"When I was here last, or rather, when we last talked back in Novgorod," Harald addressed Yaroslav, "you said that if I proved worthy of her, I could have Elizabeth as my wife."

Yaroslav's eyes narrowed.

"I don't remember that," he said slowly.

"Even if you don't remember," Harald continued, "I'm asking you for her hand."

The Russian was silent.

"Surely I am worthy of her," Harald pressed his case.

"I will consider the matter," Yaroslav agreed.

Before the Duke reached a decision, he was faced with another issue, one Harald knew nothing about, but in which he might prove useful.

Boris had gone on a trip south, exploring ideas for new goods we could trade. I knew I was taking a risk letting a freed slave go back to the area of his birth and that he might not return, but if he was to work for me long term, he needed my trust – and this was a test of that.

He did, however, return, fresh with possibilities, but also fresh with news from Constantinople. I quickly took him to Yaroslav.

"Usually there is no trouble between Russians and Greeks," Boris told him, "but the Byzantines have changed the tax system and now we are paying more than they are."

Yaroslav smiled.

"You're complaining about a cut in your profits, are you?"

"No, there's more," I protested.

"A fight started in the main market place," Boris explained. "It wasn't me! With my body, I pick fights with no one and I get out of the way when one begins."

"Go on." Yaroslav was serious now.

"It got really nasty, several traders from both sides were involved, insults, fists ... and then knives." He paused. "A merchant from Kiev was killed."

I mentioned the name and the Duke nodded.

"I know this family," he responded. "I will give some thought to what to do. The insult cannot be ignored."

Nothing more was said, but I did wonder if Yaroslav asked Harald what he knew about Constantinople. He clearly had some deep discussions with him, perhaps on that matter, but certainly on the matter of Harald's request for Elizabeth.

A few days later, we heard that wedding preparations were put in hand.

"Do you hope to marry one of Yaroslav's daughters?" I asked Edward.

"I try not to think about it," he admitted. "They are all nice girls, but I believe the Duke will be careful about their marriages." He paused. "Wulfgar, I have no kingdom and with Edward's accession, I am still unlikely to become King of England."

"If he produces no sons," I argued, "you are next in line."

"But he is still young and is apparently healthy. There is no reason why he should not marry and father a child."

He looked at me sadly.

"I don't think I am important enough for Duke Yaroslav," he said quietly, "but he may still use me in his political games. I have little choice, Wulfgar."

There was evidence of those political games the following year.

CHAPTER 40

Much happened in the year of our Lord 1043. Harald had gone north with his bride and we heard rumours he had joined forces with Swein Estrithson against Magnus. We thought that strange, but knew Harald had his own way of doing *everything*, so we should never be surprised by what we heard concerning him.

On Easter Sunday, Edward had been crowned King of England, with the ceremony taking place at Winchester. We had greeted that news with quiet acceptance.

We also had news from Hungary.

"You know Peter's been trying to get the throne back," Andrew said, "and getting help from Henry and the Germans. Well, he's finally done it."

"The people had got disillusioned with Samuel," Levente added, "and that gave Peter the opportunity."

"But Peter won't change, will he?" I questioned. "Won't the Hungarians hate him as much as before?"

The brothers looked at each other and grinned.

"That's what we think," Andrew confirmed. "This could be it. I'd give it two years at the most and then ..."

They laughed in unison.

"Then one of us will be king," Levente added.

"It looks as though the Duke's gamble over Andrew's marriage might pay off," Edward said, when we were alone. "He's planning another one now."

"For you this time?"

"No, not me. He's hoping Henry of Germany will marry his daughter, Anne."

"Really? That's a bit bold, isn't it?" I was surprised.

"Yes, but not impossible. The Duke is putting Russia on the world stage. He's about to send a delegation to Germany."

"I got the impression he was also raising an army," I ventured.

"I think something is afoot and he's involving Prince Vladimir. We'll find out eventually."

I wondered if the young men would be called upon to fight under the leadership of the Duke's son, but nothing was said.

Another wedding occurred and one that delighted me. Boris had found a girl who looked beyond his poor physique to the fine man that he was. She was a Kievan, so any concerns I had that Boris might abandon me and try to go back home were put aside. He now had a very good reason to make Kiev his permanent home. He moved out of my counting house and set up a new home with his lovely wife.

Prince Vladimir appeared in Kiev. He was usually in Novgorod, making sure all was well for his father in the north of the country. He had waged a very successful campaign against some tribe in the far north, and Russia now controlled the Gulf of Finland, much to his father's delight. The prince was now put in charge of another campaign, this one aimed at the south.

Whether the death of a noble Russian merchant really required a massive army and a revenge attack on Constantinople was probably irrelevant. Yaroslav was either truly outraged or saw the man's death as a good excuse to wage war on the capital of Byzantium. I was very unsure, not only of his motive, but also what he might gain. A better deal for us traders? Land on the Black Sea? Religious independence? The Byzantines appointed the bishops for Russia. I was genuinely puzzled and also very pleased Edward and Edmund were not part of this army.

So Prince Vladimir set off with a huge number of ships down the River Dnieper and a vast army, and while he was away, we heard news from the north. We heard that the son of Thorkell the Tall (yet another Harald, I think!) had been murdered, but Magnus had beaten Swein Estrithson in a battle in Slesvig, southern Denmark. We weren't sure what had happened to Harald, but thought he was probably still alive – and still plotting somewhere. As far as we could tell, he had not won the throne of Denmark; that seemed to belong to Magnus, news Wulf and Edie were very pleased to hear.

Yaroslav was impatient for news from Germany, as well as Constantinople.

"Wasn't Henry connected somehow to Cnut?" I asked Edward.

"Cnut had links with the Germans," he confirmed. "He had an alliance with them and managed to get his daughter married to Henry."

"That would have been Gunnhild, his daughter by Emma?"

"Yes, that's right, but the marriage didn't last long and Henry is probably looking for another wife, as he only has a daughter from his first marriage." He paused. "I think, Wulfgar, the marriage didn't last because it really didn't work. It was arranged when Cnut's daughter was still very young."

He looked at me, a little wistfully I thought.

"At least Andrew and Anastasia knew each other well," he commented. "And that's why they are happy together."

News came from Constantinople before it came from Germany. We heard the naval attack on the Byzantine capital had failed, with huge losses, though Vladimir had survived.

We heard more details very much later. The Russians had managed to take the Byzantines by surprise, but the leader, Emperor Constantine IX Monomachus, had quickly assembled his own fleet and a battle had taken place in a part of the Black Sea called the Bosphorus. The Russians had lost, the enemy being aided by Greek supporters and an ill-timed (from our point of view!) storm. We also heard that any suspected Russian sympathisers, especially merchants and Varangian mercenaries, had been arrested and, in the main, deported. Some captured Russian fighters had fared far worse, because their right hands had been cut off and displayed on the walls of Constantinople. Others had been blinded, which was a traditional punishment for rebels. In the end, very few of our forces made it safely back to Kiev.

Disappointed at the failure but not knowing its extent, Yaroslav tried to put on a brave face. He needed good news from Germany, but he didn't get it.

The delegation to the German court returned. Henry was not interested in marrying Anne; the refusal was polite, but very clear.

"We believe he is looking to the west for a new bride, rather than to the east," the messenger reported.

"So, we're not good enough for him!" Yaroslav raged and stamped his fist on the arm of his chair. "I have made Russia a great nation. Can't he see that?"

There was, of course, no answer to that. The messenger coughed nervously.

"King Henry acknowledges that Russia is a great nation," he replied. "He admires the way you have turned Kiev into a worthy capital, for he has heard tell of its beautiful buildings."

Yaroslav sat back in his chair and let his arms relax.

The messenger cleared his throat again.

"It is because of his great esteem for you that he has made a different offer."

Yaroslav raised his eyebrows.

"A different offer?"

"He does not offer himself as a groom for your

daughter, but ... but he offers his kinswoman as a bride for your son. That is the message he has entrusted to us."

There was a nervous silence.

"His kinswoman?" Yaroslav said slowly. "His daughter is far too young, so who is this relation of his?"

"She is the daughter of Luidolf, Margrave of Westfriesland, who is the half-brother of King Henry."

Yaroslav was silent.

"We were instructed to bring the lady with us on our return to Russia."

The Duke leaned forward.

"You mean to tell me that Henry refuses my daughter, but instead he has sent his kinswoman here, believing I will agree to her marriage to Vladimir?"

The messenger shifted his position uneasily and glanced at the ground.

"Well, I plan better things for Vladimir than a mere kinswoman of the German King." Yaroslav's voice did not falter. "But I see he has sought to give me no option and if I send her back, there could be trouble."

We all held our breath. No one wanted war with Germany when we were still coping with the failure at Constantinople. Yaroslav looked around his court and I'm sure he could see every eye was pinned on him.

"I will not send her back," he declared. "I don't want to make an enemy of the German King, but she won't marry Vladimir." He paused. "Instead, she can marry Edward."

CHAPTER 41

"This German lady will make a very suitable bride for our English prince," Duke Yaroslav stated.

Edmund gasped, but Edward made no sound. I saw him purse his lips slightly and he grew a little pale, but he was not about to make a scene.

"Where is she?" Yaroslav asked the messenger.

"About two days' travelling from Kiev. I have ridden harder, in order that there was no delay in your receiving the news."

"Two days. Ah, well, Edward shall have to wait to see the woman he is to marry. I presume she has a name."

"The lady's name is Agatha."

As soon as the court gathering broke up, we met as a family.

"It's outrageous!" Edmund cried. "You should at least be able to see her before making a decision."

"She is on her way," Edward responded. "The Duke has been put in a difficult position."

"But you could refuse!" his brother protested.

Edward sighed.

"I don't think I can," he said slowly. "The Duke has been very kind to us. He has given us a home for fifteen years. Edmund, we are under an obligation to him."

Edmund snorted.

"Well, I wouldn't marry a woman I hadn't seen. She could be fat and ugly."

"Edmund, that isn't helpful," Frida chided.

She took Edward's hand and squeezed it briefly.

"My darling boy, I know this is hard. It is part of the cost of being an aetheling. There is privilege, but there is also responsibility."

"I know that, Mother, and I shall marry Agatha."

Wulf and Edie, now both of marriageable age, simply stared, concerned, but somewhat bewildered.

"If I did not marry her, the Germans might wage war and that wouldn't be good."

"Edward, if she is old and ugly," I interposed, "don't marry her and I will personally fight in any war provoked."

"Bless you, Wulfgar, but it won't come to that." Edward managed a smile. "I doubt she is old. She is like a niece to King Henry, so may well be younger than me."

"If it were me," Edie whispered, "I'd be scared."

We looked at her.

"I mean, she might be my age, so how would I feel if Duke Yaroslav had sent me to the German court to marry ... someone? I wouldn't speak the language. I wouldn't know the customs. The man I was destined for might be old and fat."

"Edie's right," Wulf added. "Agatha is coming to a foreign country and she doesn't know that Edward is tall, well-built, handsome, athletic, and above all, very honest and good."

"That's some testimony!" Edmund spluttered.

"But it's true," declared Wulf.

Edward leaned over and ruffled his half-brother's hair.

"I'll take the praise," he laughed, "and you're right about Agatha. In fact, she thinks she's coming to marry a Russian prince and probably end up as Duchess of Russia. Instead, she's getting an English aetheling, who is a long way from being in a position to make her Queen of England."

"We still haven't heard that King Edward has married," I reminded him. "You are next in line, unless they want another Dane, which they won't."

"I don't look too far ahead," Edward answered. "The next thing on my horizon is ... is marriage to Agatha."

The two days of waiting for the full delegation to return to Kiev were tense. I don't know if there were any private conversations between the Duke and Edward; he certainly didn't tell me of any. The aetheling was trying hard to appear relaxed and submissive, but I guessed he didn't really feel like that inside. It would certainly have been a different matter if Edmund had been singled out. He showed no signs of wanting a wife and therefore being restricted to one woman. I had given up reproving him for his licentious behaviour, but I was thankful he was very discreet. Frida and I never talked about it.

When Agatha finally appeared at court, my heart went out to her. As Edward had said, she was expecting to marry a Russian prince, not an English aetheling, and no one had warned her of the change of plan. She was paraded into the hall, accompanied by an older woman, who had some ability to communicate in the Russian court. Agatha herself was veiled.

"Welcome to Kiev!" Yaroslav greeted them. "You've had a long journey and it is good that you are safely here."

"We thank you for your greeting," the older woman said. "I am Lady Helga and I accompany Lady Agatha here."

She looked around at those of us who had gathered. Yaroslav had restricted the welcoming group, but it was still substantial.

"I believe you know already that King Henry has, in his goodness, sent the Lady Agatha to be a bride for your son, sire," Lady Helga continued.

"Yes, we had notice of that," Yaroslav responded, "but my son is not available."

Lady Helga's eyes grew wide with shock.

"However, we are grateful for King Henry's offer," the Duke continued, "and we do not wish him to be in any way offended. There is another man, who is a suitable groom for the German bride."

Lady Helga now looked really alarmed and her eyes were flitting backwards and forwards over us courtiers.

"We have in our court a very worthy spouse, a young man who has been with us many years and has proved his valour." He paused. "He is not Russian though; he is English."

Lady Helga gasped very slightly.

"He is Prince Edward, the son of Edmund, King of England, and therefore an heir to the English throne."

He signalled Edward to step forward. He was pale and I was sure he was shaking a little, but he bore himself like an aetheling and kept his head high.

"Will Lady Agatha remove her veil?" Yaroslav's request was really a command.

All eyes were on Agatha, and I could hardly breathe. I found Frida was clutching my arm, totally unaware that her grip was tight.

A pair of small hands emerged from her cloak and Agatha slowly lifted her veil to reveal her face. I felt Frida's grip loosen and heard her sigh.

We were looking at a slim young woman, possibly not even as old as our Edie. She was very pale and her huge hazel eyes looked up at Edward, who was considerably taller than her.

"Lady Agatha," he said bowing.

She responded with a curtsey and a modest lowering of her head, before she looked back at her groom. She had appeared rather colourless and plain, but now she smiled – a shy, tentative smile, which brightened up her face.

"Now the introductions have been made," Yaroslav declared, "we must ensure you are settled into your room, and, when you are ready, we will eat together."

Everyone began talking at once and servants appeared to take the baggage the Germans had brought. Irene came forward to take charge of the two ladies and show them where they would stay.

"She seems very young," Frida whispered to me.

"She is certainly not old and ugly," I responded. "When she smiled, she had a sweet face."

"I do hope she will make him happy. Exile is so hard for him and Edmund. They need some joy in their lives."

I looked at her lovely face and smiled. Frida was nearly fifty now and little lines had appeared at the edges of her eyes, but to me she was still beautiful.

"If they are half as happy together as we are," I commented, "they will both know much joy."

"Yes, Wulfgar," she answered, squeezing my arm.

At the meal, Yaroslav had seated Edward and Agatha together, but I could see they didn't say much and Lady Helga was having to act as an interpreter. The language was clearly going to be a problem.

Later, I had the opportunity of talking to Edward.

"The Duke is confident King Henry will not be affronted," Edward told me. "It is a very difficult situation. The Germans have not acted well."

"But you have a bride! What do you think of her?"

"She has a pleasing face and good manners," Edward began. "But I don't understand what she says and she doesn't understand me." He paused. "I think I must teach her English. If ... if I ever do go back, my wife and ... any children will need to speak English."

"It's good that she has Lady Helga with her. Has she known her some time?"

"Yes, for many years." He smiled. "Lady Helga assures me Agatha is a virgin and a lady of honour. She also says she is kind and very spiritual. She is, of course, of the Catholic Church."

"She will find Russia very strange, but perhaps she will find it easier to be married to an Englishman, who has a Catholic background, than to a Russian, who knows only the Orthodox church."

"Wulfgar, I believe God has given me a good wife and I am grateful to him. You have set me an excellent example of how a man should treat his wife – with love and tenderness. I hope to do the same. Agatha is only 18 and I am 27. She will look to me to help her find the way through this tangled world we live in. For that I will need the Lord's help, but I believe he will give it to me." He grinned. "There is no need to go to war."

We laughed together and in my heart I felt sure all would be well.

CHAPTER 42

For another year, little changed in our lives. Edward and Agatha settled into married life and although it took a long time for them to find fluency in their spoken language, it was clear there was an ease between them. I often noticed him giving her an encouraging smile. At other times, she would entwine her fingers in his, unaware that I saw her. It reminded me of the tenderness his father had shown towards Frida in the brief time they had been together. Edie had early on made a determined effort to be a friend to Agatha and I frequently saw them giggling together over something.

I said nothing to Edward, as that felt like prying, but I did notice that he and Agatha often came into the room laughing together about something and that pleased me, because Edward was a serious young man and it was good to see him laughing sometimes. Indeed, Agatha exuded a zest for life prompted, I believe, by her faith. She had embraced her new life in Russia calmly and her new husband joyfully and proved to be an excellent influence on the aetheling.

The German King did not complain that Agatha had married Edward and not Vladimir. He had found for himself a bride in the west, Agnes of Aquitaine. Also Yaroslav was like a cockerel with a fresh plume of feathers, when he announced he had done a deal with France. Anne, originally destined to be Queen of

Germany (he hoped) was now to be Queen of France, a country I believe Yaroslav considered to be superior to Germany.

Lord Valgar might have quoted one of his sayings, but the words of a psalm came to my mind: "The lines have fallen for me in pleasant places, yea, I have a goodly heritage". God was blessing us all.

Even Andrew and Levente were not discouraged, because reports from Hungary told them Samuel Aba had been killed and Peter was making himself even more unpopular.

In the year of our Lord 1045, news from England confirmed what we had expected – King Edward had found a bride.

"It's taken him a long time," Edward commented. "He's been King for well over two years."

"He's made an interesting choice," I remarked.

"Or the woman's been forced on him!" Edmund suggested. "Her father's very powerful, isn't he?"

"He's certainly a survivor," I agreed. "He backed the wrong side on the death of Cnut, but managed to ingratiate himself first with Harold Harefoot and then with Harthacnut, before wheedling his way right into the royal family once Edward was king."

"You remember him, don't you, Wulfgar?"

"Yes, but I don't think I'd recognise him now, after nearly thirty years."

"I bet he's fat and greasy," Edmund suggested.

I smiled.

"He can certainly afford to eat well," I agreed, "and he's fought no wars for quite a while. He's been busy producing children, warrior sons and eligible daughters."

"How old will Edith be?" asked Edward.

"Not twenty," I speculated. "Godwine married a couple of years before Wulf and Edie were born, and Edith has at least two older brothers."

"And Edward?" queried Edmund. "He must be about forty."

"Still capable of fathering a son though," his brother reminded him. "And if he does, we won't be going home."

The aethelings' hope of going home might be faint, but it wasn't so for Andrew and Levente.

"You will not believe what Peter's done now!" Andrew exclaimed. "He's given King Henry of Germany the golden lance."

"What does that mean?" I asked.

"It's the symbol of Hungarian sovereignty," Levente told us. "In effect, he's made Henry King of Hungary."

"Why?" Edmund wanted to know.

"King Henry helped him get back the throne," Levente replied, "so he's now at Henry's beck and call."

The brothers looked at each other and then at us.

"We think our time is fast approaching," Andrew said. "It can't be much longer before they invite us back. We've already had letters suggesting it."

"But we don't want to make the mistake of going back too soon," Levente added.

"Like Olaf in Norway," Edward agreed.

"Exactly. We need to know we truly are wanted."

While they waited for their invitation, we waited for another event. Agatha was expecting a child, and Edie was as excited as if it had been her own.

"Edie, my love, do you want me to find you a husband?" I asked.

"I'm not bothered, Father. I don't really want to marry a Russian and soon there will be a little one for whom I can help care."

Neither Wulf nor Edmund showed any interest in having a wife, but probably for different reasons. Edmund liked the casual relationships he formed, which meant he wasn't tied down. Wulf spent much of his time practising horsemanship, swordplay and archery. I told myself there was plenty of time for them all.

Occasionally, we had news from elsewhere.

"We think my son-in-law, Harald, may come to an agreement with Magnus," Yaroslav told us one day. "They have been fighting each other, but it makes more sense to rule Norway and Denmark together. That way they could keep Cnut's nephew, Swein Estrithson, at bay. I am urging him to make peace."

"Magnus has no son, has he?" Edward asked.

"No. If something happened, I think Harald would take the throne and Elizabeth would become a queen. Do you hope for a son, Edward?"

"Naturally, but if Agatha gives me a daughter, I shall love her too."

"She is very calm," Yaroslav commented.

"My wife has great faith. She trusts God and believes he will bring her safely through childbirth."

"I've heard she spends much time in prayer."

"Yes, she does. She also reads the Scriptures, including reading aloud to our child."

"I never did such things," Yaroslav scoffed.

Edward simply smiled. I had a feeling he also read Scripture to this baby, and I was sure he and Agatha prayed together. This was one of the reasons they were so close. They had had to work at their relationship, but all the effort was worth it. I suspected Yaroslav saw his wife much more in terms of a child-bearer than as an equal partner. The news from England was that King Edward and Queen Edith were, we were told, as "one person dwelling in double form", but as yet there was no news that she had conceived.

Agatha was very close to giving birth when some Hungarians arrived at the Russian court, claiming to come from leading men in that country.

"We know these names," Andrew admitted. "What news have you brought?"

"There has been an assembly at Cenad with many people crying out for deliverance. The lords have seen the suffering of the people and ask you to come and free them."

Neither Andrew nor Levente spoke.

"We swear this is true. The whole country pledges you its obedience and calls on you to defend them against the fury of the Germans."

"The whole country?" Levente queried.

"We swear, as soon as you enter the land, every Hungarian, as if of one heart and one soul, will join your flag and submit themselves to your rule."

"We need time to consider this," Andrew declared.

The visitors were brought some food and drink and we did our best to entertain them, while the two brothers consulted each other. After about an hour, they returned with an answer.

"There are here in Kiev a few of our fellow countrymen, whom we know well and trust," Andrew told the envoys. "Levente and I have decided to send two of them to Hungary to find corroboration of your story. In the meantime, you will remain at court."

The envoys looked a bit surprised, but there was nothing they could do. Andrew and Levente had, in effect, put them under house arrest in Russia.

"We've got to be sure," Levente told us privately. "We think this could be a trap and that we will be killed the moment we step onto Hungarian soil."

"If we do go back, we hope you will come with us to fight for the freedom of our country," Andrew added.

"Oh, yes!" cried Wulf.

He had long been hoping for an opportunity to put his skills to the test. Frida still thought of him as a boy, but, of course, he had been a grown man for several years and had passed the age of 22. He would go, whatever his mother said. I was fairly sure Edmund would too.

Edward, at present, was totally taken up with the impending birth. He was waiting for a baby, and Andrew and Levente were waiting for the return of their fellow Hungarians. The baby arrived first.

Poor Agatha was in labour for several hours, with Edie keeping us informed of her progress, or, rather, lack of progress. We were all praying, I'm sure. It took me back to the birth of the twins and I noticed Edward was mirroring my behaviour all those years ago – the restless pacing, the lack of appetite, the anxious look.

Then the screams we heard through the walls told us something was happening and an hour later Edie came with the news a girl had been born.

"Agatha is very weak, but her women do not think she is in danger," Edie said.

I heard Edward give a deep sigh and he appeared to mouth a prayer.

"The baby's ... perfect," Edie added, and promptly burst into tears.

We gave no thought to Hungary for the next few days, as we rejoiced in the safe delivery of this little one. Edward and Agatha named her Margaret at her baptism. He didn't appear at all disappointed.

We were therefore taken a little by surprise when Andrew and Levente came to us in great excitement.

"Our emissaries are back!" they cried in unison.

"Hungary is already in a state of rebellion," Levente explained. "Foreigners are being massacred and churches burned."

"It's been confirmed," Andrew added. "We're sure of huge support if we go now. It isn't a trap. You will join us, won't you? We will be brothers in arms against the enemy."

"Yes, I will fight with you!" answered Wulf.

"So will I," declared Edmund.

"I'll fight too," I added.

"Edward?" Andrew addressed the aetheling. "Will you come?"

Edward looked first at Agatha and then across at Edie, who held the tiny bundle that was his daughter.

CHAPTER 43

"Well, Edward? We've often talked of this opportunity," Andrew said. "Surely you'll come and fight with us in Hungary."

Edward still hesitated. Then Agatha spoke up.

"This is their moment of destiny," she declared. "You have been brothers in exile. Edward, *you* cannot go home – yet – but they can. You must go with them."

He shifted his position and looked from her to Margaret to Andrew and back to Agatha.

"Trust in our gracious Lord," Agatha urged. "We shall pray he keeps you safe. Your cause is just, so he will not fail you."

"Brother, you must come," Edmund said. "We all stand together in this."

Edward lifted his head fully and faced Andrew.

"I will come," he said firmly.

So we went – within a few weeks. Money had come from rich nobles in Hungary, enough to pay for a sizable army. Yaroslav also gave us extra men, so we were quite a force by the time we were ready to leave. Frida was distressed, of course. All the men in her life were going into battle, something that hadn't happened before, but there was no way any of us would stay behind. The women had each other and, in the midst of them, Agatha, the youngest, proved the strongest. I marvelled at the depth of her faith and hoped she would not have to face terrible disappointment, at least not at this early stage in her marriage. I had seen the English routed at Assandun in 1016 and had wondered where God was. Frida had seen her young husband die in his prime and must also have wondered where God was. Agatha had not been touched by tragedy, nor had Edie, and these two young women would, I knew, support each other, as well as my dear Frida. They would also be there for Anastasia, because Andrew insisted she stayed in the safety of Russia.

The parting was hard, especially for Edward and me. The others were like young wolves about to set out on a killing expedition. I, too, prayed we would all return safely. I thought survival meant coming back to Kiev and settling back into our usual rhythm of life; in that I was proved wrong.

We had celebrated Christmas, but winter still had its grip upon the land. Our horses picked their way along the ice-rutted tracks which led over the mountains they called the Carpathians and into Hungary through the Uzhok pass. Sunshine and a sudden thaw greeted us and it was almost as though God was smiling on our venture. As we followed the valley of the River Tisza, we met with cheers from the people and we began to wonder if there would be any need to fight.

Then we saw our first evidence of the carnage. Villages still burned and bodies lay unburied.

"They're Germans," we were told. "The King's tax collectors. Good riddance to them!"

Even so, the stench of blood and fire clogged our throats and dampened our excitement.

"There are bands of rebels roaming the countryside," Edward told me. "That's what I've heard. And they are killing priests as well as foreigners. It's not good, Wulfgar. I didn't come on this campaign to kill Christians."

"The situation is so chaotic that King Peter's supporters may well be confused with honest Christians," I answered. "It often happens in war that people use it as a cover to settle personal scores."

"I fear there is something more," he said. "It is as though the devil himself is fighting in this war and ... and he does not fight for Peter."

His words disturbed me, but there was little we could do, because we were under the command of Andrew and Levente. We had to obey whatever orders they issued.

We came to a town called Abaujvar, which readily opened its gates and welcomed us in. In the town square, men saying they represented the masses met with Andrew and Levente and we were close enough to hear what was demanded. And "demanded" was the right word, for they claimed no one would fight under the brothers' flag unless they met their conditions. Those conditions made us sick inside.

The rebels against King Peter wanted all bishops and priests to be killed, on the basis they were German or Italian. I reckoned some must be Hungarian, but the rebels were making no exceptions. They wanted all churches razed to the ground and a full restoration of pagan worship. They weren't going to fight unless Andrew and Levente agreed.

There was a quick consultation between the brothers. Edward and I exchanged glances, both of us, I think, fearing the worst.

"We agree," the brothers declared and a great cheer went up from the crowd, but not from us.

"We are fighting for the devil," Edward whispered.

"This is more than simply a physical fight," I answered quietly. "St. Paul says we fight against the spiritual hosts of wickedness in high places. For the present, the dark forces are part of our army. Keep praying, Edward."

"I will," was his determined response.

When the fighting began, it was impossible to ask any questions. As the army moved across the country, we found ourselves dealing with the opposition in the way every army does, and, even though our consciences were troubling us, we killed as we were commanded. We did see some churches being destroyed, though I think we managed to avoid being part of the force that did the deed. There was no glory in this war and, if we survived, each of us would have to account to God for our part in it.

We tried to stick together as a foursome, and even in the thick of fighting, I usually knew what was happening to my son and to the aethelings. I had no wish to report to Frida that any of them had been killed.

Early April saw us approaching a ford through the great river Danube, at a place called Pest. We made camp on our side and we could see crowds gathering on the other bank, where there appeared to be a large town.

I'll never forget what happened next because it was the stuff of nightmares (and I still have them). We saw a man travelling towards the ford in a cart, but some of our troops crossed over and began pelting him with stones. He was clearly elderly and incapable of fighting back. Indeed, I could see him raising his arm and making the sign of the cross, so I guessed he was a bishop.

As my eyes scanned the terrible scene, I spotted another man, who was also being stoned.

"This is the devil's work," Edward breathed. "Those men are Christians. Come on, Wulfgar."

He mounted his horse and I hurried to mount mine. I followed him to where Andrew was surveying events.

"Andrew, I can't stand by and let these clergymen be stoned to death," Edward declared.

The prince turned to face him and I saw tears in his eyes.

"You can't save the two being stoned," he responded, "but look over there. I recognise those men. They are bishops, Bestrick and Beneta. You have my permission to try and rescue them from the mob. God go with you, my friends."

We were off and I soon realised Edmund and Wulf were following. I shouted back to them what our mission was.

As we splashed through the ford, we could see most of the mob's attention was focussed on the other two victims, but some soldiers had seen Bestrick and Beneta and guessed they too were for killing. So I found I was fighting our own men. I struck at some with the hilt of my sword, hoping simply to wound and knock them out of action temporarily, rather than kill, but I suspect the others were not so tender.

Edward managed to get Beneta over his horse and was turning back to our camp. Bestrick was in deeper trouble, as he had been slashed by a sword, but between us, we managed to rescue him and get him onto Edmund's horse. We all raced back, forded the river and sought out Andrew. His personal force surrounded the victims, and the devil-driven fighters couldn't get close.

"Thank you," Andrew said. "At least we have saved two of the bishops."

"And the others? They're bishops too?" I asked.

He was quiet for a moment.

"They are in heaven now," was his reply.

CHAPTER 44

The four of us had survived with only minor injuries, but Bishop Bestrick was in a bad way. Both men were kept safe and attention was given to their wounds, but before the day was out, Bestrick had joined the other two bishops in heaven. Andrew gave orders Beneta was to be guarded and should suffer no further harm.

I grieved at the day's events. We had rescued two bishops, one of whom had died, but our soldiers, yes, ours, I am ashamed to say, had killed huge numbers of people, many of whom I guessed were Christians. The slain were not all German or Italian; I'm sure simple Hungarians lay slaughtered on the banks of the river, whose waters were stained with blood.

"It is crucial we take the town on the other bank," Andrew explained. "Our capital is Székesfehérvár and lies beyond further west. We hear Peter is on his way to block our progress."

The next day saw a great clash, as Peter's forces arrived. Both sides wanted control of the town and both sides therefore fought like wild animals. I lost sight of my family members, as I tried desperately to keep alive myself. From my horse I had the advantage of height over the ordinary foot soldiers, but many of the enemy were also on horseback and all of us were vulnerable to arrows, which came at us through the sunshine.

At the end of the day, neither side could claim victory and I was reminded of the battles I'd seen my King fight against the Danes. Often, under cover of darkness, one side would slink away, but that didn't happen here. The next morning, Peter's forces were still here, bristling to fight. In the hours of bloody slaughter and mayhem that followed, I realised Peter had edged himself into a position to claim the town, but he was thwarted. The people would not open the gates to him.

We now pressed our advantage, as we saw he and his troops were discouraged by this setback. It gave us a new impetus, and with Andrew and Levente at the heart of the battle, shouting encouragement, our army pushed the enemy back and their forces began to splinter. By the end of the day, they were in retreat.

"We mustn't let the King escape!" Edward shouted to Andrew.

"Don't worry! I have that covered!" was the reply.

Back at the camp, we could take stock. Wulf had had an arrow in his shoulder, but its head had been removed and the wound dressed. Edward's mail showed evidence of the hard fighting, but had no deep cuts and those he'd taken had been washed. Edmund, somehow, was totally unhurt. I praised God I hadn't lost any of them. As for me, I had taken a blow to my thigh and was now struggling to walk, but I could still ride a horse.

"Levente has been wounded," Andrew told us.

He himself appeared relatively unscathed.

"Is it serious?" I asked, for I sensed from his tone that he was concerned for his brother.

"It's not good," he replied in a quiet voice. "Pray for him, Wulfgar. He doesn't know our Lord."

"What of King Peter?" Edward asked.

"I think he realises he's beaten," Andrew replied, "and my guess is that he'll make for the border with Austria. I have sent a force to ensure he never leaves the country."

"We are therefore on the brink of victory?" Edward exclaimed.

"I believe the town will open its gates to us tomorrow." He paused. "But we need to stop the killing. There is no reason for it once Peter is overthrown and ... I'm sure you'll be pleased to hear ... I won't continue a wholesale slaughter of Christians."

We were pleased to hear that, but I wondered how he could achieve it. Many had fought for him only on the basis that Hungary would be a pagan state. How could he keep control if he went back on his word?

As Andrew had anticipated, he was welcomed into the town and we were able to progress and take the capital unopposed. He paid off some of the wilder elements of his army and they disappeared back to their villages. He still had the troops which had accompanied him from Kiev, but these were under his control and more disciplined in general. He made sure they were well fed and comfortably housed in makeshift tents outside the city walls. We occupied the main court complex, where Levente was receiving the best care available.

About a week passed before we could be completely sure of victory. Confirmation came in the form of Peter himself. It was a terrible sight. His captors had gouged out his eyes and he was therefore virtually carried into the city to be presented to Andrew, who promptly had him locked away. He was given food and some care, but he had lost the will to live and he was in agony through the wounds inflicted on him. No one mourned when he died on the fifteenth day of April. We had won the war and Hungary was rid of its tyrant, but what next?

As the news filtered through the country, so men arrived to talk to Andrew and Levente. These were the leading nobles, those who had survived the bloodbath that Hungary had experienced. Andrew welcomed them alone, as Levente was in no fit state to receive visitors. We were not privy to most of these meetings.

"Perhaps we can go home soon," Edward mused.

"You mean back to Kiev?"

"Oh, Wulfgar, I realised I called Russia home," he exclaimed. "That is because that is where my darling Agatha is, with our dear daughter." He looked at me wistfully. "I must remember that England is my true home."

We had sent word to Kiev that we had all survived, but there was certainly an anxiety on the part of Edward and me to return quickly. However, we felt we couldn't do that until Hungary's future was clear.

About three weeks after Peter's death, as we shared a meal with Andrew, we heard what he planned.

"You will be aware of the many visitors I've been receiving at court," he began.

He dug his teeth into a chunk of roast meat and we had to wait until he had eaten it and taken a mouthful of wine as well.

"They have been the leading men of the nation, those who have the power to affect the future." He paused and looked round at us. "You won't be surprised to know that they want to restore our royal house to the throne, as worthy descendants of King Stephen."

"That's what we've fought for!" Edmund exclaimed. "If they didn't want you, we'd carry on the battle."

"The battle's over, Edmund," Andrew said smiling. "The country is anxious for peace after so many years of war and strife."

"How many has it been?" Wulf asked.

"King Stephen died in the year of our Lord 1038, so nearly eight years."

"That is a long time," said Edward quietly.

"So who will be King?" I asked.

"Levente is older than I am, but ... but he is a sick man. Also he is a pagan and the nobles are very clear they do not want a pagan king." Again he looked round at each of us, as though trying to read our thoughts. "They want me to take the crown – and they want me to rule as a Christian."

There was an intake of breath from someone.

"Can you do that?" I asked. "I mean, you've won the war by promising a pagan state and by having the support of those greatly opposed to Christians."

"I will do it," he said firmly. "I will set this nation on the road to greatness once again. Levente and I have talked. He knows how things are. He said to me yesterday, 'Andrew, your God has won. I admit defeat.' He does not share my faith, but he knows that Hungary's best path is to walk with the God of the Christians."

"With God's help, you will do it," I predicted.

"Thanks, Wulfgar. I'm grateful to you all, because you have risked your lives in a strange cause, for you did not know Christ would triumph in the end. So I wish to reward you."

He took a sip of wine and then replaced his goblet on the table.

"I will have lands at my disposal," he told us. "I can easily grant you an estate. Please, accept my offer to come and settle here in Hungary."

CHAPTER 45

There was a stunned silence for a moment.

"An estate of our own?" Edward gasped.

"Yes, Edward. You would not be dependent on anyone's charity. You would not be living with a king breathing down your neck, because it would be away from the capital, out in the country somewhere. You have seen what a beautiful land Hungary is. This would be a good country in which to bring up your daughter."

"Freedom," said Edmund. "We'd be free to live our own lives."

"You could make a good life here," Andrew asserted. "We will go on hoping you go home to England, but if you don't, this will be a good place to live. I'm including all of you – Wulfgar, Wulf, Edie, as well as Edward and Edmund."

"I like the idea," Edmund declared.

"So do I," Wulf added. "Father, there are bound to be trading opportunities here for us."

I smiled at his enthusiasm.

"As long as I am with my family, I'll be a happy man," I said.

I looked at Edward.

"What are you thinking?" I asked him.

"To have the freedom of our own estate would be a blessing, I believe," he said quietly. "I hope Agatha agrees, for it would be a very different life from living at court."

"I need to bring Anastasia here," Andrew remarked. "I want her at my side when I am crowned."

"Yaroslav will be a happy man," I laughed. "His daughter will be Queen of Hungary!"

Andrew's offer was the subject of much discussion over the next few days. We decided that Edward and I would return to Kiev with the Russian fighters and begin the process of preparing for the move.

"Agatha will do whatever you suggest, Edward," his brother declared. "Where you go, she'll go. Hungary opens up all sorts of possibilities for us."

I was sure Edmund had in mind more women to conquer, but perhaps our own estate might encourage him to settle down. Wulf was happy to stay in the capital for the time being and await our return.

"I'll begin talking to the traders," he told me, and winked. "We are all going to have to get used to speaking Hungarian," he added.

"We'll learn quickly, if there is trade involved!" I laughed.

I expected he might have made several deals in the weeks I would be gone.

The return journey to Kiev took less time as we were a much smaller group, because Andrew had retained many of the mercenaries in case of further difficulties. He thought there could be trouble when people realised what kind of king he would be.

Our women hugged us and cried tears of relief. Frida needed constant reassurance that we had not left behind Edmund and Wulf because they were sick.

"A whole new beginning!" exclaimed Edie. "Fields and trees and rivers, you say. What a wonderful place in which Margaret can grow up."

Edward was amazed at how much his daughter had changed in just a few months and he enjoyed all the smiles she gave him.

"The Lord answered our prayers," Agatha said. "You are all safe and now we can have our own home. I will miss the life at court, but it doesn't matter, as long as I am with you, Edward."

Her sweet little face looked up at his and not for the first time did I praise God that he had provided Edward with such a lovely wife. She was not as beautiful as my Frida, but she had a kind and caring nature and she had become devoted to the man who had been foisted on her by the scheming Russian Duke.

Back in Kiev, I took the opportunity of going into the church of St. Sophia to give thanks for our delivery from danger. Yaroslav had begun building it in the year after we had all arrived in the city and it was not yet finished, for it was a massive stone building with thirteen cupolas, the domed turrets we had only seen in the east.

Now I stood before a huge mosaic of the Blessed Virgin Mary, which had only recently been completed. Above me, in the dome, was the figure of Christ, and the Virgin appeared to be raising her arms and pleading with him for humanity.

"Dear God, I thank you with all my heart that you have kept my family safe, here in Kiev, but especially in Hungary. Forgive me for the wrongs I did and the Christians I killed unwittingly. I pray I may never have to fight on the same side as the devil again."

I stayed there in prayer for some time before I felt I was again at peace and ready for this new phase in my life. As I left the church, I noticed the Duke had had a mural painted, which depicted him and all his family. He was presenting a model of the church to Christ. I had to smile. Yaroslav was someone I was never likely to forget.

I had mixed feelings about leaving Kiev. We had been in Russia eighteen years, so it had very largely shaped the lives of Wulf and Edie; they barely remembered our life in Sweden. It was here we had buried Hild and Edith, faithful servants to the end.

Russia, for me, had been my making, because it was here I had become an independent merchant and not simply Lord Valgar's trusted colleague. I still traded with him and we both did well out of being in different countries. Boris could maintain that relationship, of that I was confident. He, poor man, wept when I told him we were leaving; he always maintained I had saved his life. I tried to comfort him with tales of all the new things I would find to trade from the new country.

By the time we returned to Hungary, the summer was well advanced. We travelled through a green and lush land; our women were seeing it at its best and certainly had no complaints. Anastasia, of course, travelled with us and we were therefore well guarded, for Yaroslav insisted she had some of his most trusted warriors.

We settled first in the capital, Székesfehérvár, and Andrew gave us a house there, which was always to be ours, even once he had found us a suitable estate. Levente, we learned, had died during our absence and had been given an appropriate funeral for his beliefs. Wulf had spent some time with him and told us Levente's attitude to Christ had softened, but he feared to commit himself lest he offended the pagan gods he had always served. Andrew told us he had written to his other brother, Béla, who was still in Poland, telling him of Levente's death and inviting him to return to Hungary and enjoy the restoration of their true place in society.

"I have an estate for you," Andrew told us late in the year. "It is in my gift for there is no heir and I'm sure it will be a good place for you to live. It's Nadasd in the far south."

The name, of course, meant nothing to us and before we took everyone there, Edward and I went to look at it to see what work needed to be done to make it truly habitable. We did not see it at its best, as the countryside

314

was coming under the grip of winter, but there was enough for us to be more than content with King Andrew's gift.

We all moved to Nadasd in the spring of the year of our Lord 1047. So we are here, in this green and beautiful land that is Hungary, and we now have to try and make this our new home.

PART V – HUNGARY

CHAPTER 46

Our first task on arriving in Nadasd was to make the buildings into a real home. Work had been carried out during the winter to repair walls and clear away rubble. Hungary was by no means a peaceful country, so Edward and I agreed the walls should be strengthened and the only access into the main complex of buildings was to be through a substantial gatehouse. We had in our mind's eye the fortifications Yaroslav had made at Kiev, including his great gate, but ours was something much smaller and simpler, though still effective, we hoped.

The site was on a hill to the west of the village of Nadasd, and small rivers, more like streams really, ran both sides of the hill. A watermill stood on one of these.

"Surely, Wulfgar, there is enough water here for more than one mill," Edward suggested.

"Yes, I should think so, though we need to remember that the melting snow has increased the water level. It will drop in summer."

Nadasd was not the only village. Our estate comprised several, of which Nadasd was the largest. So we had over seven hundred people who looked to us as their lords. The land was good for farming, so we found there were horses, cows, pigs, goats and over a thousand sheep. The land and animals were cared for by a mixture of freemen and those tied to us in service. Even the freemen were obliged to surrender to us a fixed percentage of their produce, both crops and animals. There were also bee-keepers, who kept us well supplied with honey, as well as the usual range of skilled artisans, such as tanners, blacksmiths, carpenters, metal workers, potters, millers, bakers and coopers. Fishermen and fowlers brought us food locally trapped, and a couple of extensive vineyards made sure there was always a good supply of wine.

"I could almost feel we were in England," I remarked, as I gazed over the green valleys.

"You helped manage my father's estate there," Edward remarked. "I'll need your advice, Wulfgar."

"His estate near Newbury was much smaller than this and I was only a lad then, but, as a family, I think we can pool our talents and try to make the best of these rich resources."

"The villagers will look to us for protection," Edward reminded me.

"There isn't room for everyone in this castle, so we'll need to teach them how to defend themselves and provide them with weapons."

There was no need for protection that year, as the country was war-weary and none of our neighbours were inclined to attack.

The coronation came in early summer and by it Andrew made it very clear he was a Christian king. Three of the country's bishops had survived the killing, including Beneta, and Andrew intended them to crown him. The Byzantine Emperor supplied a crown, which was a truly magnificent object, being of gold with enamelled plaques. The ceremony marked a new beginning and was soon followed with a declaration that the laws of King Stephen were to be revived. We were back in a land where the Pope held sway and the worship was in Latin. Agatha was delighted, for this was her heritage. The rest of us soon got used to the different way of worshipping and were simply thankful that Hungary was now trying hard to put its pagan past behind it.

Nearby we had a church in need of repair, but that was soon done. Frida and Agatha set about making and embroidering hangings, altar frontals and vestments.

We were beginning to build good relations with the local people. Edmund took upon himself the task of training young men in warfare. He organised the making of weapons and then had regular times of practising with them. He was far happier doing this than overseeing the counting of sheep fleeces!

News came through to us – eventually, for we were a long way south of the capital. Wulf had made his home there and was building up good trade links for us. He would send us snippets of information as they reached him.

One day, towards the end of the year, his letter brought us great sadness.

"Wulf writes there is news from Norway," I reported. "Word has passed through to Irene from Astrid, and Boris has forwarded the information because he knew we'd want to know."

I looked across at Edie in particular and she picked up straightaway that something was wrong.

"Magnus," she said. "He's about my age and was very young when he went back to Norway to be King; we heard he'd done well and even gained the name Magnus the Good. But Elizabeth's husband, Harald, he wanted to be King of Norway." She looked at me with troubled eyes. "Harald hasn't killed Magnus, has he?"

"No, but the news is that Magnus has died – of natural causes, it's believed."

She burst into tears, for she still remembered her little playmate, even though some thirteen years had passed since he'd left the Russian court.

"So young," murmured Frida. "Younger than my Edmund was when he died."

"Wulf adds that Harald is now undisputed King of the whole of Norway."

"And another of the Duke's daughters has become a queen," Agatha added.

So our first year passed and we all agreed it was good to have our own estate. Andrew's court moved around the country, so we soon found ourselves hosting him and his companions for several days. We had to supply local men who knew the best places for hunting, and the courtiers vied with each other as to the number of beasts and birds they had caught. The feasting was sumptuous and we were glad the estate was so fruitful, for vast quantities of food and drink were consumed. In the evening, there was also singing and story-telling, alongside conversation which centred on horses and clothes.

"I have put in hand a horse-breeding programme," Andrew told us. "I wish to breed the finest horses in Europe and to be the envy of my neighbours."

This was not a subject that excited me, but I could see from the reaction of Edmund and other young men that the project was becoming an obsession.

The other subject, that also held little excitement for me, was the matter of dress. Andrew was importing very costly materials from Italy and Byzantium, and also furs from Russia, and these courtiers all wanted to be almost as well-dressed as the King. I was interested in the trade aspect and I knew that Wulf was making sure we benefited from this desire for beautiful material, but it was not in my nature to flaunt my presence with bright colours and jewels. Edward and I made sure our women were fashionably dressed, but both he and I tended to wear plainer clothes.

"If you ever become King of England," I remarked, "you will have to get used to wearing more elaborate outfits. The news I hear from home is that Queen Edith ensures her husband is impressively dressed in embroidered robes of many colours."

"If it ever happens," Edward laughed, "I shall delight in dressing according to my new status."

Occasionally, Edward and Edmund joined Andrew and his court at another estate in Hungary and in that way remained very much at the heart of the nation. Edmund loved these times and revelled in the hunting and feasting, and no doubt found a willing serving girl in all the places he visited. Edward knew it was important to be there and so fulfilled his duty, but he was at his happiest when at home with Agatha and Margaret.

Wulf, though an aetheling's half-brother, was not an aetheling himself and was more detached from court life. When the King held court in the capital, Wulf was often there, meeting many of the high-born men and women of Hungary – and more than holding his own, for he had learned when to speak and when to be silent. Most of his time was absorbed by pursuing our business interests, but on one of my visits to the capital, I found he'd had time to woo.

"Her name is Maria," he told me. "Her father was a nobleman, but was killed in the troubles."

"You obviously like her," I commented. "Are you serious enough to marry her?"

"She has little by way of a dowry, but that's not what's bothering me."

"What is then?" I asked.

"What happened to her while Peter was King."

CHAPTER 47

Wulf sighed.

"We only heard snippets about life in Hungary while Peter was King," he said. "We knew he treated King Stephen's widow with disdain and cruelty. He was arrogant and greedy and had about him men who were equally arrogant and greedy."

He paused, but I said nothing.

"He had little control over these retainers," Wulf said at length. "Indeed, he didn't care what they did, for he set them an example of evil."

He cleared his throat and I could see that what he was sharing was very painful.

"His court moved around, as Andrew's does," he continued. "That is the Magyar way. But visits were very different from visits by the court of the saintly Stephen. The host's wife and daughters were ... were to be enjoyed, as well as the hunting and feasting."

He looked at me and I saw the grief in his eyes.

"Maria was raped several times," he whispered, and turned his face away, so that I would not see any tears. "She was only fourteen the first time it happened."

"This was typical of life when Peter was King?" I asked.

He nodded.

"Some girls are so hurt by their experience that they have joined the nunnery Andrew has built. They simply cannot bear for a man to touch them."

"How this country needs healing," I sighed. "And Maria ... You think marriage might not work?"

He nodded again.

"I'll pray for you, son. May God show you the right path. Be tender with her and take your time."

The following year we met Béla for the first time. Andrew had invited him to return, but it had taken nearly two years of persuasion. The King made his brother a duke and gave him authority over about a third of the kingdom, in areas of Hungary known as Slovakia and Romania.

By then I had met Maria as well and I could see how gentle Wulf was with her. I often saw them laughing together, which I took to be a good sign. I wasn't surprised when he announced they had decided to marry.

"I am trusting the Lord that our relationship will work," he told me. "We bring out the best in each other. With all the tough bargains I have to make, Maria touches the softer part of my heart, and I encourage her to be strong and brave and not let the past ruin her future."

"Are you planning to marry here, in the capital?" I asked.

"Yes, I'd like you and Mother and Edie to be here, but it will be a quiet celebration. When ... when we're more used to being married, I will bring her out to Nadasd to see the estate."

He was 24 and Maria a little younger, and I felt sure they would find their way in the world. In the meantime, Edward and Agatha let us know another child was expected and that gave Edward a good excuse to spend much of his time at home.

So it was that, in the year of our Lord 1049, Agatha gave birth to her second child.

"We have named her Christina," Edward told Frida and me. "Now Margaret will have a little sister to play with."

"And Edie another baby to nurture," Frida laughed.

"Not a boy," I said quietly.

"No, Wulfgar, but Agatha is fit and well. There may yet be a boy." He paused. "We have not heard that King Edward yet has a son."

"You're right," I agreed, "and it is more than four years since he married Edith." I looked him in the eye. "You are still the next in line." I paused. "But I think you are enjoying running an estate here."

"I am," he confessed. "If I never return home, I will still feel that my life has not been wasted. But I cannot forget that I am an aetheling. What do we know of what is happening in England?"

"We get scraps of information, but I think I need to do something more positive. I need to find someone through my business contacts who is based in London and can send us news on a regular basis. The English need to know where you live!"

"So they can come knocking on my door with an invitation," he laughed.

"It could happen," I assured him.

Wulf and Maria came out to Nadasd and spent a couple of weeks with us. I saw Maria holding baby Christina and wondered how things were between her and Wulf. He said nothing, so I kept quiet. They seemed at ease in each other's company, but I thought I saw a look of sadness in Maria's face as she cuddled the tiny child.

In view of all that was happening at Nadasd, it was some months before I had cause to visit the capital. As usual, I made my base at our family house, which Maria had made more homely since their marriage. She was out somewhere, but I found Wulf was at home.

"I think you'll notice some changes," he told me.

"In business?"

"No, at court."

I raised my eyebrows.

"For one thing, Andrew has taken a mistress."

"No! I don't believe it! He's meant to be a model Christian king," I declared.

"He says it's part of the Magyar tradition for kings to have other women, as well as a wife."

"What does Anastasia say?"

"She's furious, but can't do anything about it. The court, in general, seems to back Andrew."

325

"I'm disappointed," I admitted. "I thought he would put Christ first and yet he commits adultery."

"There's more," Wulf continued. "One of the old traditions that many are happy to revive is that of high-born ladies choosing a lover."

I stared at him.

"I'm warning you, Father. You are still young enough to attract the attentions of a princess."

He laughed, but I could see he was serious.

"When I go to court, I take Maria with me. That way I'm left alone, but you will be there without Mother, so watch it!"

I was glad he had warned me. To begin with, I mingled with the courtiers in the usual way, discussing trade in general and what the latest fashions were in particular. I made a mental note of materials and finery I needed to source.

We sat to eat a good meal of roast wild duck, goats' cheese and a fine Italian wine. As I drank, I couldn't help remembering what hatred there had been for Italians when we arrived from Russia. Importing excellent goods from Italy was one of the changes that had occurred.

Another was the attitude to relationships. No one mentioned Andrew's mistress or mistresses (I wasn't sure if he had more than one), for at this meal Anastasia was making her presence very obvious. I gathered she had been trying to stop the moral decline, but most of the courtiers were enjoying the sexual freedom.

I felt someone come and sit next to me. Then I smelled the perfume and knew it was a woman. I turned slightly and greeted her with a brief smile. At a quick glance, I couldn't easily judge her age, but her voice was that of a mature woman.

"You are Lord Wulfgar," she said softly. "I've heard much about you. You fought well for the King and now you supply him with fine materials for his clothes."

"I trade in silk and cloth and all sorts of fabrics," I answered.

I could feel her thigh against mine.

"You are far from home, so you must be lonely," the soft voice continued.

"There are you wrong," I asserted. "I'm not lonely. I'm not in need of company."

"Spring is here, but the nights are still cold. You have no one to warm you."

"I have a wife and am more than content with her. She is a great blessing."

"But she is not here," the woman persisted.

At this point, I turned to look at her properly. Her eyes were heavily made up, her headdress covered her hair, but from the lines near her eyes, I guessed she was in her forties. As she caught my eye, she smiled coyly and sat more upright in order to emphasise her ample bosom. I was not even tempted.

"I would never be unfaithful to my wife," I said firmly and saw the flicker of annoyance on her face.

I turned back to talk to others on the table and she soon moved away.

Back in Nadasd, Frida was horrified by my news.

"This is no way for a Christian court to act!" she cried. "I remember King Aethelred was reputed to have mistresses and he was despised for it and denounced by the bishops."

"We are part of court life, living as we do on an estate which is the King's gift," I responded, "but we can limit our involvement there."

I thought it best to warn Edmund, but was not surprised by his reaction.

"I can look after myself, Wulfgar," he declared. "I have plenty of experience. Edward might have trouble coping with alluring princesses if he didn't have Agatha with him, but I'll be fine."

I did wonder if he was over-confident, and events later in the year showed I had been right to be concerned.

CHAPTER 48

The year of our Lord 1050 brought the first serious trouble with aggressive neighbours. King Henry of Germany had never been happy that his puppet king, Peter, had been defeated. Henry had lost Hungary and it grieved him. Now he sought to invade.

Edmund took from Nadasd some of the men he had trained to fight, as Andrew needed help and it was a good opportunity to put their skills to the test, as well as support our benefactor. In the end, there were a few border skirmishes, but nothing very serious.

Edmund stayed on in the capital as I think he found Nadasd a bit quiet and he relished mixing with other young men at court. I heard he celebrated his 33rd birthday with some fine food and plenty of wine.

A couple of months later, I was in the capital myself with strict instructions from Frida to take back news of Edmund.

"He's asleep," Wulf told me, on my arrival at the house.

"It's nearly noon!" I exclaimed.

"This is typical," my son responded. "Mother will want to know he's well, but you may not want to tell her everything."

I felt my stomach turn over.

"What's he been up to?" I asked.

"Can't you guess? We both warned him about the women at court, but it didn't take long for Princess Anna to capture him."

I sighed deeply.

"I happened to be there and saw it all," Wulf continued. "Edmund had had plenty to drink, so his defences were lowered. She began simply talking to him. Part of his charm is that he is an English prince; everyone knows that."

"How old is this woman?" I wanted to know.

"Mid-thirties, maybe. She could be a bit older than Edmund. These women make their faces up, so it's difficult to tell."

"And she's a princess?"

"She's related to Andrew in some way, but I'm not sure how. You know how complicated these family relations are."

"Go on."

"She began stroking his hair and his beard, and you could see he was enjoying himself and making no effort to resist her. Then she ... she unlaced her bodice and pulled his hand inside. She is a woman with ample breasts. By then, he was hooked."

"And this ... this relationship has persisted?"

"Oh yes, but she is very much in charge. Edmund lives here, but when she wants him, she sends for him. It is as though he's attached by a rope and she simply tugs on it and he goes meekly to her bed. She clearly gives him a good time and must be very demanding, for he comes back here at first light, exhausted, and then sleeps for several hours."

When Edmund woke, he discovered I wanted to talk to him.

"Oh, I know Mother won't like it," he declared. "You don't have to tell her, Wulfgar."

"I don't, but that doesn't stop me being concerned. She's not some serving girl."

"You're right there! She has the most wonderful body and has taught me ... quite a lot. Her bed is sumptuous, very comfortable, and with rich hangings. This is far better than pushing a girl up against a wall in an alleyway."

"What happens if she gets pregnant?"

"It's not likely," he responded. "She's had lovers before me and never conceived a child." He winked at me. "Besides, we're not at it *all* the time."

I could see it was useless to argue with him. He thought his actions had no consequences and was enjoying the moment. I wasn't sure what to tell Frida!

In the end, I told her very little, simply assured her Edmund was well. Wulf promised that he'd let me know if Edmund got into any difficulties, both of us wondering if the other lovers of the Princess might prove jealous, though we weren't sure if they were still at court.

So the rest of that year passed quietly. Princess Anna did not conceive, but Agatha did, and I think we all hoped that, this time, it would be a boy.

In the year of our Lord 1051, Edmund again took a large group of fighting men from Nadasd, for this time Henry of Germany was more serious in his invasion of Hungary. He headed for the capital, presumably working on the basis that if he captured that city, the rest of the country would fall, but he underestimated Andrew and Béla, who worked together to repel him. The German soldiers were soon running for their lives, discarding armour and goods to speed their flight.

"Andrew tries to negotiate with King Henry," Edmund told us, "but the German King is an arrogant fool and thinks he can conquer us."

Agatha gave a slight smile when she heard this.

"He thinks of everyone as chess pieces that he can move at will," she commented. "He is the Holy Roman Emperor, so he thinks he has God on his side and everyone should bend to him."

She laid her hand on her greatly swollen abdomen.

"But we won't, will we, little one?"

She smiled across at Edward.

"I was one of his pawns, but, as it happened, his moving me to Russia was very good."

"You captured the heart of a king-in-waiting," Edward laughed.

"Checkmate!"

"What is the news from England, Wulfgar?" Edmund asked.

"Nothing very much, according to Alfred."

"He's your merchant friend?"

"Yes. We have managed to work out a way to get letters to each other, using merchant friends along the way. Alfred writes to me about political events, as well as trade opportunities. Godwine and his sons all hold positions of considerable power, but their sister shows no signs of giving birth to an heir."

Shortly after this, Agatha gave birth to a boy and there was huge rejoicing. At last!

"We are naming him Edgar," Edward declared, "after my father's grandfather, who was a great King of England. Maybe one day he too will be its king."

The news of Edgar's birth was almost as good as Edward being invited back to England. I began to grow more confident that would happen, for who else could succeed to the throne?

Then events late in the year again put our return in jeopardy.

"Alfred writes that there is trouble between Earl Godwine and the King," I reported. "He says that accounts disagree, but something happened in Dover and Godwine was ordered to ravage the town but refused, which is tantamount to treason. A council has been called and he says he will write again when there is further news.

He adds there are rumours the King is under pressure to put his wife aside and take another."

There was also trouble in Hungary's capital – not a military invasion this time, rather something more personal affecting our family. The King summoned Frida to court.

"But why?" she demanded.

"I don't know," I answered. "He doesn't say. We will no doubt find out when we get there."

Wulf was not at home when we arrived and Maria explained that he was away in the east and had been for a couple of weeks, though she expected his return imminently. If she knew anything about our summons, she was keeping quiet. We immediately went to see Andrew.

"I am really sorry that I felt the need to summon you in this way," Andrew began. "You've probably guessed it's about Edmund."

"Edmund?!" Frida cried. "What's happened?"

Andrew looked briefly at me, but I gave no sign of having guessed what was coming.

"He is at the centre of a scandal," Andrew said.

CHAPTER 49

"Scandal?" gasped Frida. "What do you mean?"

"He has been carrying on an affair with Princess Anna and now she is pregnant, but he is refusing to marry her."

Frida almost fell into my arms and began weeping.

"Why is he refusing?" I asked.

"He claims the child is not his," Andrew replied, "but we both know Edmund. He has never wanted to be tied down, to be fettered by marriage."

I bit my tongue. Here was Andrew condemning Edmund for his loose morals and irresponsible ways, and yet the King had at least one mistress and I'd heard rumours of more than one illegitimate child.

"He must marry her," Frida asserted through her tears. "I cannot have disgrace brought on my family."

"I shall expect that by tomorrow you will have persuaded him to do so. Come back then."

We were dismissed. I was seething, but there was nothing I could do. Andrew's hypocrisy angered me, but, at the same time, I knew Edmund had been courting trouble and he now had to pay the price for his indiscretion.

Edmund was not in the house, but Wulf was.

"You know what's going on?" Frida asked.

"Of course, the whole court has been talking about it," Wulf replied. "I was going to write, but had to go east on urgent business."

"Oh, this is terrible!" she moaned.

"Edmund claims the child is not his," I mentioned. "Is that possible?"

Wulf raised his eyebrows and smiled wryly.

"Hardly. He's been her only lover for about a year."

"A year?" screamed Frida and, turning on me, added, "Did you know?"

"Yes," I admitted reluctantly.

"And you didn't tell me!" she accused.

"What was the point?" I countered. "It might all have blown over, like a storm on a lake. You know he doesn't usually have long-term relationships with women."

"She wasn't letting him go," Wulf remarked.

He had the attention of both of us.

"Edmund was away earlier in the year, fighting the Germans," Wulf explained. "When he came back, Princess Anna was very relieved, as she feared he'd be killed or wounded. And she became very possessive. In fact, I've hardly seen him. He's been with her constantly for the last few months."

"So there's no doubt he's the father?" I queried.

"None at all. I think he's been in her bed every night until she announced she was pregnant. Then he hot-footed it back here and hasn't been near her since." He paused. "I'm not surprised Andrew summoned you. I'm sorry I didn't warn you."

"He must marry her," Frida declared.

When Edmund appeared late in the day, he found us waiting for him.

"You know why we're here," Frida stated.

"I can guess," he muttered.

"You will marry her, Edmund. I will not have our family disgraced."

"I'm not a child. I can make my own decisions."

"This is a matter of family honour. If you don't marry her, you can leave this house and I will ensure you are sent no money from the estate."

I saw the shock on his face – he hadn't expected that!

"I'm serious," Frida continued. "You will do what is right by this woman. You have until the morning to make your decision."

With that, she grabbed my hand and pulled me out of the room, leaving Edmund somewhat stunned.

By the morning, Frida was having doubts.

"I can't abandon him, Wulfgar. I can't," she moaned.

"Let's see what he says first," I suggested. "Don't let him think you might back down or he will wriggle free."

She kept calm and gave no indication of her aching heart.

"Well, Edmund?" I asked. "Will you marry Princess Anna?"

"Alright, yes, I will," was his unenthusiastic response.

"And you'll be faithful to her?" Frida added.

"I won't promise that! Who knows how I'll feel in a year or so?"

I sighed and inwardly confessed my doubts. A relationship based on little more than physical attraction didn't bode well, but, perhaps, I wondered, the birth of their child might bring about some greater sense of being a couple committed to a future together.

Wulf took me on one side the next day.

"It's ironic, Father. Edmund doesn't want to be a father, but is going to be. I would like to be a father, but ... nothing is happening." He cleared his throat. "Maria didn't tell me, but she conceived a child as a result of one of the rapes, but the child was born dead. We wonder if that is why she has not conceived a child by me."

"I'm really sorry to hear that," I said.

"But we are still happy together and if we never have children, then at least we have each other."

I was struck by the contrast between his relationship with Maria and Edmund's with Princess Anna and I promised to pray for them.

We stayed in the capital until the marriage had taken place, but were then happy to return to the peace of Nadasd and enjoy the late autumn colours of its many trees.

Our "peace" was disturbed, however, by news from England.

"Alfred writes of an amazing turnaround in the fortunes of Godwine and his family," I reported.

"You said he was in trouble with the King and that a council was to be called," Edward remembered.

338

"There was a second council at which Godwine was outlawed."

"Outlawed! That is serious!"

"Godwine has gone to Bruges and his son Harold to Ireland, while other family members have left too. And Edith ..." I looked round at their attentive faces. "King Edward has put his wife in a nunnery and taken to himself all her land!"

There was a stunned silence.

"How terrible for her," whispered Frida. "After all we've heard she's done for him."

"There are rumours she conceived a child some time ago, but it never developed and she miscarried," I reported. "She has not conceived since." I suddenly thought of Maria. "It is thought the King will take a new wife," I added.

"Who may give him a son," Edward concluded.

I met his eyes and I guessed we shared the same thought – his hope of return would be crushed again.

The year of our Lord 1052 is one I prefer to forget, but never will. It is good we do not know what lies in the future.

"I see you have heard from Alfred," Edward said.

"Yes, he writes that this spring there was an unusual visitor, Duke William of Normandy," I answered.

"Why should he be in England?"

"That's a very good question! I think he is waging war somewhere, so there is speculation he came asking for military help. He is, of course, related to the King's mother, but that didn't do him any good. Edward is not a king who is very willing to help others in their wars."

"Didn't we hear he refused to help Swein Estrithson in his war with Magnus?"

"Yes. That's some years ago now, but his policy doesn't seem to have changed. Duke William went home to Normandy, and very soon afterwards the King's mother died."

"You would remember Emma, wouldn't you, Wulfgar?"

I pictured again Aethelred's widowed queen flirting with the incredibly young Cnut. She had certainly made a good marriage there and had seen two of her sons on the throne of England.

"Yes, but I haven't seen her for nearly 35 years."

"We felt her influence," Edward snorted.

"She cannot try to kill you now. Indeed, I cannot see that anyone would try to kill you. You and Edmund are the only aethelings who could be considered as the King's successor."

I didn't know how soon that would change.

CHAPTER 50

Princess Anna gave birth to a girl in the middle of May and I took Frida to see her new grandchild, who had been named Elizabeth.

"She is very small," Anna commented, as she handed the child to Frida to cuddle.

I thought how small the twins had been. This little one was about the same, yet they had survived, so perhaps she would too.

I left the women to talk babies and went in search of Edmund. I found him polishing his sword.

"We're expecting more trouble," he warned me.

"The Germans again?"

He nodded.

"But we'll be ready. Andrew has a good system of spies."

I sat beside him and watched him work.

"So, you are a father," I said at last.

He gave me a slight smile.

"For better or worse," he replied. "Actually, marriage is alright, in that I am always in her bed. She can't send me off to our house like she used to."

"I hope you find she is a companion as well, and perhaps also a friend."

"We get on best when we are not talking," he grinned, "when we are making love. We are good at that." He winked at me. "She has a wonderful body, which I'll be

341

able to enjoy again very soon, I hope. Marriage isn't that bad after all."

I sighed. I knew from my own experience that there was more to marriage than what happened in the bed and I hoped Edmund would learn that too – eventually.

War came in the summer, with the Germans laying siege to a town in the Slovakia region. Wulf kept us informed as best he could and so we heard the enemy had been defeated in an unusual way.

"Wulf says Henry was using ships to besiege Pressburg," I told the family. "But in Andrew's army was a skilful swimmer of the name of Zotmund. He is able to hold his breath for a very long time."

"So what did he do?" Edward asked.

"It seems Zotmund swam under the ships and so damaged them that they sank."

"Oh, well done, Zotmund! I hope Andrew rewards him."

"That was very brave," Agatha commented. "I hope he survived."

"Yes," I replied. "He was able to report back to Andrew and then they watched as the leaking ships gradually keeled over and sank, with all the German supplies going to the bottom of the river. Henry has had to go home again, with his tail between his legs. The Pope has apparently been involved, trying to establish peace between Germany and Hungary."

"I'm sorry, Agatha, but it's your relative who is the

aggressor," Edward commented.

"There's no love lost between me and my uncle," she responded.

Edmund had not been injured in any fighting and was back home with Anna and Elizabeth, so Frida was at peace, and at our meal that evening, we toasted Zotmund the swimmer.

By early October, we had news of a different kind, but which also caused us to celebrate.

"A letter from Alfred," I declared, and began to look at its contents.

"You're smiling, Wulfgar," Edward said.

"Godwine is back in favour!"

"Really?"

"He returned to England with a considerable number of warriors, and the English didn't want a civil war, so he's been forgiven. King Edward has given him the kiss of peace."

"And his sons? And Edith?"

"All restored. And, yes, Edith is back as queen. So, Edward won't be taking a new wife."

I grinned at Edward and he grinned back.

"No rival aethelings," I stated.

Our celebration was muted and, as it happened, short-lived.

There was a banging on the gates, urgent, attention-demanding. A messenger was quickly admitted.

"Lord Edmund!" he gasped. "He's very ill."

Frida grasped the man's arm.

"Ill! What's wrong?"

"The pox."

She screamed and I went to hold her. She sobbed in my arms.

"Take me to him!" she managed to say through her tears.

I nodded to a servant and soon we had horses and provisions for our journey.

"It's very dangerous," Edward warned. "You will be at risk, Mother, for you could get it."

"I don't care. I will die with him if necessary."

Edward looked at me and I shrugged my shoulders. We knew there was no point in arguing. I risked my life too, but I would do that for Frida.

We set off with our escort and, after two days, we came to Edmund's house. We were quietly admitted; indeed the house was eerily quiet.

"Where is he?" demanded Frida.

"I will take you to Princess Anna," a servant whispered.

We were ushered into the main hall. Anna sat nursing her daughter and weeping. Frida went close.

"Anna, Anna." She touched the woman's shoulder. "How is he?"

"Gone!" wailed the Princess. "My beloved is gone!"

She dug her face into the baby's shawl and her whole body shook with grief.

Frida seemed turned to stone.

"Gone?" she breathed. "You mean he's ... he's dead?"

Anna continued to weep, so Frida looked at the women who attended her. Their pale faces and red eyes told us the truth, as they gently nodded their heads.

"Then I must see him," Frida declared.

"We have buried him," one of the women responded. "The pox is so dangerous that he was buried the day he died."

Now Frida began to wail and I had a hard time trying to stop her from becoming hysterical. I had seen her weep for her first husband, Siferth, and seen her weep for her second, King Edmund, but this was different. Now she wept for her son and I felt powerless to help her.

We spent only two days there, enough to get some rest from our journey and to see Edmund's grave. I barely had time to catch up with Wulf. I found that he and Maria were well and doing what they could to stay that way.

"He was my brother," Wulf sighed. "He was a good brother too. How cruel that his life has been cut short through illness – after all the battles we fought."

"There is suffering all around us," I commented, rather lamely. "But you have some good memories."

"Mother must be devastated."

"She is. I'm not sure how to console her. I have never seen her so struck down by grief."

"Just go on loving her, Father, as you always have."

That is what I tried to do, but in vain. We returned to Nadasd, but Frida was withdrawn and silent, reluctant to do anything. She rarely spoke and hardly ate. I began to be seriously worried for her health.

We tried to raise her spirits by having the children near her. Margaret and Christina were very good with her and tried hard to get her interest. She refused to play with Edgar, who was now an engaging toddler.

Within weeks, she had taken to her bed.

"She has lost the will to live," I said to Edward.

"I know," he answered. "You must prepare yourself, Wulfgar. I do not think she will last much longer."

He was right. She faded away in front of our eyes. I tried to hide my distress from her, but, alone, I would weep, angry at my helplessness.

"Wulfgar," she whispered one day, as I sat by her bed.

I took her hand. It was icy cold and the veins stood out, for it had little flesh on it.

"You have been a good husband," she said, and briefly opened her eyes to focus on my face. "You have given me much happiness," she added.

"I have always loved you," I answered. "My life means nothing without you."

"Servant, husband, father," she murmured. "Look after Edward."

"I will ... and Wulf and Edie. Don't leave us, Frida."

My words were lost, I think, for she seemed to have fallen asleep and this time she did not wake.

CHAPTER 51

I was inconsolable. Frida had been at the centre of my world for more than thirty years. I didn't know how to live without her.

We buried her by the little church and I spent much time at that spot, frequently putting fresh leaves in lieu of flowers on the disturbed earth. It was the depth of winter and the bare soil distressed me. When spring arrived, wild grasses would reclothe the ground, but I felt that life had ended for me too and nothing could ever cover the emptiness in my life.

"Why did she give up?" I asked Edward, as we sat at the table one day.

He was quiet for a while.

"I think we have to face the fact, Wulfgar, that Edmund was her life." He reached over to lay his hand on my arm. "My father's death was devastating and then she found she was with child. It was as though her husband lived on, within her, in the new baby. She called him Edmund and he was like a replacement for the wonderful man who had died."

I looked at his serious face and saw the understanding and compassion in his eyes.

"He always mattered more to her than I did," he admitted, "but I don't think I minded. You were a special friend to me long before you married Mother. You gave me value and, yes, you loved me."

"Surely she loved you too?"

"Not in the same way that she loved Edmund. But, as we know, she indulged him. However, I don't mind that she never indulged me, as I think it has made me a stronger person."

"You have been a good son to her."

"And you have been a good husband."

"She never loved me like she loved your father."

"I know, but she respected you and valued you. You made a big difference to her life. You could not have loved her more or done more to help her through her losses."

"Except I could not save her after the loss of Edmund."

"None of us could," Edward consoled me. "She is at peace now. She does not have to face growing very old and not seeing her son grow old too."

Edward was right, but I still found it hard to go on living. He made sure I was kept busy with physical work on the estate and working on the accounts and, of course, there were journeys to the capital to visit Wulf and Maria. We never visited Princess Anna again, for baby Elizabeth only lived for a few months, and going to that house of death was more than I could bear.

There was another death in the following year, that of Godwine. He had collapsed at a feast in the presence of King Edward and died soon afterwards. Alfred gave his date of death as 15th April.

His death meant nothing to me. Long, long ago he had been an important part of our lives, but he had taken one path, while we had taken another. A result of his death, Alfred said, was that his son, Harold, had grown in power and was now the King's right-hand man. I was too numb to care.

Another year passed and the gentle love of my family began to have its healing effect. I would never forget Frida, but the pain of her death had lessened and the wound was not so raw. I began to take more interest in the world outside Nadasd.

"It is perfectly right what the Pope is doing," Agatha declared. "They are wrong."

I had just come into the hall and seated myself. Margaret, now eight, had come and sat on my lap.

"Who is wrong?" I asked.

"The Patriarchs in Constantinople, those who lead the Eastern Church," she replied.

"What have they done?" I wanted to know.

"They use leavened bread in the Mass," was her answer.

"Do you remember that, Wulfgar?" Edward asked. "In Kiev, we received bread risen by yeast and were told it symbolised the presence of the risen Christ."

"But the Mass replicates the Last Supper," Agatha countered, "and the bread used there would have been unleavened, because it was a Passover meal, remembering the escape of the Israelites from Egypt."

"So have I got this right?" I said slowly. "In the Mass, the Eastern Church uses leavened bread and the Western Church uses unleavened bread." I paused. "Does it matter?"

"Of course, it does!" Agatha cried. "The Eastern Church should follow the Pope."

"As we do," Margaret whispered to me. "The Pope is our Lord."

"The two Churches are on the verge of schism," Edward explained.

"Over bread?" I said in surprise.

"And other things," he added.

"The East does not use Latin," Agatha stated, "but that is a universal language."

"The East uses Greek," Edward informed me.

"A crucifix should show Christ dying," she continued. "He was human, he was one of us. We must never forget he died for us."

"The art in the East is different," Edward responded, in his effort to help me understand. "A crucifix rarely shows the dead Christ, but the Christ in glory, the overcomer of sin and death."

"But the truth is that Christ is both human and divine," I argued. "He took our sin upon him on the cross and died in our place, but the cross is also the place of victory, his death being the moment of triumph. These are but two parts of the whole."

Agatha looked at me crossly. I was aware she had firm views and that her early and formative life had been spent in Catholic Germany, whereas Edward and I had enjoyed the riches of the Eastern Church for many years before our move to Hungary. I sensed her influence on her eldest daughter.

"They are puppets!" Agatha sternly declared. "The Patriarchs in Constantinople are puppets of the Byzantine Empire, but the Pope is above politics and is the true successor of St. Peter."

I caught Edward's eye and read there my own view that this was not a battle worth fighting here in our hall.

"So there is a serious danger of schism?" I asked.

"We think so," Edward acknowledged, "but Hungary will stay true to the Pope."

"As it should!" was Agatha's final word and I noticed little Margaret solemnly nodded her head.

"I have in mind building a new bridge, which would mean travellers aren't dependent on the ford," Edward told me, and I smiled at the way he had changed the subject. "I'd like to show you where I think it could go."

Margaret slipped off my knee.

"Father needs your help," she said solemnly.

Building the bridge was a good project and Edward even involved Edgar, though he was only three.

"He needs to learn from an early age what is expected of a lord – and perhaps a king. The local people are calling it the Bridge of the Three Princes, so you are royalty now, Wulfgar."

We had laughed together over the name, but soon had cause to be more serious about the word "princes".

"Edward, I have a letter from Alfred," I said, "and he has news of a decision made at the Whitsun meeting of the Witan."

I looked at him and grinned.

"They are sending a delegation to establish contact with the son of Edmund Ironside!"

CHAPTER 52

"At last!" cried Edward. "The Witan acknowledges I exist and that I am a true aetheling."

"This is what we have been hoping for all these years," I acknowledged. "Every time there was a change of king, you were overlooked, but now that Edward has no son, who is to succeed?"

"Harald they call Hardrada of Norway? Swein Estrithson of Denmark? Who are these men?" Edward laughed. "Are they English? No. They are not aethelings."

"There is no one more suitable to succeed than you."

"And do they know where to find me?"

"Oh, yes, I have made sure Alfred has told enough of the right people."

"They know too that Edmund died?"

"Yes, they know that."

"You have done well, Wulfgar."

"But Hungary is not a country with which England has any diplomatic ties," I warned. "No Englishman would be sure of how to find it."

"So what will happen, do you think?"

"I really don't know. The King will appoint some envoys, but how they reach us ..." I shrugged my shoulders. "How would we find our way to England? We have come to Hungary by a very strange and circuitous route. The way would not be through Russia. I would use my trading contacts and probably have to travel through Germany."

"We'll face that issue when the envoys arrive," Edward responded. "We are assuming they will invite me to return to England." He grinned. "And, of course, I will graciously accept their invitation."

We feasted well that day. Agatha and Edie were full of questions about England and the three children listened in amazement. It was hard for them to imagine what was about to happen.

I say "about to happen" and to begin with our departure felt imminent, but several weeks passed before another letter came from Alfred.

"He says the King has chosen two clergymen as his envoys," I told everyone. "Bishop Ealdred of Worcester is one. Alfred says the Bishop has travelled to Rome in the past and therefore has some experience of Europe. The other is Abbot Aelfwine of Ramsey, who represented the English church at the Council of Rheims."

"What else does he say?" Edward asked.

"Nothing of relevance to their task," I answered. "He is not even sure they have yet left England."

"We must be patient, Edward," Agatha urged. "They will arrive, but it will not be tomorrow."

"Or even this month," he responded.

"Let's hope it's this year," I laughed.

Weeks slipped into months and Christmas came with no news of the envoys. Alfred knew no more in England than we knew in Hungary. The whereabouts of the English delegation was a mystery.

Andrew's court came for one of its visits in the early spring of 1055 and we shared with him our puzzlement.

"From England, the most direct route is through Germany," he informed us. "The journey would not take six months to accomplish."

"So where are the envoys?" we asked.

"My guess is that they are in Germany."

"Awaiting better weather for travelling?"

He snorted.

"It's more likely Henry has taken them prisoner."

"Prisoner?"

"I don't get on with Henry, as you know," Andrew said. "He's tried to conquer Hungary and failed. In the past I made overtures to him, even said I would pay an annual tribute if he would acknowledge me as King, but he hates me and acts like a big bully. As Holy Roman Emperor, he thinks he can do what he likes."

"You have spies in his court," Edward said. "Can they not find out what has happened?"

"That's a good idea, Edward. I'll see what I can do. But your English envoys were naïve if they thought going to Henry would give them easy access to Hungary."

A few more weeks passed and then news came from Andrew that the Bishop and the Abbot, together with their companions, were indeed at Henry's court in Cologne. They were *not* prisoners, well, not officially. Henry had greeted them warmly and heaped honours and gifts on them – and not lifted a finger to help them reach Hungary. Rather he had very cunningly distracted them. His archbishop, a man named Hermann, had inveigled the two English clerics into studying in depth the ecclesiastical organisation of the German Church.

"I do not believe this!" Edward cried in exasperation. "King Edward sent them to find me and they have allowed themselves to sit in Cologne doing ... doing something totally irrelevant to their mission. Are these men fools?"

"Andrew says it is thought the clergymen are under the impression that Henry is trying to make contact with Hungary," I added.

"Does it take six months to make contact with a country with which you share a border?" he demanded. "It's ridiculous! Cannot they see he is making fools of them?"

"Why does King Henry not tell them that he won't deal with Hungary?" Edie asked.

"Diplomatic reasons probably," Edward explained, calming down slightly. "In the past, he was married to King Edward's half-sister, Gunnhild, though that proved disastrous. He's married now to Agnes of Aquitaine. But he won't want to upset the King of England."

"A few years ago," I said, "Henry had trouble with the Count of Flanders. Other countries joined in, some backing Henry, some backing the Count. King Edward decided England should back Henry, probably because

Flanders was a haven for some English exiles and also gave refuge to Scandinavian pirates. So, there's another reason why Henry wouldn't want to upset Edward. He was probably extremely embarrassed by the arrival of the envoys and has been desperately trying to avoid helping them, whilst still appearing to be friendly."

"Oh, I'm sure my uncle can do both things at the same time," Agatha declared. "He really has no quarrel with my dear Edward, but he won't help him because he lives in Andrew's kingdom. He's a stubborn fool!"

We now had some idea of what was going on, probably more idea than they had in England, for Alfred kept telling me there was no news at all. At least we had discovered the whereabouts of the envoys and why they were stuck in Cologne.

"I cannot see a resolution to this, Wulfgar," Edward confessed. "How can the Bishop and Abbot find me here, if Henry offers them no way of travelling through his country?"

I shook my head in frustration.

"I agree," I said. "I cannot see how this can be resolved."

A whole year had passed since the news had reached us of the delegation to find Edward, and our joy at that news had long since departed.

Late in 1055, Alfred wrote to say the envoys had returned to England, having failed in their mission. I wrote back to tell him what had really happened, but he was simply a merchant, not even a member of the Witan, and there was nothing much he could do.

Our hopes had been crushed again.

CHAPTER 53

We did our best to celebrate Christmas, but there could be no denying that a cloud of disappointment hung over us and in particular over Edward.

"My father was King of England," he said to me one day in early January. "I have been born into a royal family and yet all my life, I have been unable to act as such."

"But think how long the present King of England had to wait. Much of his time was spent in exile," I reminded him. "Edward must often have wondered if he would ever receive the crown. He had to wait nearly forty years, and see others crowned in his place."

"I will be forty in a few months' time," he answered sadly.

"And you have had an interesting preparation for kingship. You have been at the court of Olof in Sweden and then you were schooled by Yaroslav in Russia. You have seen different styles of leadership and fought many battles. You know a great deal about war and peace and kingship."

He smiled slightly.

"Wulfgar, you have been such a rock in my stormy life. I have learned much from you too, especially about loyalty."

"Don't give up Edward," I urged. "Remember, there is no heir in England."

Finding an heir, however, did not seem to be a pressing matter for England during that year. Alfred told me how there was trouble with the Welsh and that was keeping the King and his thegns busy.

There was also trouble in Scotland. The king there was Macbeth, but Malcolm and Donald, the two sons of the previous king, Duncan, whom Macbeth had defeated in battle, had sought protection in the English court, and Edward was now trying to secure the Scottish throne for Malcolm.

Our life in Nadasd continued as usual, for there was little else we could do. Then, in October, we had a glimmer once more of hope.

"Wulf tells me that news from Germany has been greeted with great rejoicing in the capital," I informed the family.

I looked across at Agatha.

"It concerns your uncle," I added.

"Henry? What stupid thing has he done this time?" she asked.

"He's died."

There was a stunned silence.

"Died?" she whispered. "But he is only the age of my dear Edward."

"He was taken ill," I reported. "There is no suggestion he was injured in battle, though he's been fighting a fair few in various parts of his empire. He knew he was dying and asked his nobles to accept his son as his successor."

"He's but a boy!" Edward cried.

"So others will govern for him, I presume," was my comment.

The next day, Edward sought me out and surprised me by his proposition.

"The news of Henry's death has been in my mind ever since you told us," he said, "and it is as though God is laying something on my heart."

"Like what?"

"When the envoys were sent from England two years ago, they were detained by Henry in Germany," Edward continued. "He didn't tell them he had a quarrel with Hungary, but we think that's why they never reached here. Henry was simply being malicious, trying to get his own back on Andrew."

"Yes. He kept them in Cologne and gave them no opportunity to journey through his empire to reach us."

"He's dead now." Edward grabbed my arm. "Don't you see, Wulfgar, everything has changed?"

His eyes were bright with excitement and I could feel his hand was shaking.

"I'm going to get Agatha to write to Agnes, asking for permission for English envoys to pass through Germany."

"Edward! Are you serious?"

"Absolutely! Agnes may refuse, but if we do not ask, we'll never know."

"It's a bold plan," I acknowledged, "and certainly one worth trying. You think Agnes may have a different attitude to that of her late husband?"

"It's possible, Wulfgar!"

I could not have stopped him if I'd tried. He believed God had given him this idea and he was going to pursue it. Whether Agatha shared his enthusiasm, I don't know. Edward wrote the letter in her name and she used her seal on it before it was despatched. I hope it contained appropriate words of condolence.

Now we had to wait. The dark days of winter did nothing to raise our spirits. Then, just before Christmas, a reply came from the German court.

"Agnes has considered our request and consulted her nobles and..." Edward looked up from his reading and smiled broadly, "... and has no objection to allowing envoys to visit us in Hungary, if they come again from England."

"That is wonderful news!" I cried. "Well done, Edward. Your idea has worked."

"But now we need the English court to send some fresh envoys," he declared. "Wulfgar, you need to get Alfred to do his part in London."

"I'll send a letter *now*," I declared, and did.

Through the icy months of January and February, we heard nothing. The water was frozen in the troughs and it was as though our lives were frozen too, waiting for good news to thaw them and bring us hope.

Then we heard.

"Alfred says envoys have been despatched. Their mission, endorsed by the Witan, is to seek out Edward, son of Edmund, and invite him to return to England."

"And *this* time," Edward declared, "they will reach us."

They did – in early April, as the trees were bursting into new life. It was as though the long winter of exile was at last coming to an end and a wonderful return to our homeland was imminent.

The delegation was led by a cleric, aged about forty.

"I am Wulfstan, prior of the monastery at Worcester," he told us. "It was my bishop who tried to make contact before, but he has sent me on his behalf."

"You are very welcome, Father," Edward said. "I do not know Worcester, but my step-father, Wulfgar, does."

"Ah, really?" he queried, turning to me.

"I was there at the time when Swein Forkbeard had conquered England," I replied. "My lord Edmund was in hiding in the monastery at Evesham, and Bishop Wulfstan was a great help to us in finding out news."

"Bishop Wulfstan. Ah, he was my uncle. I am named after him. A wonderful man, I think you will agree."

"Yes, I have vivid memories of him. He was fearless in his denouncing of England's sin and thought the Danes' conquest of us was God's judgement."

"But did he not serve under the Danes?" Edward asked. "Was he not one of Cnut's bishops?"

"Ah, yes," Wulfstan agreed, "but he was able to ensure that King Cnut upheld the laws of King Aethelred, so he used his position of power to good effect. We are called upon to be wise."

He looked around at us.

"Lady Agatha, I believe you are from Germany originally."

She nodded.

"And your children have all been born in Hungary?"

"Margaret was born in Russia, but was only a baby when we came here," she replied.

"And you, Lord Edward, you left England as a child?"

"I was only in my second year."

"Even you, Lord Wulfgar, have not been in England for nearly forty years."

"That's right. We went first to Denmark, for the aethelings' lives were at risk. Then to Sweden, where we spent several years. Edward was, I think, about twelve or so when we went to Russia, and we've been here in Hungary for about ten years."

Wulfstan frowned slightly.

"You will need much wisdom," he said quietly. "England has changed since you left."

CHAPTER 54

"It is a relief that your English is so good," Wulfstan commented. "I feared we might have difficulty communicating."

"Edward's mother insisted her children spoke English," I explained.

"Of course, there was another son, was there not?"

"My brother Edmund was a tiny baby when we left England," Edward answered. "He died of the pox over four years ago."

"Any children?"

"A daughter, but she died too."

"And your mother?"

"She died soon after my brother. She had married Wulfgar back in Sweden, so I have a half-brother, Wulf, and a half-sister, Edie."

"You will all come to England?"

"Yes," said Edward firmly. "We are a family. We have been through much together."

"But none of you knows England," Wulfstan commented. "Not the land it is now under King Edward."

"We understand he has brought peace," I said. "I remember attacks from Danes and pirates, but there has been less of that, we hear."

"Attacks from the east are few and those from the west have been contained," Wulfstan agreed, "but there are tensions and divisions within the kingdom."

"Among the thegns?" Edward asked.

"Ah, yes, and the most powerful man of all is Harold Godwineson. You will need to make a friend of him."

For me, some of the excitement of the invitation to return was tarnished by his words of warning. I suddenly felt I did not know my homeland at all. I might speak its language, but I would be a stranger to its customs – and especially to its politics. I feared we might be entering a land of marsh, where we had to seek out places of dry land on which we could stand without sinking, but I said nothing to Edward, as I did not want to spoil his joy.

We easily accommodated the Prior and his companions. They needed to stay for several days, as we made arrangements to leave Nadasd. Wulf and Maria joined us, bringing all their belongings from the capital. I had asked Wulf if he wanted to stay in Hungary, but he was determined to come to England, and Maria would go wherever he went.

The children were excited, but puzzled, for they had little concept of the world beyond our estate. Margaret was now about eleven, Christina seven and Edgar five. Margaret took the opportunity offered by having a cleric among us to ask him questions.

"We should obey the Pope, shouldn't we?" she stated.

"Of course," Wulfstan replied. "He is the head of the church on earth."

"But those in the East refuse to do so. That's wrong, isn't it?"

"Yes, it is wrong."

"So there has been a schism between the Eastern Church and the Western Church," Margaret added.

Wulfstan raised his eyebrows, glanced across at Agatha and smiled.

"I see, Margaret, that you are well versed in the matters of the church."

"Yes and it is wrong that there is division," she declared. "Christ would have us be one body, but the Eastern Church has broken the unity. They should repent and return to the true church."

I could see the Prior had not expected so young a girl to have such clear views, and over the next few days I often saw him asking her questions, as well as seeking to answer those directed at him.

Eventually, all the arrangements had been made. Andrew was to provide us with some of his bodyguard to ensure we had a safe journey. We were sad to leave Nadasd, which had been such a haven of peace after so many years of exile and living on the charity of rulers, but Edward had trained a steward to run the estate and Andrew was happy with the plans that were in place.

We did not anticipate ever returning, but we realised our journey was into the little known, and it was good to know Nadasd could still be a haven for us if necessary.

Andrew paid us a last visit.

"Edward, my brother," he exclaimed, hugging him to his chest. "You helped me win my kingdom and I will never forget the courage and help you and your family gave."

"You came home and were crowned," Edward replied, as Andrew released him. "I'm going home and hope, one day, to be crowned – and without having to fight for a kingdom."

"It is a very different situation," Andrew agreed, "but being a king is not easy. You will need God's grace and God's wisdom – and his protection from those who wish you evil."

"I don't think anyone wishes me evil," Edward laughed. "I am to be the saviour of the English, for they want to be ruled by an Englishman, and not a foreigner."

Andrew glanced at me and I read in his face something akin to a warning. Was Edward being naïve, a little over-confident? I hoped not. I genuinely hoped we would be met by joy on the part of everyone in England.

I had no idea we were so far from our destination. We went first into Germany and stayed several days with Agnes and so were able to thank her for the part she had played in making our return possible.

We also stopped in Bruges, a place that had given refuge to English exiles in the past, before making our way to the coast for the crossing to England.

None of us adults had been on a sea voyage since Valgar had taken us to Novgorod. Edward remembered that, but Wulf and Edie struggled to recall it. Agatha, Maria and the children had never been on the sea before, and I remembered my own nervousness all those years ago, when we had fled from Queen Emma. My dear Frida would be so thrilled that we were returning. She had never lost hope of Edward being England's king, but the death of her dearest son had sapped her of any will to see that hope fulfilled. I confess I shed a few tears as I boarded the ship.

Our Hungarian escort left us at this point, and with all our family and the Prior's delegation, we filled two boats. The weather was typical of August, warm with a few clouds visible, but we had not proceeded very far, when the cloud increased and the wind strengthened.

"It looks like a rough crossing, Wulfgar," Edward remarked.

"The waves never bothered you as a child," I responded.

He looked at the darkening sky.

"I was not then a husband and a father." He frowned. "Surely, Wulfgar, the Lord will get us safely to England – after all that has happened?"

Suddenly, I was again at Assandun, where King Edmund, through treachery, was defeated by Cnut. Then I was in that room at Glastonbury, listening for the last breath of my dying King and hearing the weeping of his distraught wife. And I knew that what I thought God would make happen did not always come to pass.

"Pray, Edward!" I shouted, as the wind whipped at the sail and the boat lurched through the waves.

Oh, God, I thought, we cannot all die now. Do not crush England's hope – and ours. Save us, I beg you!

We clung to each other as well as to the boat – and came through the storm. By the time we reached the River Thames, the worst was behind us and none of us had perished, though Agatha and Maria had been sick.

The sun reappeared and its heat soon dried our wet clothes. We could see the mud flats and marshes that lined the river and the richness of the bird life.

"England is beautiful!" Edie said, snuggling up to me, as though she were still a child. "Are you happy to be home, Father?"

"Very."

I smiled at her.

"But we cannot expect our lives to be as they were in Nadasd," I warned.

"I know," she answered, "but I do not mind as long as I can still care for Margaret, Christina and Edgar."

As we came nearer to London, we could see how busy the riverside was and the huge number of boats.

"Where are we mooring?" I shouted to the captain.

"Greenwich!"

We were coming full circle. We had left here in the dark in September 1017. Our return though was in broad daylight, with the sun making the river glitter and the sound of English voices shouting to each other.

Edward was the first out of the boat. He leaped down onto the quay, stretched his arms out wide and stood tall, breathing deeply the warm air.

"Wulfgar, we are home!" he shouted.

"At last," I sighed, and began to laugh.

The exile was over.

E N D S

If you have enjoyed this book, please email the author at fenflack@btinternet.com.

Historical note

The Anglo-Saxon Chronicle, the major source for the history of this period, records that on 30 November 1016 Edmund died. It does not say how he died. This has led to speculation that he may have been murdered. Henry of Huntingdon, writing about 1128, claimed the son of Eadric killed Edmund as the King sat relieving himself, the fatal blow being a dagger into his bowels. Henry is known for his sensationalism and I have chosen to have Edmund die naturally, though readers will note I have used the rumoured murder in my story.

There is little of which we can be absolutely sure with regard to what happened after the death of Edmund Ironside; incidentally, this nickname is not recorded before 1057. The only definite fact is that his son, Edward, was living in Hungary at the time of his recall to England. How he got there is the subject of debate.

The sources are various chronicles, some near-contemporary, some written much later. These accounts do not always agree, so I have tried to make sense of what seem to be the facts. I am indebted to "The Lost King of England" by Gabriel Ronay (published by The Boydell Press in 1989), but I have not followed this slavishly and I disagree with some of what he says.

Edmund Ironside had a son called Edward and also another son, who is generally thought to be named Edmund. Which was the elder? Were they twins? Anglo-

Saxon kings did not have a tradition of naming their sons after them, so logically I think Edward was the first-born. Almost certainly, the second boy must have been born posthumously and it would be natural for him to be called Edmund after his dead father. Much later in life, a bride was found for Edward, not Edmund, which seems also to point to his being the older son. We do not know the name of their mother; only one chronicler calls her Ealdgyth and he may be confused. In my first book, "Ironside", I gave her the simpler name of Frida, so I have called her Frida in this book too. We do not know what happened to her, as she is never mentioned, but surely she must have gone into exile with her tiny children, unless they were ripped from her breast, as one story suggests? I also think she would have spoken English to them in the hope that one day they would return.

The servants, Wulfgar, Hild and Edith, are all fictional, but it seems likely the widow of Edmund Ironside and her babies had companions on their travels. Their benefactor is named as Walgar, a Danish nobleman. I was told the Danes pronounce a W as a V, so I have called him Valgar. His "sayings" come from "The Sayings of the Vikings", a translation of the Hávamál, by Björn Jónasson (published by Gudrun Publishing in 1992).

Some Chroniclers claim Cnut sent the aethelings to Sweden with a "letter of death", which meant the king there was meant to kill them – quietly. Ronay claims Edmund Ironside's wife was Swedish, but gives no source for this claim. If she was Swedish, the King of Sweden was unlikely to kill her children! I think she was English anyway. Olof, the Swedish King, was related to Cnut through marriage, so the "letter of death" is possible. In view of Walgar's involvement, I've had him help the aethelings to escape from Cnut and I have not pursued the "letter of death" suggestion.

I have called the countries involved in this story by their current names, e.g. Denmark, Norway, Sweden, Russia, Hungary and Germany. A thousand years ago, people may have used different names. Sweden had only recently been created by the union of the Goths and the Svear and I could not find its name. Russia was the land of the Rus. Castle Reka, Nadasd, is the traditional site of the aethelings' home in Hungary. I have included some maps to help readers appreciate something of the political pattern, as it is not the same today.

The tribute demanded by Cnut in 1016 was £72,000. This could be roughly equivalent to £350 million today and clearly an exorbitant amount.

The travels of the aethelings were so amazing that my plot was supplied and I have simply tried to bring it alive and make it feasible. I have not altered any known events, but have, of course, added to them. You may think things happened in a different way; they may have! That is the joy of historical fiction.

Fen Flack